BLOOD & ASHES

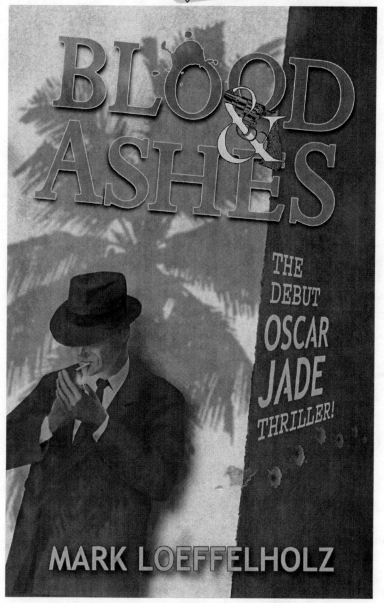

THE DEBUT OSCAR JADE THRILLER!

MARK LOEFFELHOLZ

Outskirts Press, Inc.
Denver, Colorado

Blood & Ashes
The Debut Oscar Jade Thriller!

V2.0

Outskirts Press, Inc.
http://www.outskirtspress.com

ISBN: 978-1-4327-5934-6

Library of Congress Control Number: 2010928202

PRINTED IN THE UNITED STATES OF AMERICA

For **Tom Loeffelholz**, my dad…
Without whom there would be no Oscar Jade

Miami Beach, Florida – December 9th, 1941

1
Fumble-Foot

The stranger took Oscar Jade by surprise—that was the worst part. Worse, even, than the white-hot pain as Jade dropped to one knee, angry with himself because he had no one else to blame.

He figured the stranger would have been watching closely as Jade got up from the outdoor table he'd been sharing with the dame at the beachfront Pelican Bar & Grill. He'd probably taken note of the way Jade's left foot turned inward, and the obvious limp, as Jade made his way past the other tables to where the stranger stood. He would have made a quick and casual appraisal of Jade's lean, lanky height. The stranger probably missed the unusual thickness of the wrists, the wiry power hidden in those long arms, and the measured determination of the approach. He would have been confident in his judgment that Oscar Jade was easy game.

The stranger was broad-shouldered, thickly muscled and obviously very powerful beneath his expensive grey suit with its telltale bulge under the left armpit. His hat was angled forward, the stiff brim nearly hiding his sharp, dark eyes. The wide nose had been broken at least once, the chin was pointed, the smile a little too self-satisfied. He was probably in his late thirties.

Jade passed beneath the red and white striped canvas awning of the Pelican's open-air frontage and stood next to him. The stranger leaned back, his elbows resting on the ancient wooden tavern bar. He slowly turned his gaze upward to meet Jade's eyes.

"Hello," said Jade.

"Hey," he replied lazily.

"Anything I can do for you?"

"I doubt it, junior." His smile didn't waver as he stared over Jade's shoulder at the brunette at the table. She was in conversation with Claude Applegate, the owner of the Pelican: a huge, square-jawed, white-haired, lean giant of a man. Both of them returned the stranger's stare.

"Is there a problem?" asked Jade easily.

"It's none of your business, fumble-foot."

Jade smiled pleasantly. "Actually, it *is* my business now."

And so the stranger had quickly stepped forward and stomped down on Jade's club left foot, and Jade dropped to one knee and cursed his own stupidity.

He looked back at the table; Myrna's mouth was open in surprise. Claude took a step toward the bar. Jade raised an open hand, and Claude stopped in mid-stride.

The stranger leaned down, grabbed Jade by the collar of his shirt, and whispered in his ear. Jade noted the distinct Brooklyn accent. "If you're smart you'll stay out of it, gimp."

He let go of Jade and stood up. He smiled at Myrna and Claude, and tipped his hat. Then he turned and walked away. Emerging from beneath the Pelican's awning, he strolled toward the corner of 15th Street and Ocean Drive, where a line of cars were parked at the curb alongside the stuccoed south wall.

Jade stood up quickly. He reached across the bar and grabbed an unopened bottle of beer from a tub that Claude had recently filled with ice. By this time the stranger was perhaps thirty feet away. Jade held the bottle firmly by the neck in his right hand, stepped forward, and threw it overhand, putting all of his weight behind it. The bottle completed one revolution end over end in midair before it hit the guy at the base of his skull and bounced upward in a lazy, looping arc. It didn't break until it hit the sidewalk—exploding with a *pop* of foam and shards of broken brown glass—and by that time the guy in the nice grey suit was sprawling forward on his face. His jaunty hat fluttered to the ground beside him.

Jade was upon him in no time. He rolled him over onto his back, and stepped on the stranger's neck with his bad foot. Only those who knew him well would have noticed the slight twitch at the corner of his mouth as Jade accepted the pain with the familiarity of an unwelcome relative.

The guy blinked up at him in disbelief, his constrained breaths whistling between bared teeth. Jade opened the guy's suit jacket and pulled a Colt .45 semiautomatic from a leather holster under his arm.

"Nice piece," Jade remarked, and stepped down harder. The breathing stopped altogether. He pulled back the hammer, and jammed the barrel directly between the stranger's bulging eyes. "Just so you know," he said, "I don't like assholes."

Half an hour earlier, as he'd stared out at the water and wished he had someone else's head on his shoulders, Jade's biggest problem was a screaming hangover.

A view from the beach is like having a good, long look at *forever*. The sea and sky meet at the horizon, somewhere distant, and you aren't meant to see what happens beyond that point. Just as well, Jade thought as he gazed at the endlessness of the Atlantic Ocean. There was a storm raging over there, and he would have no part in it. The knowledge burned in his belly like a bad meal.

He lit a cigarette and watched a few scattered bathers approach the edge of the water, where green waves lapped gently against the sand. A handsome woman in her early forties and a dark-haired twenty-something beauty herded four young boys, ranging in age from toddler to adolescent, toward the water. The three older boys romped into the surf. The youngest plopped down in the wet sand, and giggled as the sea washed across his lap.

Jade took a drag on his cigarette, watched that little boy and wanted to trade places with him. Too many beers, a night spent with a redhead whose name he could not remember, and less than four hours' sleep added up to an ugly morning filled with regret. The woman was gone, thank God, but the regret—and a thumping headache—lingered. Still, there was nothing to be done…except, perhaps, contemplate the first beer of the day. He glanced at his watch. It was 11:30 AM. Jade folded his arms on the table and laid his head down. The laughter of the kids splashing in the surf, the rustling of the palms in the cool breeze, and the gentle crashing of the waves all had their effect. Sleep began to claim him.

"Lady here to see you, Oscar." Claude's gravelly voice carried a hint of Chicago.

"Not today," Jade mumbled. "Tomorrow."

"I need your help, Mister Jade." It was a silky voice, assertive, yet somehow fragile in its urgency.

Jade cursed softly, his eyes still closed, and tried to figure a way out.

"Is he hungover, or still drunk?" she asked.

Claude hesitated. "Well, miss…"

"Does it matter?" Jade asked, looking up and squinting against the brightness of the day. She had long, dark brown hair that was done up to perfectly frame her face, which was full of freckles. She had big, widely set brown eyes, and a delicate pixie's nose. Her dress was a conservative navy blue, like you'd see on a secretary in a doctor's office, or maybe in church. A fleeting glance down revealed a nice, slender figure, with smallish, highly placed breasts and a narrow waist. She had dimples in her cheeks, which probably deepened when she smiled. But she wasn't smiling at the moment.

"It matters to me, Mister Jade," she said, setting

down the large suitcase she'd been holding. "If you're busy curling up inside a bottle, I'll take my business elsewhere." She leaned over and took the cigarette out of his hand—the ash had nearly reached his fingers while he dozed—and ground it out in the ashtray on the table.

Jade smiled in spite of himself. The bird had class. "Just what is it that you need my help with, Miss..."

"Mrs.," she corrected him. "Mallory. Myrna Mallory."

"Well, then, Mrs. Mallory?"

She hesitated and glanced at Claude, who still hovered nearby, holding a table rag in one oversized hand. Then she looked at Jade. "It's my husband."

Jade sighed, and lit a fresh cigarette. "I don't do matrimonial work, Mrs. Mallory."

Claude rolled his eyes as he grabbed a chair and pulled it out. "Have a seat, ma'am." She thanked him and sat down. He gave Jade a look and withdrew, shaking his head.

Jade went on, "I can give you the names of several private investigators, very good men, over in Miami who are experts—"

"You misunderstand," she said. "My marriage is already over. Or it may as well be. What I need is...well..." Her voice trailed off. "I'm really not sure *what* I need, to be honest."

Ah, Jesus. Jade forced a smile. "Why don't you start from the beginning?"

She looked him in the eye. "I'll pay you for your time," she said stiffly. "Even if you refuse."

"Want a smoke?"

"No thank you."

"Please go on," he said.

As she spoke, she looked past Jade, or perhaps *through* him.

"I was working as a teller at the Madison Bank," she said. "I'd been working there since just after I graduated high school. I don't want you to think that I—that I never had any other..." She glanced away, and frowned. "I was engaged once, when I was twenty. I thought he cared about me, and we...I thought we would...but it never happened."

Jade stifled a yawn, and tapped the ash off his smoke as she continued.

"My mother always told me that if you weren't married by the time you were twenty-five...well, I never believed *that*, of course. But time goes on, and I was twenty-nine when I met Horace. He came in every day of the week to make deposits and cash checks. He asked me to dinner.

"He's older than me, Mister Jade. Fifteen years older. But he was kind. He was a gentleman. He made me feel like I was someone special." She paused and looked at Jade, as if she expected a rebuttal of some sort. When none came, she said, "I just want you to understand why things happened as they did."

Jade shrugged.

"We'd only been seeing each other for a few weeks when he proposed," she went on. "It was all so fast, but it seemed right. It *felt* right. He was a good businessman, and he made a lot of money. He said I should quit my job, because real ladies shouldn't have to go to work every day of their lives. He said I'd never want for anything, that I'd never have to go to work for anyone ever again. And so we got married. Not in a church, like I wanted, but at the courthouse. He had an employee there as a witness. One of my girlfriends from the bank stood up with me. I wanted my mother to come down from Tallahassee, but he said he wanted to get married as soon as we could. He said he'd make it up to her." She looked away. "I should have known better."

"You said he *was* a good businessman," said Jade.

"Did I?" She seemed surprised.

"What does your husband do for a living?"

"He manages the Caribbean Hotel, on Collins Avenue."

Jade whistled. "Nice place," he said. "Big."

"It makes a lot of money," Myrna said. "Conventions, trade shows." Jade raised his eyebrows, and she smiled again. "I'm a woman, Mister Jade, but I used to work at a bank. I saw the deposits."

"But something's wrong."

She nodded. "Everything was fine for a while. Better than fine. It was almost perfect. Horace would come home after work and I'd make dinner. He loves the radio. We listened to Fibber McGee and Molly, and Jack Benny. He was happy. We were happy. He actually talked about wanting children..."

Her voice caught, and her eyes welled with tears. "And then, about two months ago, it all just stopped. One night he just stopped coming home at five o'clock, like he used to. He would come home at nine o'clock, then ten or eleven...and then it was after midnight. It got so I stopped trying to keep dinner warm for him, and then stopped setting a place for him at the table. Then, one night he didn't come home at all.

"I went to see him at the hotel the next day. They wouldn't let me into his office." Myrna's mouth became a thin line. "Well, I'm afraid I made quite the scene at the front desk. And finally he let me in.

"He looked terrible. His face was swollen. He had a black eye and a fat lip, and he was still wearing his clothes from the day before. Of course I was horrified. He told me that he'd been having 'business trouble.' I asked him what he meant, and he said he couldn't talk about it. He told me not to worry, and said he'd be home for dinner. Then he hurried me out the door."

"What did you do?"

"I didn't know what to do," she said. "I was frantic. I went straight over to the bank to talk to Betty—she's my friend, the one who stood up with me when I got married. I asked her if the deposits from the Caribbean Hotel were as big as they used to be." She met Jade's eyes. "You probably think I'm crazy."

"Not at all," Jade said. "I would have done the very same thing."

"Betty told me that the deposits were as big as usual. Maybe bigger. It didn't make any sense. So I knew that Horace really meant that *he* was in trouble. I think it's gambling."

"What makes you think so?"

"We followed baseball all summer: DiMaggio's hitting streak, Ted Williams hitting four hundred…"

Jade smiled, and exhaled a lungful of smoke. He was starting to like her.

"But Horace loved the Dodgers most of all. He'd

talk for hours about Leo Durocher and Pee Wee Reese, how Brooklyn was going to win it all and make the Yankees look like saps. So of course we listened to the World Series, and when the Dodgers lost the fourth game, Horace just went and lay down, without saying a word, and he didn't talk the next morning. And then the Yankees won the series...well, that's when everything changed. He started to ask me about every quarter I spent at the grocery store. That was when he started staying out late. Then he stopped coming home at all."

"Before that, did you have any indication that he was gambling?"

"No...but then he never talked to me about anything that happened outside our home." She avoided his gaze, and watched the people on the beach.

"Mrs. Mallory..."

"I began seeing another man," she said quickly. "Quite by accident. Horace asked me to go to the post office to mail a few letters, and that's where I met Peter."

"Peter who?"

"I'd rather not say," she said. "There's no reason to drag him into this. It's not his fault."

"With all due respect, ma'am," Jade said tiredly, "All I can tell so far is that you're in an unhappy marriage. I'm sorry about that, but it's not anything I can help you with."

The words began to spill from her in a torrent; she seemed to build momentum as she went along. This Peter guy had asked her out for a cup of coffee, and she'd agreed to go. He was even older than her husband. He was also charming and polite, and took an interest in everything she had to say. They talked for more than an hour. One thing led to another, and they began to meet for lunch on weekdays. He took her to places around town she'd never been to before. Myrna was happy to be able to get out of the house—she had lost contact with most of her friends in the months she'd been married, and Mallory never let her invite them over.

"And then one day, he took me to the Crab House, and we…" She stared down at her hands, which fiddled with the metal clasp of her purse. When she looked up, her face was flushed, but she smiled as she met Jade's gaze. "I excused myself, and went to the ladies' room. He followed me in, and locked the door behind him. We made love right there." Her stare was challenging. "Does that shock you?"

Jade tried to imagine this woman, with her conservative blue Sunday church dress hiked up and her perfect hair coming undone, her back up against the wall in a public restroom. It was an interesting picture, but Jade didn't indulge her. "I don't shock too easily," he said.

"We met that way a few times. Always in a public place, where we might get caught at any time. But we never were." She shook her head, but the smile remained. "I knew it was wrong, but I did it anyway. It was just so long since I'd felt happy. And I didn't even feel guilty about it. Not at first. Then, about three weeks ago, Peter said I should ask my husband for a divorce. He said he wanted to marry me.

"It surprised me. I told him I'd think about it. And then I guess I panicked. I stopped meeting him. He telephoned my house several times, and I finally told him that I couldn't go on with it. I hung up on him. It was the last time we talked.

"Horace hardly talked to me anymore. But when he did, it was always about money. He yelled about how much I was spending on bread and eggs, or whether a dress I was wearing was 'another new one.'" She smiled ruefully. "I can't remember the last time I thought about a new dress. About two weeks ago he came home—in time for dinner, for once—and he was very quiet. I didn't have anything ready, so I thought I'd make him an omelet. While I was cooking, he came into the kitchen and started asking me about my mother."

"Your *mother*?"

"Well, my mother's money. How much did she have, did my father leave an estate behind after he died, that kind of thing. I said it was none of his business how much money my mother had—or didn't have. We had a terrible fight. He told me I was selfish and stupid…then he asked me where I had been going during the day. He said he'd been coming home in the afternoons and I was never there."

Jade frowned. He put out what was left of his cigarette.

Her eyes filled with tears once again. "I told him I went to the library, that I went for walks on the beach, and to the matinee. I told him I was dying at home every day without any friends, which was the truth. But I didn't tell him everything. How could I?"

Jade nodded.

"He said he didn't believe me. He said he knew exactly what I'd been doing. I told him I wanted a divorce. He laughed at me, and said it didn't matter! I told him I was leaving, and he said that I could run as far as I wanted, and that didn't matter either. 'Till death do us part,' he said."

"He actually said that?"

She nodded. "After that, we didn't speak at all. He came home on time for dinner, and I cooked for him. We listened to the radio, but we didn't pay any attention. At least, I didn't. Then the day before yesterday, Horace left his briefcase at home. I went to put it in his study, and it..." She looked Jade in the eye, and gave him a sly smile. "Let's just say it *accidentally* fell open. I picked up the papers, and I found this." She opened her purse, took out a few sheets of folded paper, and handed them to Jade.

"My husband has taken out a life insurance policy on me, Mister Jade. Fifty thousand dollars."

Jade looked at the documents. He sat back in his chair and allowed himself a moment to let this sink in. "You think he intends to do something?"

"I don't know what to think," she admitted. "But I'm frightened. I left our home today, and I'm not going back."

Jade studied her for a long moment. "Have you gone to the police?" he asked.

She shook her head. "My husband has a lot of friends who are policemen. They'd laugh at me. And I'm not exactly innocent."

"That's different," Jade said impatiently.

"Is it? Do you think a woman who cheats on her husband is going to get any sympathy from his friends?"

"Do you have a lawyer?"

"No," she said. "Do *you* know a good one?"

"I might," Jade said.

"Well, my husband knows them all."

"Why don't you ask this Peter guy for help?"

"I can't." She looked down. "That was a mistake, the whole thing. I know that now. I can't go on with it."

A moment of silence passed between them. The palms moved in the breeze. "Well?" asked Jade finally. "What do you want me to do?"

"I want protection," she said, "and I'll pay for it."

Jade rubbed his eyes. "This isn't as easy as all that," he told her. "I can't just be your personal bodyguard. You won't be able to afford it—and even if you could, it's not what I do."

"I understand," she said. She dabbed at her eyes with a handkerchief she took from her purse. "I want you to find out why my husband is in money trouble. I want to know why he wants to be paid fifty thousand dollars if I die."

She reached forward and took one of Jade's Lucky Strikes out of his pack. Jade lit it for her, and she took a long pull. The breeze snatched the smoke away.

"Then I want you to convince him to give me a divorce," she said.

"Why me?"

"You have a reputation for doing the right thing," she said, putting her handkerchief away. "I've been told that you can be trusted. And that you don't give up. That's what I'm looking for."

Jade looked out at the horizon. No answers there; just sea and sky…and forever.

He said, "Here's the thing, Mrs. Mallory. This won't be cheap, and it won't be easy. I'm going to have to spend a lot of time, and talk to a lot of people. And I'm going to have to give some of these people money. It can add up."

"How much money?" Myrna asked.

"Twenty dollars a day for my time," Jade said. "Plus expenses—that'll be the money I have to give to other people, or if I have to travel—"

She opened her purse and pulled out a wad of bills. She peeled off a bunch of twenties, recounted them and handed them over. "Here's three hundred dollars to start."

Jade took the money and counted it, hoping he'd managed to hide his surprise. He put it in his pocket. "Mind if I hang onto the insurance policy?"

"Help yourself."

Just then Claude reappeared at the table. He bent down and whispered in Jade's ear. "Lady's got a tail."

Jade turned around and looked. There stood the stranger, staring intently at their table—eyes sharp, hat tilted forward, elbows on the bar.

Jade got up, and went to say hello.

2
Lunch at the Pelican

Jade pulled out the hood's wallet. He was Nino Valletti from New York, according to his driver's license—and his P.I. ticket, which allowed him to carry iron in the state of New York. Jade had allowed Valletti to sit up, but was keeping him covered with the .45, which he held at his hip, the barrel squared up on the well-dressed man's chest.

Valletti tried to stand up, and Jade corrected him with a subtle movement of the gun barrel. "Just sit tight, tough guy. You're already hurt. There's no need to be a hero."

Claude ambled over, afforded Valletti a dangerous stare, and whispered in Jade's ear. "I called the cops."

"Good," said Jade in the same whisper, and nodded in Myrna's direction. "Get her out of sight, would you?" Claude nodded. Once they were gone, Jade returned his attention to the goon on the sidewalk.

"Who are you working for?" Jade asked him.

"What's your beef?"

"None of your business."

"You have no idea what my business is," said Jade. "Or else you wouldn't be trying to muscle me on my home turf. Ask around, and you'll find out."

Valletti gingerly prodded the back of his head. His fingers came back bloody. He wiped them on his pants. "You're gonna get yours," he said evenly.

"That what you do, Nino? Make sure people get theirs? Well, maybe this time it doesn't work out that way. What brings you to the Pelican? Why pick a fight here?"

Valletti looked like he wanted so say more—plenty more—but he just stared back at Jade. "I got nothing else to say."

A long moment passed. Most of the beachgoers and passers-by were going about their business. The handful still watching were those who knew Jade, and he had every confidence the story would go his way when the paperwork was written up.

Valletti looked around nervously. He had to know the cops were on their way. He'd be thinking about his options. Was he going to make a move? Probably not, Jade decided. He'd have noticed the way Jade stood well out of arm's reach; the way the gun remained steady on the center of his chest. He'd probably decide that he'd already made enough mistakes for one day. But Jade hoped Valletti would make a move. His foot was still screaming at him, and he had an overwhelming urge to backhand the Colt's barrel across Valletti's teeth and watch a few of them spill out onto the sidewalk next to his fancy hat.

"Nice suit," Jade remarked. "Bet it cost a lot."

"So?"

"So do all your boyfriends dress as pretty as you do?"

Valletti's face bloomed with crimson fury. He got to one knee.

"That's right, you moron," Jade hissed between clenched teeth. "Come and get it."

A cruiser from the Miami Beach P.D. pulled to a stop behind Valletti, and he froze. He looked at Jade, eyes blazing, and sat back down. "You're a lucky son of a bitch," he said.

Jade laughed.

A second police car pulled up behind the first. Two uniforms got out of the first car, and Captain Allen Billings got out of the second.

Billings was in his mid forties, and although slight in both height and build—Jade had always figured he'd weigh in at about 125 with a couple of rocks in his pockets—no matter what the situation, he'd always somehow been big enough. His badge gave him all the weight he'd ever need.

"Well, well, well." Billings walked briskly over to where Jade stood guard over Valletti. "I was in the neighborhood when the call came in: trouble at the Pelican." He looked from Jade to Valletti and back again. "Imagine my surprise," he said dryly. "Bit early in the day to be bouncing drunks, isn't it, Oscar?"

Jade handed him Valletti's gun and wallet. "I'd like to swear out a complaint against this musclehead, Captain."

"That right?" Billings walked around and took a look at the back of the goon's head. "What's the gripe?"

"Assault," Jade replied. "And bad manners."

"Oh, dear." Billings was deadpan. "What's your story, Mister"—he checked the wallet—"Valletti?"

Valletti pointed at Jade. "He hit me in the head with a beer bottle."

Billings stared at Jade for a long moment. "Say it ain't so," he said finally.

Jade told the story, beginning at the point where he asked Valletti if there was a problem, leaving out any mention of the woman. "The point is, Captain, this guy was making Mr. Applegate nervous."

By this time Claude had emerged from the Pelican, and stood beside Jade.

"That right, Claude?" Billings asked, the hint of a smile playing at the corners of his mouth. "This fellow make you nervous?"

"Yessir," Claude said, delivering his lines as well as ever. "His behavior was alarming, disturbing, and disruptive to my clientele."

Billings looked over at Herman 'Babe' Baker and Paulie Ryan, the two morning drinkers who were propped up at the far end of the bar, nursing their beers, looking utterly indifferent to the proceedings. "All *two* of 'em?" he asked.

"That's right, Cap'n," Claude said. "Mister Jade went over and greeted this guy, and he went and stomped on Mister Jade's foot for no good reason. Mister Jade was just defending himself."

"What a f—" began Valletti, but Billings cut him off.

"You'll get your chance to make a full statement, Mister Valletti."

A dark green Plymouth pulled up behind the

parked police cruisers. The engine shut off, and a sturdy-looking young man in a dark suit climbed out. He gave the guy sitting on the sidewalk a curious look, nudged his hat back with a fingertip and asked Billings: “What do we have here?”

“Nothing much.” Billings gestured toward Valletti. “Somebody started a fight.” He nodded toward Jade. “Oscar, I’d like you to meet Detective Connor. Detective, this is Oscar Jade.”

Connor stepped forward, shook Jade’s hand with an extra squeeze, grinned broadly and flashed his shiny tin shield with a little too much self-satisfaction for Jade’s taste. “Call me Rusty,” Connor said. “I’ve heard a lot about you, Jade. You know, you’re kind of a legend back at the station house.”

“Swell,” Jade replied.

Valletti stared at Connor. “I wanna talk to a lawyer.”

“Yeah, sure, pal,” Connor said. He put a hand on Billings’ shoulder. “I can handle this.”

Billings shrugged and nodded. “Book him…but first take him to the hospital and have that head looked at.”

“I mean, I wanna talk to a lawyer *right now*,” Valletti insisted.

“You’ll get your lawyer.” Connor grinned as he hoisted Valletti up, cuffed him and put him into the Plymouth’s back seat. He backed out and pulled away, followed by the other two cops in their cruiser. Claude retreated into the Pelican.

“What’s with the kid?” asked Jade.

“Just made detective a couple months ago.” Billings chuckled. “He’s pretty bright, and he’s a go-getter. Wants to make a name for himself. Reminds me of someone else I used to know, once upon a time."

Jade frowned.

"Oscar...what the hell's going on here?"

"I have no idea," said Jade.

"Got something cooking?"

Jade shrugged. "I'm working. Matrimonial stuff."

"This have anything to do with that?"

"Good question."

"Matrimonial, huh?"

"That's right."

Billings shook his head. "You're better than that, Oscar."

"Gotta make a living," Jade said.

"Word around town is that times have been tough."

"Times have been tough for everybody."

"You could've stayed on the force, you know."

"I'm not a desk man, Al."

Billings frowned. "No shit," he said, got in his car and drove off.

The Pelican's twenty-five-foot-long tavern bar—and the fixture behind it, which held row after row of both premium and cheap spirits—had been carved from old hardwood from the Black Forest of Germany in the mid-1800s, and had crossed the ocean at the turn of the century, as Claude happily told every newcomer to the establishment who would listen. It had spent its first several decades of service in a tavern in Raleigh, North Carolina, before Claude had purchased it on the cheap in 1929 during the throes of a federal liquor prohibition he had been rightly convinced could not last forever. If furniture could talk, Claude would say to his customers with a wink, this bar would certainly get one hell of a lot of people in serious trouble. Oscar Jade, sitting on his usual barstool, would surely be one of those people.

He checked his watch. It was 1:00 PM—about a half hour since the cops had removed Valletti from the premises, an hour and a half since he'd first met Myrna Mallory, about twenty-four hours since the '4-F' had become official. At least his hangover was gone.

"...And in the world of sports, Cleveland Indians star pitcher Bobby Feller has announced that he has enlisted in the United States Navy," the radio announcer said. "The news had baseball owners reeling at their meetings today in Chicago..."

"That's bad news for the Indians," Claude observed as he drew a beer from the tap and slid it toward Jade.

The lunch crowd was lighter than usual, just like the traffic on Ocean Drive. It had been the same yesterday, when they'd sat with a few regulars and listened while Roosevelt declared war on Japan. Everybody was on edge. There was talk about what the war was going to do to the vacation business in South Florida. And in-between the grim news breaks on the radio, where the death toll at Pearl Harbor got bigger each hour, the Hit Parade played on; songs like "White Cliffs of Dover," "Take the 'A' Train" and "I Don't Want to Set the World on Fire" gave a temporary illusion that everything was okay.

But it *was* an illusion. The world had gone crazy, and everyone knew it. The headlines shouted: ENEMY PLANES NEAR NEW YORK. The Associated Press said that "hostile aircraft" were reported "two hours out of New York City at noon today." On the other side of the country, San Francisco had blown its air raid sirens twice during the previous night. Japanese planes had reportedly been spotted over Panama. The Canadians said the Japanese had forces just off the Aleutian Islands, near Alaska. Berlin radio said the Japanese were advancing in northern Thailand toward the Burma Road. Meanwhile, Hitler had promised Japan that he'd have control of the French Vichy naval fleet by the end of the year. A senator from Florida announced that it was "just a matter of time" before congress extended the declaration of war to include Germany and Italy. Given all this, it felt better to talk baseball.

"Of course the navy took Feller," Jade said disgustedly. "They want the Yankees to get to the series again next year."

"You know, you're gonna have to quit being sore at the navy pretty soon." Claude nodded toward Jade's foot. "You shoulda known they'd be taking all the kids first...the young bucks who can run the hundred yard dash. Paper says they were turning away four out of every five guys, for cryin' out loud."

"Yeah." Jade stared into his beer. "Right."

"All right, you win." Claude shrugged. "I won't

talk about it no more."

"I appreciate that." Jade took a bite out of the ham salad sandwich Claude had made him, and washed it down with a long drink of beer. "How's our guest?"

"She's lying down. In the spare room."

Jade filled his friend in on what she'd said. "What do you think?"

"I think she's on the level," Claude said. "Scared, for sure. Plus, you got the muscle from New York. There's something going on here."

"I figured her for hysterical until she grew a tail. That son of a bitch isn't playing around."

"She might be right about the gambling angle," Claude said. "Makes sense. People get stupid with that stuff."

"Must be a whole *lot* of money if this Mallory guy's getting his face rearranged. Local boys don't want that kind of heat."

"Yeah, but out-of-towners won't give a shit." Claude wiped down the bar while he talked. "They can make a mess, and then leave. You better be careful, Oscar. New York's the major leagues."

"Something doesn't square up," said Jade. "If Mallory is the one who owes the money…" he paused and looked at Claude, who looked like he was thinking the same thing. "You think they want to grab her, or—"

"Or at least they want Mallory to know they can if they want," Claude finished.

"But they won't know she's running away from her husband."

"Won't matter, will it? They'll figure Mallory will

pay to get her back. If he can't pay, then…"

Jade remembered the desperation in Myrna's voice—and the tears, which had irritated him at the time. There was nothing worse than a woman bawling. It always made him feel as if he was being manipulated. "She needs protection, all right," he said. "But not just from her husband. There's something else."

"What'd you ask for?"

"Twenty a day."

Claude raised his eyebrows.

"I was trying to put her off," Jade said defensively. "How was I supposed to know she was going to show me three hundred? And it looks like there's more where that came from."

"Maybe you should have asked for thirty."

"Maybe you're right…and you know what's funny? If that asshole had stomped on my foot before she paid me, I'd probably be doing it for free."

Claude grinned. "And you don't do matrimonial work."

"Never again," said Jade. "No more peeking in hotel windows for a living, no matter what. This is different."

Claude's grin faded. "Yeah. I think it is," he said, and hung the bar rag on a hook. "You know, if her husband can find her anywhere, he can sure as hell find her here. And so can the out-of-towners."

"Yeah," Jade agreed, and finished his beer.

Upstairs in the spartan, single-room flop where he lived, Oscar Jade positioned the stiff leather holster in the small of his back, inside the waistband of his trousers. He drew his snub-nosed Smith & Wesson 'Military & Police' .38 Special, swung out the cylinder and used the ejector to kick the six rounds of ammo into the palm of his hand. He put them on the nightstand, cleaned and oiled the weapon, swung the cylinder closed, aimed the piece and smoothly squeezed through six empty *clicks*. Then he reloaded it and returned it to the holster. He put on a tan suit coat and a dark brown fedora.

"So, it's business as usual, right?" Claude said with a wink when Jade reemerged from the door behind the bar. "No undesirables."

"Absolutely. Which reminds me..." Jade reached into his pocket and withdrew the money Myrna had given him. He counted off five twenties and put them on the bar. "Put that on my account."

Claude picked up the cash and stuck it in his pocket. "Thanks, boss."

"Sorry about wasting that beer."

"S'okay," Claude replied. "I charged you for it."

3
Sole Beneficiary

Oscar Jade owned a cream-colored Ford roadster convertible, which he'd bought brand new in 1935 with every cent he'd had at the time, and which continued to consume every spare dime he collected. It came out the third year Ford had put out the Flathead V-8: a big engine on a small chassis, with good acceleration from a dead stop and an ability to run full out for hours on end. Jade had a friend in the police garage who'd been a willing accomplice in modifying the car for speed over the past few years, as money allowed: a dual exhaust system, an over-bored block, outsized pistons, an enlarged carburetor, and finally a custom-modified McCulloch supercharger. A racing suspension and custom brakes had been added a few months ago, and Jade was now reasonably confident that the Ford could get him out of anything he might get himself into. He knew for a fact that it was faster than any police car in Miami-Dade County, and he drove it with practiced abandon.

Jade heaved open the garage door to Ocean Drive, got into his car and fired up the engine, relishing the throaty-deep rumbling of the roadster's dual exhaust. A few moments later he was motoring past the emerald-green grounds of the municipal golf course on Lincoln Road, top down, the dry December breeze tugging at his hair. He turned right on Lenox and parked in the middle of the block, in front of a modest commercial building that hosted—along with a shoe store and a realtor—a small office with the words "Mutual Trust Insurance Company" painted on its smoked-glass door.

Its front desk was attended to by a severe-looking older woman Jade guessed might well have taken San Juan Hill alongside the Rough Riders, had she only been born a man…which appeared, upon further inspection, to have been a near thing. "Good afternoon," she said, the civility of her greeting served out in a single, precisely measured teaspoon. "How may I help you?"

"Hello. I'm interested in purchasing a life insurance policy. I've been told to ask for Mister Halliwood."

Chester P. Halliwood was a thin, round-shouldered man who was probably forty years old but looked at least ten years older. He welcomed Jade into his office warmly, but cooled somewhat when he saw the P.I. credentials.

"I don't know what you're after, Mister Jade," he said. "And I'm not sure how much I can tell you. My clients expect their business with me to remain confidential."

Jade gave him an easy smile as they sat down on

opposite sides of Halliwood's desk. "So do mine," he said. "And it always does. You can be assured of my discretion."

"What seems to be the problem?" asked Halliwood, who fiddled with various objects on his desk: an ink-pen, an inscribed marble paperweight and his desk blotter, none of which he could seemingly position to his satisfaction.

Jade watched him intently, keeping his smile fixed. He waited until the insurance man looked him in the eye before he spoke. "What makes you think there's a problem, Mister Halliwood?"

Halliwood half dropped the paperweight as he set it down. He folded his hands together, where they fidgeted with each other instead. "Well, I'm not used to having private detectives asking me about my business, that's all."

"That's a nice paperweight," Jade said. "What does it say?"

"It says, 'Honesty is the best policy.'"

"What a lovely sentiment."

Halliwood looked up from the paperweight. "What…can I do for you?"

"I'd like some information about a specific policy you sold, about a week ago," Jade said. "Horace Mallory. He bought a life insurance policy, in the amount of fifty thousand dollars."

Halliwood looked up at the ceiling, as if in deep thought. "Mallory…hmm…"

"How many fifty thousand dollar policies did you sell last week, Mister Halliwood?"

"It *was* a busy week, actually." He pointed at a plaque hanging on the wall behind his desk. "I'm the number one salesman in my district, so—"

"The policy was on his wife. It named him as sole beneficiary in the event of her death."

"I don't think I recall such a transaction," Halliwood said.

"Hmm." Jade pulled the papers Myrna had given him from the breast pocket of his suit coat. "Fortunately, I have the document right here. Maybe this will refresh your memory." He pushed them across the desk. "That's your signature, isn't it? Right next to Mr. Mallory's."

The insurance man gazed down at the document. "Ah, yes, of course. Mallory. How stupid of me. How… er…did you come to be in possession of his policy?"

Jade spread his hands. "That brings us back to confidentiality and discretion, doesn't it?"

Halliwood smiled weakly. "Yes. I suppose it does."

Jade leaned forward in his chair. "Want to know what's worse than having a private detective asking about your business, Mr. Halliwood? Sending him away more curious than he was when he showed up. See, I can be pretty stubborn. What you *don't* want is for me to make you my personal hobby. I can find out things about how you do business that'll make it hell for you to open your doors in the morning. You might have all kinds of problems. Might even get audited, who knows? Bottom line is, you'll wish you'd just come clean early on, when you had the chance. So instead, let's keep this nice, okay? I can be a good friend. I might even be able to do you a favor at some point, if you treat me right. But if you sit here and try to play canasta with me, you're gonna have problems. That I can guarantee."

"There's no need for that," Halliwood stammered.

Jade smiled thinly. "I'll decide that for myself, thanks."

"Look, Mister Jade. I'll help anyway I can."

"Well, I sure appreciate that. Now, was Mrs. Mallory with her husband when you drew up the policy?"

"No, but he assured me that she was fully aware of it. I had no reason to believe otherwise."

"Was there a second policy...one on Mallory himself?"

"No—at least, not with us," Halliwood said. "I asked him, naturally, since we offer a discounted rate for multiple policies. But he said it wasn't necessary. I just assumed he already had coverage with another carrier. It *was* strange, though, now that you mention it."

"How so?"

"Well, Mr. Mallory approached me on the street at five fifteen in the evening—we close at five. He came up to me while I was locking the front door. He insisted that it had to be taken care of right away, that it couldn't even wait until the next morning. Well, I get odd customers all the time, you know, and besides, it was a good sale. So I let him in and we wrote it up. He was a nice enough fellow, but pushy—you know, a guy who's used to getting his way. If he asked me once, he asked me ten times if the policy took effect once he signed the papers and paid for the policy. Then he wanted to know how long it took to process a claim."

"That's interesting."

"Well, his check was good," said the insurance man. "Sure, it was queer, but that's not exactly illegal, is it?"

"Not exactly," Jade agreed.

Danny Pettone, as legend had it, had been a numbers runner in Milwaukee in the 1920s, working for an extended finger of the Capone organization. When things had begun to unravel for Capone (so the story went), Pettone had seized an opportunity and attempted to abscond with two weeks' take from the numbers operation in the greater Milwaukee area, which amounted to a few thousand dollars. Frank Nitti's men had reportedly caught up with him in Chicago in late December just as he was about to catch a train south with the cash. They'd ushered him out of Union Station and kept him in a basement somewhere until well after midnight. Then they'd taken him to a lot on the south side where a number of evergreens were on display for purchase as Christmas trees. They'd stripped Pettone naked and handcuffed him to the largest tree on the lot, which they then adorned with tinsel and ornaments. Nitti's men had taken turns urinating on Pettone while he shivered in the freezing-cold midwestern air, then left him alone for the night. Apparently Pettone lost two toes—the smallest one on each foot—to frostbite. Less charitable speculation was that he'd lost other things to the cold as well. He'd gotten the name 'Tinsel' because—if the best stories were to be believed—the frozen piss had caused the decorative silver strands to stick all over his body as he'd struggled vainly to free himself. Supposedly, despite being near death, he'd looked quite festive upon his eventual discovery the following morning by a young couple and their two children who arrived at the lot before the salespeople. They'd been eager to find a last-minute Christmas tree bargain. What they found instead might well have ruined the holiday for them forever.

So far as Jade knew, he was the only one south of St. Louis who called Pettone 'Tinsel' to his face—and even he only did so when he had a gripe with him.

Tinsel worked out of the back of Brumly's, a small neighborhood grocery store on 78th Street in North Miami Beach. Jade parked the roadster on the opposite side of the street and hurried across, the pain in his foot barking like an angry dog with each step. A couple of shoppers were browsing the produce baskets lined up just outside the store's front window, and they both turned to watch as Jade dodged between cars. His clubfoot always drew attention he could have done without: variations of curiosity and pity, each of which angered him equally. But he smiled amiably as he limped onto the curb. Like the pain itself, the stares were a fact of life best ignored, since nothing could be done about either one.

There was another customer inside, an older lady, over by the canned goods. Joe Brumly, the owner, was stocking the candy counter near the register. He was about sixty years old, rotund and bald, with a bulbous nose that always reminded Jade of W.C. Fields. He grinned widely as Jade came through the door. "Hiya, there, Oscar! How the heck are ya?"

"Doing just fine, Joe," he said, and shook the offered hand. In a lower voice, he said, "Tinsel back there?"

"Oh, yeah," said Brumly offhandedly. "Busy as ever." He reached over the counter and pressed a button underneath.

In the rear of Brumly's store was a tiny stockroom, with shelves of extra product waiting to be moved forward. At the far end of this room was a locked door, which was only opened when the man behind it deemed it prudent to do so. It opened now, and Jade stepped through.

It was a windowless, smoky space; a tiny, oblong room with more activity and noise than it should have been able to hold. Three tired-looking guys feverishly worked eight telephones, scribbled notes and thumbtacked them to the walls—each note a bet on a horse or dog race, a college or professional football or basketball game, or maybe a boxing match—all overseen by the slightly dumpy middle-aged man with the forever-untucked shirt. "Jade," Tinsel said, more of a statement than a greeting.

"Hello, Danny," Jade replied. "How's business?"

"I tell ya, I need more help, I need more telephones. It's just nonstop, day in and day out. Money's okay, but I'm killin' myself here, I swear to God, I'm killin' myself. I need to take a vacation."

Jade grinned. Tinsel did everything fast: he talked fast, he smoked fast, and he walked fast (it would be more accurate to say he *scurried*). He even breathed fast, through an open mouth with dried spittle in its corners, during the brief moments he wasn't talking. He also sweated profusely—even now, during the relatively cool winter months when the temperature rarely climbed into the eighties. The dried sweat had crusted into his dark shirt as jagged white stains around the armpits.

"How about taking a break for a minute," Jade said. "I got something for you."

"Yeah, sure, yeah." Tinsel wiped a filthy rag across his moist forehead. "Don't mind if I do."

Out on the street in front of Brumly's, Jade offered him a cigarette and they both had a smoke. Along with the Lucky, Jade handed him a twenty-dollar bill. Tinsel tucked it away without comment.

"Know anything about a guy named Horace Mallory?" asked Jade.

"You kidding?" Tinsel took several quick drags on the cigarette, puffing like a steam locomotive. "Everybody in the business knows Mallory. He's into everything, in a big way."

"That's what I hear. How much do you know?"

Tinsel grinned slyly. His false teeth were as unconvincing as the black rug on top of his head, or the dyed black pencil-thin mustache on his sweaty upper lip. "How much do you *want* to know?"

"I want to know how much money he owes to guys like you," Jade said.

Tinsel burst out laughing. "That's good," he said. "That's rich."

"How do you mean?"

"You are kidding, right, Jade? I mean, you gotta be kidding."

Jade stared at him.

"Okay, okay. Sorry. Normally I assume a guy like

you's in the loop on stuff like this. Thing is, Mallory's one of the biggest players in town. Not as a customer, though. You know he runs the Caribbean Hotel, right? Well, what you see ain't everything you get, if you know what I mean."

"Pretend I *don't* know what you mean."

"He's got an operation," said Tinsel. "A nice one, too. Gambling, all kinds, plus broads...in every price range."

"I heard he lost a lot of money on the World Series," Jade said.

Tinsel was smug. "If he did, he ain't the only one. I figured Brooklyn might take 'em, too. But I wasn't dumb enough to bet on 'em myself, so it was a pretty good series for me. Never bet against the Yanks."

"Maybe it was a *lot* of money," Jade said, more to himself than to Tinsel.

"Whatever Mallory lost on the Dodgers, he ought to be able to afford it. The guy's lousy with cash. The bottom line is, Mallory don't owe people. People owe Mallory."

"So does Mallory have a boss?" Jade asked him.

"Sure he does. Everybody's got a boss," Tinsel said darkly. "But who knows who?"

"See if you can find out." Jade pulled out another twenty and handed it to him.

"Jesus," Tinsel said. "I don't know, Jade. Mallory's not one of the local boys. He's competition. Word is he's got out-of-state backing. I wouldn't know where to start."

"Sure you would," said Jade, handing him a third twenty. "I'll check back with you in a day or so."

"Yeah, yeah, okay," Tinsel said nervously. "I'll

see what I can do."

"Anything else you can tell me? I hear he stays out late. Any idea where he spends his leisure time?"

"You mean, when he's not counting his money?" Tinsel grinned, obviously feeling more buoyant with fresh greenbacks of his own in his pocket. "One of my boys tends bar at the Marmalade Club at night. He sees Mallory there all the time, sniffing around one of the dancers. Young broad named Greta."

4
The Caribbean

They'd started to build hotels bigger in Miami Beach a few years back, especially along Collins Avenue. Instead of two or three floors, they were eight or ten stories high, changing the look of the town and casting new shadows across the beach in the afternoon and evening. These hotels were in the new style—Jade had read about it once in *Life* magazine, without much interest—'Modernist,' it was called: rounded corners and windows, fancy carved stonework and streamlined ledges. They were mostly white, but were trimmed in pale colors like pink, blue and yellow. The Caribbean was one of these. Nine stories tall, white, trimmed in seafoam green and topped with a curving parapet that looked like the sail of an eighteenth-century sea vessel, it was an impressive joint that caught your eye as it faced the Atlantic over the roofs of the smaller buildings along the beachfront. As more and more of the big hotels sprouted up like weeds, more and more of the old beach went away.

Jade circled the block twice before parking near the corner of Collins and 19th Street. He bought a newspaper from a stand, sat down on a nearby bench and pretended to read the paper as he watched the traffic moving through the hotel's front door, where uniformed valets and bellhops attended to cars arriving beneath a curved ledge. Atop this ledge, the word *Caribbean* was proclaimed in sweeping fancy neon tubes, which made the hotel's name glow bright green after the sun went down.

After about twenty minutes Jade got up, tucked the paper beneath his arm, and made his way around the corner. He found the entrance to the alley and made a pass by the hotel's service entrance and loading dock, where a tough-looking guy in a suit stood watch. He was maybe twenty years old, stupid and mean looking, built like an oak tree from the ground up; narrow at the waist and broad through the shoulders, with a neck like a bull and confident dark eyes beneath a protruding brow. He gave Jade a wary stare; Jade gave a friendly nod and limped past.

He rounded the far corner of the hotel and stopped there, his back to the wall. Over the course of just a few minutes, three cars came and went, either dropping off or picking up. It was an unusual amount of movement for the rear of a hotel at this time of day—Jade checked his watch; it was 4:40 PM, just starting to get dark—and he figured it would get a hell of a lot busier at night. The very fact that Mallory had muscle guarding the back door was a dead giveaway.

On either side of the Caribbean's foyer were bas-relief stone friezes depicting old sailing ships arriving on tropical shores with palm trees and flamingos. The lobby itself was clean and expansive, with a bright terrazzo mosaic floor and colorful murals of beach scenes on the walls. To the right of the front desk, a curving stairway disappeared into the ceiling. A silver metal-and-glass hand railing cascaded down its perimeter like a frozen waterfall.

Jade approached the desk and gave the serious young man at the front desk a wide smile. "I'd like to see Mister Mallory, please."

The response was quick, easy, and well practiced. "I'm sorry, but he's not available. Would you like to leave a message?"

"No thanks," said Jade. "I'll try back later."

He stepped off to one side, unfolded his newspaper and read for a couple of minutes until someone else approached the desk and engaged the clerk's attention. Then he simply turned and headed up the stairs. When he got to the second floor he reached into his pocket, took out his keys and carried them casually in his hand, just as any guest of the hotel might hold their room key.

He walked the length of the second floor hallway, past the elevator. At the opposite end was a doorway marked 'Service Stairs.' Jade opened the door and stepped through. It was a narrow, utilitarian stairwell with painted metal handrails and a naked light bulb on the wall above the landing. Jade leaned over the rail and gazed up the narrow space between the flights of stairs, which extended the height of the hotel's interior, and then looked down into what would be the building's basement. He watched for hands on the railing, and listened for any sign of traffic in the stairwell. There was none. He waited for a couple of minutes, then went downstairs.

He came out into the empty first floor hallway. The door at the end of the hall would be the service entrance to the alley, where the muscle was standing guard outside. Jade opened the door and said, "Hey, Mac."

The guy turned around. His eyes narrowed and he stiffened up. Jade knew he recognized him from the alley.

"This is my first time here," said Jade. "Where's the fun at?"

"Who the hell are you?" the guard demanded. His hand went inside his jacket.

Jade raised his hands. "Easy, there, Tom Mix. The boss sent me by to check on the security situation," he said smoothly. "Don't worry, you did fine. Can't say the same for the guy up front. Gonna have to have a talk with him…and he ain't gonna like it." He took out his pack of Luckies, tapped two out and handed one to the guard, who—after giving him a good, long look—left his rod in his coat and took the smoke. Jade lit it for him, and then his own. "Been rumors that things have gotten sloppy. That's why I'm here."

"Who says?"

"Boss hears stuff, that's all. If he doesn't like what he hears, he sends me down to have a look-see, and check things out. That way, things get fixed before they get worse. God forbid somebody drops the ball for real, know what I mean?"

"What boss you talking about?"

"Mallory's boss," replied Jade. "Why? Who'd you

think I meant?"

"Never mind," said the muscle-head uneasily.

Jade took a drag on his smoke and grinned. "See? That's good. You're testing me. That's what I'm talking about. We need guys who ain't afraid to use their brains…'course, some of 'em ain't got any, but there you go."

"Well, *nobody* gets by me," the muscle-head said.

"And I can see why. What's your name?"

"Freddie."

"Nice to meet you, Freddie." Jade extended a hand, and Freddie shook it. "So how's business, anyway?"

Freddie jerked his head toward the hotel. "They don't tell us stuff like that. But it's been slower the past couple days, that's for sure. You know, with the war, and all."

"Yeah, sure, that figures. Any action at the tables?"

"Not much. Better at night, and on the weekends."

Jade nodded, and wondered how far he could move the ball downfield. "Well, I don't have to catch the train until tomorrow morning," he said. "Food any good?"

"Hell, yeah. Best steak dinner in town."

"Think I'll have any luck at blackjack?"

Freddie grinned. "Don't see why not. The boss's boys always do pretty well."

"So where is it?" asked Jade. "Top floor?"

Freddie's brow creased with uncertainty. "You don't know where it is?"

"Hey, cut me some slack, would ya? I just got into

town. Never been here before. I always check the outside before I go inside. Makes sense, don't it?"

It looked like Freddie had some lingering doubt, and Jade prepared himself to make a move if things went south. The most obvious one would be to take Freddie here, put a gun in his back, and demand to be taken to Mallory's office. Or he could play it rough, make the guy miserable until he spilled the beans, tie him up and stow him in a janitor's closet. That would buy him a few minutes, but he wouldn't have any spare time to see the setup.

But finally Freddie shrugged. "Yeah," he said. "Sure. Fourth floor."

"What room?"

"All of 'em."

Jade was impressed. "Really?"

"Yeah. 'Course, most of 'em are for the broads. But you got cards in 401, 403 and 405; craps in 402; roulette in 404. You get the idea. Take the elevator to four. The guy who meets you is gonna tell you it's a private party. Just give him these numbers..."

"Forty-two, thirty-nine, fifty-six," Jade said to the burly, olive-skinned goon who stood in front of the elevator door when it opened. The guy was a few inches taller than Jade, and outweighed him by at least a hundred pounds.

"Good afternoon, sir," he said, and stepped aside.

It might have passed for a private party if you

were a dim-witted tourist down from Hoboken for a week's vacation, or a sap who'd just pressed the wrong elevator button. Anybody else with eyes could see that something was going on. A Tommy Dorsey tune played softly from a jukebox next to a full-service bar. The lights were turned down low. Guys in nice suits, with slinky dames on their arms, swilled champagne and smoked cigars. Jade bought a beer at the bar, and took a long drink.

Freddie was right. Things were slow now, but they were expecting more traffic any time. Rackets that didn't make big money were never this well staffed. Right now, employees outnumbered gamblers two to one.

The doors to the rooms with games stood wide open, guarded by watchful guys in suits who looked Jade up and down. He gave each of them a nod and a stupid grin: *That's right, pal. I'm just another mark, and a lame one at that. You can relax.*

He followed the telltale jingling and jangling of coins. The slot machines, two rows of six lined up back to back, had a room of their own. An old lady wearing a feathered hat that looked like a bird's nest was working three of them with feverish purpose. She gave Jade a wary gaze as he tried one of the machines on the opposite side. He fed it a nickel and pulled the handle. Nothing. One of hers paid off, nickels clattering happily into a metal receptacle. She gave him a knowing, superior smile. Jade tipped his hat and moved on.

He sipped his beer and watched a few hands of poker in one of the card rooms, the only one with any activity: six guys playing very intently, with a large pile of cash in the center of the table and no attention to spare for the half-dozen spectators. A skinny guy with a red bow tie lost five hundred bucks without blinking an eye, and pulled more money from his wallet.

The two blackjack rooms were unoccupied, but held eight kidney-shaped tables, four in each, the green baize awaiting the coming night's business. The dealer at the table nearest the door asked Jade, "Care to try your luck, buddy? Minimum's a buck." Jade shrugged and took a seat. He got a jack of clubs and a five. Fifteen. The dealer had the ace of spades showing. Jade took a hit, and the dealer threw him an eight. Bust. The dealer took his dollar. "Try again?"

"Sure," Jade said casually. "Why not?" He put down one of Myrna Mallory's five-spots. He got a four, and the king of hearts. Fourteen. The dealer had a two of clubs showing. "Hit me," Jade said. The dealer tossed him a three, to make seventeen. "I'll stay."

The dealer drew himself the ace of hearts, then a nine. He paused, glanced at Jade, and drew a seven. He turned over his facedown card: the three of clubs. Twenty-two. The dealer paid out five dollars. "One more?"

Jade took the ten bucks off the table and tucked it into a pocket. "No thanks," he said.

In another room, there were four people shooting craps on one of the two tables. Three people huddled around a roulette wheel in another.

The last stop in his reconnaissance was room 406. Jade smelled the rich blend of perfumes from a mile away. An elegantly dressed middle-aged woman who once upon a time must have been a real head-turner—and who used every available means to maximize what she had left—met him just inside the door. Six very attractive young women, in various shapes, sizes and colors, sat in chairs along the wall behind her.

"Hey there, sweetie," she said. "See anything I can do for you?"

Jade looked at each of the girls in turn; only a couple of them looked him in the eye. They were all pretty, but it was a tired, hollowed-out kind of pretty—the kind that wouldn't last long at the rate they were using it up. If you looked close enough, you could already see the cracks beginning to show, revealing a grim desperation that crouched, like a beaten dog, behind their painted-on smiles. It was the sort of thing you never see at midnight, when you're drunk...but it wasn't midnight, and Oscar Jade wasn't drunk.

"Not today, thanks," he said.

Jade took the elevator to the first floor and headed toward the front of the hotel. He figured the manager's office would be behind one of the two doors marked "Private" that he'd noticed near the front desk, and it was, but he picked the wrong door first and interrupted a mousy-looking accountant shuffling papers in front of an oak filing cabinet. "What the—" the mouse stuttered, but by then Jade had closed that door and entered the one across the hall, moving as quickly as his limp would allow, passing by the secretary who tried to slow him down with an ineffectual “Sir, sir, he’s not in…er, he’s busy…” as he strode past her desk with a quick smile and opened the door with the engraved brass plate that said ‘Manager.’

The man who looked up from his desk might have been a car salesman or a politician, but was obviously comfortable in his pressed white shirt and brown suspenders. The knot of his tie was snug and perfect at his collar. His suitcoat hung on a wooden valet in a corner of the office. The lingering green discoloration around one eye hinted at the bruising Myrna had talked about.

“What the hell do you want?” asked Horace Mallory. His voice was casual, but his eyes told a different story. “I don’t know you,” he said.

“You will,” Jade said, closing the door behind him. “Nice place you’ve got here, Mister Mallory. Looks like a real moneymaker. How much do you take in during a good week?”

“What—what do you want?” Mallory asked again. He grasped the rear edge of his desk with both hands. “I don’t have anything here.”

“Why do you think I’m here?” Jade asked him.

“I…don’t have any idea,” Mallory said.

Which was probably true, thought Jade, and suddenly he understood. Mallory was terrified. He looked like a guy who thought his number was up.

Jade looked him straight in the eye. “I don’t believe you,” he said. “I figure you probably have a few ideas…and none of them have a happy ending. Am I right?”

"Tell him I'm good for it," Mallory stammered. "I don't know how it happened, but I'm going to find out, and I'm going to fix it. It's not going to happen again. I'm going to hold up my end of the deal."

"Talk to your wife today?" asked Jade.

The question obviously blindsided him. Mallory couldn't hide his surprise. "No," he said.

Jade gave a thin smile. "I didn't think so."

"What are you saying?" The question had a peculiar tone as it left his mouth, like a phonograph record spinning just a little too fast.

"I'm saying she won't be coming home tonight, Mister Mallory," Jade said. "She wants her life back."

Mallory reached beneath his desk, making no effort to disguise the move.

Jade's right hand went to the butt of his holstered Smith & Wesson. "Easy does it, pal. If I were here to kill you, you'd be dead already. And if you pull anything funny out of that desk, I *will* kill you. I'll explain it all to the cops, and tell your wife she doesn't have to worry about you anymore…and then I'll sleep like a baby. Understand?"

Mallory nodded.

"I'm just here to give you a piece of friendly advice. Give the lady a divorce, and let her go."

Mallory smiled and said, "If only it was that easy."

The door behind Jade swung open, and the space inside the frame was completely filled by the big gorilla from the fourth floor. The big guy held a revolver in a sure, steady hand. Jade felt like an idiot. Mallory hadn't been reaching for a piece. He was calling for help.

"Don't shoot," Mallory said. His voice, quite suddenly, sounded calm—even amused. "We need him alive."

Jade put his hands up.

The big guy stepped into the room, with Freddie, from the alley entrance, trailing behind him.

"Hello, Freddie," said Jade.

Freddie glared as he took Jade's gun. The big guy closed the door.

"You know this guy, Freddie?" Mallory had fully recovered control of the situation.

"I didn't let him in through the back," Freddie said, a bit too quickly.

"He was upstairs," said the big guy. "On four. He knew the code."

Mallory looked back to Freddie.

"He got in through the front." Freddie's voice was desperate. "He said he worked for your boss."

"*My* boss." Mallory smiled. "Is that right?"

"That's what he said."

"And that was good enough for you."

The words hung in the air. Freddie looked at his own feet. His shoulders slumped, almost imperceptibly. Then, suddenly, he stepped forward and clubbed Jade in the ear with the butt of his own gun. Jade staggered sideways and fell across Mallory's desk.

"That's enough," said Mallory. "Not here."

Jade righted himself, put a hand to his ear, and looked at his fingertips. They were red. He looked at Freddie and grinned. "Good one," he said. "I owe you."

They each got a hold of one of his arms,

straightened them out and pulled them back, taut. Jade was lifted nearly off the floor. His good right foot could support his weight, on tiptoes, but his bad one could only reach the floor on its outside edge, and it howled at the strangely placed weight burden. The pain coiled up his leg like an angry snake and nested at the base of his skull, where it threatened to eat his brain whole. For a single, hateful moment, Oscar Jade could think of nothing else.

The big guy jammed the barrel of the Colt between Jade's shoulder blades.

"Go out the back." Mallory's tone was dismissive. "Take him to the place. When I get there, he'd better still be able to talk—and it's not just me who says so. Get it?"

"Yeah," the big guy said. He and Freddie manhandled Jade toward the door.

"And make it fast. I don't want a floor show out there."

"We'll talk again," Jade said to Mallory as he was hustled out the door.

"You bet we will," said Mallory as the door closed.

Jade was dragged quickly down the hallway, toward the door to the alley. Whatever "the place" was, Jade was certain he didn't want any part of it. Mallory had said they needed him to be able to talk. Hopefully that meant they wouldn't be too quick to shoot him.

"Oh, God," he said, as they got near the back door. "Jeez, guys. Hold on a second, would you? Can't you see I got a bad foot, here? Gimme a second..."

"Shut up," said the big guy, who kept him covered

with his gun. Freddie opened the door, and they moved out onto the concrete loading dock. Night had fallen. A single light, surrounded by buzzing insects, illuminated the rear entrance.

Jade allowed his foot to give way, forcing Freddie to carry more of his weight. Freddie let him go, and Jade fell to his knees between the two men. The cry of pain was only half show biz. He let his head hang low, but watched carefully out of the corners of his eyes, measured the proximity of his targets, and began to gather his focus and resolve.

"Goddamn cripple," Freddie said disgustedly.

The big guy had the Colt's barrel about six inches from Jade's head. He glanced over at Freddie and said, "Go get the car. I'll—"

In all likelihood, the big guy had intended to say that he would keep an eye on Jade while Freddie fetched the car, but he didn't finish the sentence, because Jade had already grabbed at the big guy's crotch, clutched his testicles firmly, squeezed with everything he had, and yanked sharply downward.

The big guy's jaw went slack, and he made a soft "aaaaah" sound as he dropped to his knees. The Colt Police Positive fell out of his hand, forgotten. Freddie was fumbling with Jade's .38. Jade swung his left leg out behind Freddie's feet, and gave a quick hard shove. Freddie fell backwards off the loading dock, his arms flailing, and landed flat on his back in the alley. His head snapped back and hit the pavement with a dull thud.

The big guy was still on his knees, clutching at himself, his eyes bulging. Jade stood up and raised his right hand—stiffened like a knife blade—and brought the outer edge of it down with all the force he could muster on the offered spot between the big guy's shoulder and the base of his neck. The collarbone broke cleanly. The big guy collapsed, spilling to one side like an oak tree going down.

Jade grabbed the Colt and put it in his suit pocket. He took the steps at the end of the loading dock and limped to where Freddie still lay on his back. Freddie, looking dazed, was trying to raise himself to his elbows. Jade picked up his own gun, which was just out of Freddie's reach, and smashed it hard across the man's nose. He wiped the blood off on Freddie's trouser leg, and holstered the weapon. Then he took Freddie's gun, a Colt identical to the one the big guy carried, and put it in his other suit pocket.

"You just got your ass kicked by a cripple," Jade told him. "I think you're gonna be in Dutch with the boss."

Oscar Jade limped away, down the dark alley, in the general direction of his parked car.

5
Greta

Jade parked the roadster near Mr. Ted's, a bar on Euclid Avenue. He found a space on the street, as far as possible from the nearest streetlight, and set about cleaning up the bloody mess made by a lousy little cut across the top of his left ear. He took a half-pint bottle of Jim Beam out from beneath the driver's seat and used it to moisten the corner of a handkerchief. Jade dabbed at the wound and ignored the sharp sting, cleaning away the blood that had gotten into his hair and run down his neck. He glanced at his reflection in the rearview mirror. Not too bad—only a little on his collar, and a couple of drops on the lapel of his suitcoat. With any luck, it wasn't enough to turn any heads in a darkened room. He'd just smell like booze. Like anyone else who'd been there a while.

He took a swig of the Beam for good measure and sighed with satisfaction, relishing the warmth it gave him on the way down. He screwed the lid back on and tucked the bottle away. A panel in the driver's-side door came off to provide access to a hidden compartment. Jade dropped the two purloined Colt revolvers inside and replaced the panel. Inside Mr. Ted's, he found a payphone and plunked a nickel into the slot.

Jade called the Miami Beach P.D. and asked for Billings, knowing he'd still be there even though shifts had changed more than an hour ago. The desk sergeant told him to hold. After about a minute, Billings answered. "That Valletti fellow you roughed up this morning made bail inside an hour, Oscar. He's got pricey representation."

"I'm guessing he's got a rap sheet, too."

"Just minor stuff—misdemeanor assault, mostly, but he's been clean since '32. His shyster has a letter authorizing him to carry a piece in the state of Florida. So he's legal, as far as that goes. What the hell's going on here?"

"That's a good question," Jade replied. "I got one for you too: how big is the New York mob on the beach?"

"How do you mean?"

"Gambling. Broads."

There was a long pause. "They're around. Just like anyplace else."

Jade told him about the Caribbean. "The manager's name is Horace Mallory. Know him?"

"Can't say I do."

"Well, I hear he's got friends. You don't run an operation like that without buying some cops along the way."

"I don't like what you're getting at."

"Prove me wrong and I'll apologize," Jade said. "They're pretty damn casual about the whole thing. Smells funny, catch my drift?"

"I'll have a look-see tomorrow. What does Valletti have to do with all this?"

"I don't know yet, but I'm going to find out. Mallory's in money trouble, too—even got smacked around a couple of weeks back. Maybe that's the connection."

"Mallory, huh?" Jade knew the cop was scribbling the details down on paper. "Anything to do with that 'matrimonial' case you're working on?"

"No comment."

"I didn't think so." Billings was silent for a moment. "Tell you what, Oscar: if this guy's got his fingers in that many pies, and you get to be a problem for him—"

"Yeah," Jade said. "I know."

The Marmalade Club was on the corner of Collins and 22nd Street, just a couple of blocks away from the Caribbean Hotel. Far enough for some breathing room, but too close for comfort. Jade parked on Liberty Avenue, a block west, and pondered the wisdom of his next move. Making contact with the girl Tinsel had told him about was risky—but it probably wouldn't get any easier if he waited.

Mallory had been genuinely surprised to hear about his wife, and would not react well to the news that Jade hadn't hung around long enough to let

Freddie and the gorilla beat anything out of him. Even if Mallory didn't love his wife anymore (assuming he ever had), she seemed to mean more to him than a life insurance policy worth fifty grand, which begged the question: How much did Myrna *really* know about her husband's business? And where did Nino Valletti fit into the picture?

He glanced at his watch as he approached the front door of the Marmalade Club. Almost 7:30 PM. At least he'd earned today's twenty bucks.

Jade paid the fifty-cent cover charge at the door, and went inside. In the foyer was a large sign on an easel: *"THE MARMALADE CLUB PRESENTS: THE EXQUISITE MISS GRETA VINCENNES AND THE SPUN-GOLD REVUE! SHOWS AT 8:00, 10:00 AND 12:00 NIGHTLY."*

Well, that figured, thought Jade as he grabbed a stool at the bar and lit a smoke. When Mallory wasn't busy with the hotel, or the gambling and call girl operation, he was trying to make time with the Exquisite Miss Greta Vincennes. No wonder he never made it home in time for his wife's meatloaf.

Jade had only been to the Marmalade once or twice—and even then, only to make an arrest—so this was the first time he'd really paid any attention. The smell was the first thing you noticed: tobacco and perfume. It was a big room, an expansive, rectangular space with a low ceiling where recessed neon tubes provided dim light in shades of pink and blue. Two dozen round cocktail tables filled the floor, and upholstered leather booths lined two walls. The bar where Jade sat—a long, curving affair with a glossy black top and a lot of chrome—ran the length of the room. Fancy, sure, but he'd take the Pelican's timeworn, hand-carved hardwood any day. A guy couldn't get comfortably drunk in all this shiny, polished glitz.

A jazz quartet—bass, piano, drum kit and clarinet—softly played "One O'Clock Jump" on an elevated stage at the far end of the room, a background to the clutter of quiet conversation, the occasional outburst of laughter, and the tinkling of empty cocktail glasses as uniformed busboys lined them up at the end of the bar.

The place was less than half full, but this was the early show. Jade guessed the later shows would have a bigger crowd—then again, there *was* a war on, now. Who knew what that would do to business? Maybe nothing. People wouldn't want the Japs or Hitler to keep them home at night if they could help it. For two years, the newsreels and papers had shown the Nazis rolling through Czechoslovakia, Poland, France and the Netherlands, and dropping bombs on London. That the Japanese had been the ones to strike first had been a shock, but anyone who was truly surprised that the war had finally come to the States probably *ought* to stay home on a Tuesday night.

The bartender, a blond-haired young man wearing a crisp white shirt and a black bow tie, ambled over to him. "What can I get you?"

"You Marty?" Jade asked. The kid nodded. "My name's Jade. I'm a friend of Danny's. He tell you I was coming?" The kid nodded again. "Tell you what, Marty. What I need is a chance to talk to Greta."

"Jeez," Marty said with a laugh. "Get in line."

"How do you mean?"

"She's got company already." The bartender nodded toward a closed door near the restrooms marked 'Employees Only.' "It's a *cop*."

Jade cocked an eyebrow. "Who is it?"

"Don't know him. Plain-clothes, not a uniform. But they all look the same to me anyway. And they all smell like trouble."

Jade laughed.

"Your best bet is to wait until after the first show," Marty said. "See the guy in the suit over by the front door? That's Mannie—my boss. When the lights come back up, I'll call him over. While I'm talking to him, that's your chance. Follow the hallway. It'll make a right-hand turn, and you'll be backstage. Miss Vincennes' door is the first one on the left. There's a gold star on it. If you get caught, I don't know anything about it."

"Fair enough." Jade thanked him, ordered a draft beer, paid with eleven bucks and told him to keep the change. Marty nodded, and casually pocketed the ten-spot.

Jade kept an eye on the 'Employees Only' door, but nobody ever came out.

He had just finished his second beer when the quartet finished its last song at about five minutes to eight. The drum kit was broken down and quickly removed, the piano pushed behind the curtain, and a microphone on a stand placed at center stage. The lights went down, and the room got quiet.

A single spotlight illuminated the stage, where a tall, thin man with a waxy complexion and a pencil-thin mustache, dressed in a tuxedo, emerged from behind the burgundy-colored curtain. "Ladies and gentlemen," he said as he leered at the audience and motioned toward the curtain with outstretched hand, "The Marmalade Club is proud to present, for your entertainment pleasure: a glimpse of heaven, the temptress of the tease, the mistress of mystery—ladies and gentlemen, the incredible, exquisite Miss Greta Vincennes and her world-famous spun-gold revue!"

He moved offstage, taking the microphone stand with him, as the curtain opened to a round of applause.

Behind the curtain was a bigger band, a ten-piece swing outfit that went straight into "Temptation" as six showgirls in skimpy, glittery gold costumes, feather boas and tall gold and rhinestone studded headdresses danced their way to center stage, shoulder to shoulder: blondes, brunettes and redheads. They were all very lovely, with their shapely dancer's legs, fixed professional smiles and well-rehearsed moves, but they were clearly just window-dressing. When they parted in the middle, three on each side, they were quickly forgotten as the star of the show emerged and took center stage.

In each hand, she carried a very large fan made of what looked like golden peacock feathers, artfully positioned to reveal as little or as much as she chose. Initially, it was her legs—tanned, supple and perfectly sculpted—and her eyes, which even from across the room were an arresting, disconcertingly crystalline blue in the stark glare of the spotlight. She was quite tall, and her hair was golden blonde—spun gold, indeed—swept back away from her face and done up in large curls. She moved forward to the edge of the stage, her movements in perfect time to the music, as she smoothly shifted the two feather fans, affording the brief 'glimpse of heaven' to which the lascivious master of ceremonies must have been alluding: large, perfectly-formed breasts, each tipped by a golden-tasseled pasty, a narrow waist and flatly-muscled stomach, and the generous, inviting swell of her hips. The fans shifted again as she pirouetted, ballet-like, and there was the delicate curve of the small of her back, and the trailing edge of the glittering, golden G-string. There was a spontaneous, involuntary gasp from the audience, followed by enthusiastic applause and wolf-whistles, as she looked over her left shoulder and gave the room a mischievous come-hither smile.

She was the most beautiful woman Jade had ever seen—whether in movies, in magazines, or in person—the brilliant blue eyes, the high cheekbones, the fullness of her lips, the flawless line of her jaw and the longish, inviting neck. But it was her smile that reached across the room. There was a tiny yet unmistakable downturn at the corners, a hint of melancholy, which gave her an elusive fragility, and the effect was devastating. Jade had the distinct feeling that she was looking directly at him. But then, every man in the room would doubtless be thinking the same thing. That was part of the whole deal, the reason why somebody without a lot of money might pay four bits to walk through a door.

The show lasted about thirty minutes, which included two costume changes. The finale was a more conventional striptease, where she started out in what looked like a man's tuxedo and tails, like Marlene Dietrich, and ended up in nothing but the tasseled golden pasties and the glittery G-string. By the time the curtain closed and she had blown a last kiss to the crowd, Jade figured that every red-blooded man in the Marmalade Club was fully prepared to follow Greta Vincennes through the piping-hot gates of hell.

The house lights came up. Jade finished his beer in two swallows and made his way toward the restrooms. Marty, true to his word, distracted the manager and Jade slipped backstage. He knocked on the door with the gold star.

"Come in."

Jade opened the door and stepped inside. "Miss Vincennes?"

She wore a navy blue terrycloth robe and sat at a dressing table, her back to him, regarding him suspiciously in the reflection of the lighted mirror. Jade was surprised to feel his heart catching in his throat. As beautiful as she'd been from across the room, she was overwhelming up close.

"Who are you?" she demanded.

"My name's Oscar Jade," he said. "First of all, that was one great show. You should be in the big time."

"This is a private room. You shouldn't be here."

Jade held up his hands. "I don't want to make any trouble, I promise."

"One scream from me and the cops'll be here before you know it."

"Weren't the cops just here?" he asked. "Right before the show?"

"I don't have any idea what you're talking about."

He decided to let that one go. "Actually, I'm here about Horace Mallory."

The expression on her face told the whole story. There was a brief flash in those stunning blue eyes, a telling pause, as Jade watched her search for words. "Never heard of him."

Jade smiled. "Nice try, ma'am. Look, I'm a private investigator who's been hired to look into Mr. Mallory's activities, but I'm not here to make trouble for you."

She gave a short laugh that was utterly without humor. "What's the difference?"

"You tell me."

"I don't have to tell you anything," she replied brusquely.

"I think he's in serious trouble, Miss Vincennes. And that could mean trouble for anyone associated with him. Including you, I'm afraid. I wouldn't want that to happen."

"You don't have any idea what's going on," she said. "You can't possibly know."

"What I don't know yet, I'm going to find out. You can count on that."

Greta Vincennes picked up a cigarette, stood up from the dressing table, and walked over to him, her arms folded in front of her.

Jade produced his Ronson and gave her a light. She inhaled deeply, looking at him in frank appraisal. He guessed she was five foot ten, maybe five eleven. She was standing before him, just a foot away, and she seemed to radiate heat. Her nearness was an overpowering distraction. Despite an obvious sheen of sweat from her performance and the hot stage lights, she somehow managed to smell clean—or, at least, cooked just well enough to taste good. Not at all like the tired, over-perfumed ripeness of the girls on the Caribbean's fourth floor. Jade could almost feel the pulse of her heart beating from a foot away. Or maybe it was just his own. Nevertheless, it was a remarkable sensation, and he'd never felt it before.

She smiled slyly. "You're not a bad looking man, Mr. Jade."

"Nice of you to say so."

"Mmm. Tall, too. It's nice to be able to look a man in the eye...what happened to your ear?"

"I have a way with people."

"I can imagine," she said. "Who are you working for?"

"Let's just say that my client has an interest in why Mallory is looking for some quick money."

She shrugged. "Everybody wants quick money."

"Yeah, but some people *need* it. How long have you known him?"

She took another pull on the smoke, and exhaled languidly. "It's not what you think it is."

"Glad to hear it," said Jade. "He owes somebody, right? Somebody who scares him plenty. Does it have anything to do with the Caribbean?"

"You're barking up the wrong tree," she said. "Now, if I were you, I'd make myself scarce. He's going to be here any minute."

"Really? Maybe we can all have a chat."

She gave a silky laugh. "Yeah, sure. That sounds nice."

"He's here a lot, isn't he?"

"Every night. You can set your watch by him. He always comes early for the second show, has a bunch of drinks, and then…"

Her eyes darted to one side. Jade followed her glance. There was a cot in the corner of the room, rumpled and unmade.

"It's not what *he* thinks it is, either," she said coolly.

"You know he's got a wife, don't you?"

"Don't they all?" She smiled ruefully. "Don't you?"

"No, I don't."

"Well…good for you." She went to the door, opened it for him, and beckoned Jade to leave with her cigarette hand. "Should I tell him you were here?"

"That's up to you. He's probably not going to be in a very good mood." Jade paused on the way out. "I'll be in touch, Greta. That's a promise."

Jade made his way back through the narrow, cluttered backstage passageway toward the door that led to the Marmalade's main room. He opened the door slightly, took a look around the room, and saw Horace Mallory standing at the bar.

Standing next to Mallory, and still wearing the jaunty, forward-tilted hat Jade had first seen at the Pelican that morning, was none other than Nino Valletti.

Jade slowly closed the door, and found a back way out of the Marmalade Club.

6
A Situation

Oscar Jade set a canvas bank bag on the counter behind the Pelican's bar with a heavy thump. "For the collection," he told Claude, who was in the process of frying a kettle of chicken, mashing potatoes, baking biscuits, and taking care of a dozen customers. Claude nodded and placed the bag, which contained the two Colt .38s Jade had taken from Mallory's men, inside a cabinet beneath the shelf of liquor bottles. Jade nodded at a couple of the regulars, who waved back and offered slurred greetings.

Claude drew Jade a beer from the tap without asking, and Jade took it.

"The dame's gone," Claude said. "I think she left around eight thirty."

"Where the hell did she go?"

"No idea. Didn't say a word. Snuck out the back door while I was working." Claude motioned with a thumb toward the door behind the bar. "Cleaned the upstairs nice and pretty before she left, though."

"Goddamn it." Jade stood up, and moved toward the stairway door. "What the hell is she thinking?"

"Well, she's a woman, ain't she?" Claude said behind him as Jade went through the door and up the stairs.

Jade's room above the Pelican Bar & Grill was many things. It was austere, and yet comfortable. It was small, and yet big enough. It was nearly empty, and yet contained all of his worldly possessions—at least, all of them that weren't stashed somewhere in his car. Above all, the room was cheap…and Claude Applegate was, thank God, tolerant of Jade's frequent tardiness with the rent. But one thing it wasn't—at least, not often—was immaculately *clean*. Myrna Mallory had swept, dusted, straightened and put away. The bed was made. The handful of books on his shelf was neat and orderly. His clothes had been folded and neatly stacked on the room's single chair, which sat beside a battered chest of drawers.

Jade stood in the open doorway and surveyed the tidiness. He shook his head. Then he went back downstairs, and took his customary place at the bar. In hushed tones, he quickly told Claude about Greta Vincennes, and having seen Valletti—with Mallory—at the Marmalade. Claude took it all in and went back to work, while Jade sat at the bar and stewed to a slow boil. Twenty minutes and two beers later, when his friend placed a plate full of fried chicken in front of him, Jade asked, "All right. Where do *you* think she went?"

"Damned if I know." Claude gave him a fresh beer. "Maybe she skipped town."

"That'd figure," Jade muttered, and tore into his

late supper. "Think she'll be back?"

Claude hesitated. "I dunno, boss."

"Well, I think she will," Jade said. "So we'd better be ready for it. Tomorrow's Wednesday. You got Ben, right?"

"He's in at noon, like always. Gonna polish the bar brass and fix a keg line for me. Then maybe take a look at the gutters on the south side—"

"Tell you what," Jade said. "I've got something for him. And tell him there's a ten-spot in it. Give him a call and tell him to get here first thing tomorrow morning. If she comes back, I want him to camp outside, say half a block away, and keep an eye on the joint. And if she leaves *again*, I want him to tail her. I'm not gonna get caught with my pants down."

"You got it," Claude said, and thought for a moment. "Dame might be more trouble than she's worth. You sure you wanna—"

"She's paid me for a couple weeks' work," Jade said, gingerly touching his ear. "I'm gonna do the work."

"D'you think Valletti's trying to muscle Mallory?"

"I don't think so," Jade said with his mouth full. "I saw what Mallory looks like when he's scared, and this wasn't it."

"Then he's gotta be working for him," Claude ventured. "Mallory put him onto the dame. Maybe he just wants to hand her over, and then collect on the insurance."

"Maybe." Jade washed down a bite of chicken leg with his beer. "Bottom line is, Valletti's told him about us by now, you can count on that. Once Mallory finds out I'm the same guy who showed up at his office…" He didn't have to finish the sentence.

"We got us a situation," Claude said. "Don't we?"

It was about an hour later, at ten minutes past eleven, when Myrna Mallory walked through the door of the Pelican. She drifted past the bar, gave Jade and Claude a cursory, soft 'hello' and went through the door that led upstairs.

Jade followed her up the stairs and into the spare room. She must have known he was following her, he reasoned, because she left the door open for him. She crossed the room, sat down on the twin-sized bed, and gazed out the single window. She didn't look at him when he closed the door behind him, nor when he asked the obvious question—in the calmest tone he could muster. "Where the hell have you been?"

"I went for a walk," she said woodenly.

"A walk," Jade said. "In the dark, alone, for nearly three hours, after paying me three hundred bucks to protect you. That doesn't make much sense."

"I'm sorry," she replied, still staring at the streetlight outside the window. "I just had to get out for a while and do some thinking. I'm fine, as you can see. What's done is done."

"Done? Nothing's done, Mrs. Mallory—"

"Please call me Myrna."

"I could call you a lot worse, Myrna. Like maybe foolish. Or missing. Or dead."

Finally, she turned to look at him. "What are you saying?"

Jade picked up a wooden desk chair, which he placed on the floor just a couple of feet from her, turning it around backwards so that he could straddle it and rest his arms across the back. She watched his movements closely and it seemed, finally, that he had shaken her out of her numbness.

"Okay. You need to listen to me now," he told her. "And listen to me good, because I'm not kidding around here. Are you listening?"

"Yes, Mister Jade," she replied, her voice very small. "I'm listening."

Her eyes—huge, brown and doe-like—stared into his, and for a moment Jade looked into their depths and was utterly lost. With her freckles and dimples, and her unadorned 'girl next door' freshness, she was the sort of girl who would somehow still look good at six in the morning, her eyes puffy from sleep, when she got up to use the bathroom and then came back to bed. She was someone to spend your life with.

Horace Mallory—with his shady connections, hired muscle and wandering eye—must have figured she wasn't enough for him. What a fool.

Jade felt a crazy urge to take Myrna's face in his hands and kiss her, long and hard, just to see what her reaction would be—to see if she would stiffen in resistance, or melt against him, and then let the chips fall where they may. He resisted it. Instead, he managed to say: "Call me Oscar."

"Oscar," she echoed.

"Okay, that's better. For this to work, you need to trust me, Myrna. But more important, I need to trust *you*. Things might get dicey pretty quick, and I need to be sure I'm not risking trouble with the cops just to be someone's patsy. I'm not a nice guy when I get screwed over."

"I don't understand."

"I spent all day checking out your husband. I even got to talk to him. For a couple of minutes, anyway."

She leaned forward. "What did he say?"

"I'll get to that. First of all, I've got something to tell you, and I think you ought to prepare yourself, because it's bad news."

"All right."

"Your husband's been seeing another woman," he said. "A dancer."

He didn't know what he'd expected, but it certainly wasn't the laughter—a deep down belly laugh—that seemed to come from somewhere deep within her. She composed herself after a few seconds, looked at Jade, and began to laugh again.

"Maybe you should let me in on the joke."

"I'm sorry," she said, "but it was the look on your face when you said it, like it was the end of the world. I imagined he was having an affair. Probably more than one. Why wouldn't he? And when I started seeing Peter, I actually hoped he was, because that way I didn't feel so guilty."

She wiped her eyes. Jade noted the tears, and wondered about the laughter. This was why he strictly avoided marriage stuff. Once you got between a husband and a wife, no matter who suspected whom, regardless of who was caught red-handed, anything could happen—and frequently did. "I had to make sure you knew about it, that's all."

"I don't think my husband can surprise me

anymore," she said evenly.

"I guess we'll see about that." He offered her a cigarette, lit it for her, then got one for himself. "What do you know about the Caribbean?"

"I told you. He's the manager."

"You're not aware of anything else?"

"No."

He watched her in silence, until she began to bristle beneath his inspection. "What? Tell me, already."

Jade did, laying it all out for her a step at a time. It turned out she was still capable of being surprised, after all.

"What were they going to do to you?" she asked breathlessly.

"I didn't stick around to find out." He pointed at his left ear. "But they weren't going to take me out for dinner and dancing, that's for sure. And then it got a little rough. Your husband probably had to send at least one of his guys to the hospital—maybe two." He paused. "I hope it was two."

"Oh, my God."

"And it turns out the guy who was here this morning—the guy who was watching you from the bar, remember? I'm pretty sure he works for your husband, too."

Her face grew ashen.

"So there's more going on here than just your husband wanting to collect on an insurance policy, which is why I need to be sure—"

Myrna cupped a hand over her mouth and ran to the door, threw it open, and crossed the hall to the bathroom. Jade heard her retch. He picked up the cigarette she'd dropped, and snuffed it out in an ashtray.

She returned a few minutes later, pale and shaky. Jade helped her back to the bed.

"Thank you," she said. "I'm sorry…I don't know what came over me."

"No need to apologize," Jade said. "It's a bad business, all right."

"And I've gotten you in the middle of it."

"That's why we need to be on the same page. I can't have you out walking the beach at eleven o'clock at night, when I'm supposed to be looking out for you. That won't work."

"I understand." She accepted the fresh cigarette Jade offered her and asked, "So what happens now?"

"I've got to find out who your husband's in trouble with. Whoever it is, they've got him plenty scared, and guys who're scared do crazy things. Do you know who he works for?"

She shook her head, and stared out the window. "Horace talks to him on the phone sometimes. But he always takes the call in his study and closes the door."

"Well, whoever it is, he owns the Caribbean, and he has to know what's going on there—but if he doesn't, he will soon enough. I tipped off the cops tonight, so things are going to get hot for both of them. If Mallory's worried about saving his own ass, maybe he'll leave you alone…and if we can get him locked up for racketeering, your problem's solved."

She didn't look at him, still gazing at the streetlight outside. "I hope so," she said.

Suddenly Jade had an idea. "You said your husband has a study in your house?"

"In *his* house," she corrected him. "But he always keeps the door locked. I was never allowed inside."

"I can get inside," Jade said.

Mallory's house was in a very nice neighborhood just off the west edge of Miami Beach, accessed by a short bridge on 71st Street. The house, a sprawling, single-level colonial-style, was only a block from Biscayne Bay. There was a light on in the front window, barely visible behind drawn draperies. Myrna had said they always left it on when nobody was home, but turned it off when they retired for the night. Jade hoped it meant that Mallory was maintaining his active nightlife with the Exquisite Miss Greta Vincennes.

He checked his watch: 1:15 in the morning. His first day working for Myrna Mallory was officially in overtime.

She'd been appalled by his suggestion. "You can't break in! What if he catches you?"

"I'm not breaking in," Jade had replied. "I've got your key."

"But it's too dangerous! I had no idea…you've done too much already."

"I haven't done nearly enough," he said. He'd remembered the look of anticipation on Mallory's face when he'd told his men that Jade would still need to be "able to talk," whatever that had meant. "I'm looking for anything that will tell me who his boss is, or prove he knows what's going on at the Caribbean. And I need to get it done tonight, before he has any more time to cover his tracks."

"But you've already been hurt! If anything else happens to you, it's my fault—"

"Nothing's going to happen. I'll be in and out in no time."

And he needed to be, thought Jade now as he parked the roadster two blocks away, on Rue Versailles. If Mallory wasn't already home, there was no telling when he might arrive. Jade had no desire for another conversation with Horace Mallory that night.

It was a clear night, and the moon cast soft shadows on the dark street. Oscar Jade clung to those shadows as he moved along Biarritz Drive. The smell of flowers and freshly cut grass mixed with sea air fleetingly reminded him of his childhood. What would that child make of the man who now crept along a quiet street, with the intent of sneaking into someone else's home in the middle of the night? *Don't think about that. Just get the job done. You're getting paid.*

There was no car in the driveway. He looked through the window of the garage; it was empty. Good. He had time.

He went around the side of the house and into a spacious back yard that was enclosed by immaculately trimmed hedges at least five feet tall. The lawn was newly seeded young grass, which had been recently watered. Jade took care to stay off it. He took out a pair of thin leather gloves and pulled them on. Somewhere, perhaps two houses away, a dog barked. He paused for a moment, and the barking stopped. He fished Myrna's house key out of his pocket, and tried the back door.

It was unlocked, and swung silently open. He put the key back in his pocket.

The kitchen was dark, except for a shard of moonlight through the window over the sink. The next room was the dining room: a large wooden table and chairs in the center, with a matching china cabinet along one wall. The dry ticking of a mantle clock seemed unnaturally loud in the silence.

Straight ahead was the living room. The lighted table lamp sat in front of the window. A chenille sofa sat along one wall, with two matching chairs in the corners of the room on either side. On a mahogany coffee table covered with embroidered linen doilies, the latest issues of *Look* and *Photoplay* magazines patiently waited to be read. Jade gave a wry smile. He couldn't have felt any more out of place if he'd snuck into Buckingham Palace.

On the opposite side of the room, beneath a wall-mounted curio cabinet laden with porcelain and glass figurines, a large Philco console radio—from which the Mallorys would have heard about the Brooklyn Dodgers' crushing World Series defeat—sat on a narrow table. To the left was a long, dark hallway. The doors on either side of the hallway would lead to the bathroom and two bedrooms. And according to Myrna, at the far end of the hall—where a sliver of light shone beneath a closed door—would be the study.

He slowly crept down the hall and tried the door.

As promised, it was locked. He took out the professional lockpick set, which Claude had only surrendered to him after endless protestations ("You're gonna get yourself killed, Oscar"), and, very quietly, made short work of the lock. He gently opened the door...and then his breath escaped in a long sigh as he entered the study and closed the door behind him.

Horace Mallory had been home, all right—but he wasn't home anymore. And he never would be again.

Mallory's body was leaned back in the leather swivel chair behind the desk, his head thrown back and his eyes staring at the ceiling in disbelief. His arms were outflung, his palms turned upward as if in benediction. The handle of a huge carving knife protruded from his chest at a 45-degree angle, but that blow had merely been the last of what looked like a dozen or so stab wounds to his neck, chest and stomach. His expensive white shirt had gone completely red. Behind the body, a window was open, and a gentle breeze stirred the drapes.

As Jade rounded the edge of the desk he saw the massive pool of blood, which had already congealed and looked like black tar on the hardwood floor beneath the chair. Blood had also splattered across the green felt blotter, and splashed in great globs against the desk drawers, down the front of his trousers and onto his fancy wingtip shoes. Some of it had even made it to the wall behind the desk, streaming down in crimson rivulets from the many points where it had initially splashed. The ivory-colored drapes were dotted with it. Jade looked at the patterns of the splatter on the floor, some of which were marred by shoeprints: Mallory's own, by the look of it. During what must have been one hell of a struggle, at least at first, Mallory had tried to get out from behind the desk, to get away from his killer. But ultimately, he'd simply sat back down in the chair to die.

Jade reached over and moved one of the arms. No rigor mortis yet. He'd bled out very quickly and he hadn't been dead long, a couple of hours at the most. Then again, it had only been about four hours since Jade had seen him, very much alive, with Nino Valletti at the Marmalade Club.

"God damn it," he said.

Then he remembered why he was there, cursed his distraction, and began to search through a filing cabinet next to the desk, trying not to disturb the mess made by Mallory's arterial spray.

He'd only made it through the first few file folders when he heard the front door of the house burst open, followed by urgent voices and the sound of hurried movement down the hall toward the room where he stood, poised over a freshly murdered corpse.

7
Playing With Fire

For a split second, Jade froze where he was, one hand frozen in the act of paging through manila folders, the other suspended over the holstered .38 at the small of his back. As the footfalls grew nearer, the scales in his mind weighed the probable consequences of staying versus running, given the fact that he didn't know who he would have to deal with in the hallway outside, or what their intentions were.

Instinct took over. He dashed to the door, and locked it just as someone on the other side tried the knob.

Oscar Jade rounded the edge of the desk, taking care not to step in the sticky pool of black blood. He leapt for the window behind Mallory's body and dove cleanly through. The drapes brushed past his face. The moist soil with the still-sparse, delicate new grass rushed up to meet him.

He landed hard on his left shoulder and

somersaulted. Momentum brought him upright, and his bad foot hobbled him miserably as he veered to the right, crossed the lawn as fast as he could and launched himself at the hedges, which suddenly seemed impossibly high. He rolled over the top of them, pointedly ignoring the stabs of the clipped branches as they tried to snare him halfway across. As he hit the ground on the other side of the hedgerow, in the back yard of Mallory's neighbor, he heard the wood of the study door finally splinter and give way, followed by exclamations of surprise.

"The window!" somebody shouted, but by then Jade had painfully vaulted the picket fence into the next yard, and had stretched his lame gait to as near 'running' as he would ever achieve. The pain in his foot thumped along with his lurching, stumbling steps and his racing heart, and he stowed it away in the back of his mind. He'd remember it—and deal with it—later, when he had the time.

A dog barked again, this time comfortably distant. Jade guessed the animal had belonged to a neighbor somewhere on the other side of Mallory's property. Not knowing which way Mallory's presumed killer had gone, the pursuit had taken multiple directions, and one of them must have run afoul of a backyard guardian. Jade grinned through his agony and kept going.

A few moments later, he reached Rue Versailles and crawled into the roadster. He had to use both hands to lift his now-worthless left leg, and its wretched foot, into the car. He slammed the door shut, gunned the Flathead V-8 into life, gritted through the excruciating use of the clutch pedal, and accelerated into a fishtailing U-turn escape from the Normandy Isles, shifting quickly through the gears as he howled across the short bridge on 71st Street and into the welcoming maze of Miami Beach's nighttime streets at seventy miles per hour.

As usual after hours, the Pelican's open-air frontage was buttoned up with hinged accordion-style shutter panels when Jade put his car in the garage at a little past two in the morning, but there was still a light on in a downstairs window. He found Claude alone at the bar, drinking a scotch on the rocks and working on the ledger book. Without looking up, Claude said, “Trouble?”

Jade knew his limp was more pronounced than usual. His clothes were covered with dirt and grass stains, and certain things simply didn't need to be said. Then again, certain things did.

“You could say that,” said Jade as he went behind the bar and drew himself a beer. “I was here all night. Right?”

“Right,” said Claude.

“In fact, I got drunk and went to bed after dinner, say around eleven, because my foot was still bothering me from that muscle-head stomping on it yesterday morning.”

“Okay.”

“You don't know anything about the case I'm working on.”

“Not a thing.”

"Myrna Mallory didn't spend the night here."

"Check."

"And she won't be here tomorrow morning…even if she *is*."

"'Course not."

"I'm going to bed."

"'Night, boss."

Upstairs in his room, Jade peeled off his filthy clothes and drank the beer down in three long swallows. In the bathroom across the hallway, he stood in a steaming hot shower for five minutes, then turned off the hot water and let the bracing cold water cascade over him for thirty seconds. From the medicine cabinet above the lavatory, he took out a bottle of surgical alcohol and did some proper first aid on his ear.

Wearing only a towel, he opened the door to the spare room. In the light from the hallway he could see Myrna lying on the bed, her back to him, the covers drawn up to her bare shoulders. He watched her breathe regularly for a full minute, and wondered if she was actually asleep. Softly, he closed the door.

Back in his room, he turned off the light and tossed the towel on the chair. He climbed into bed and stared at the ceiling. At some point, before the glow of the rising sun began to peek from behind the drawn window-blind, Oscar Jade fell into a fitful sleep.

At 7:30 AM he brought a tray of coffee to Myrna's

door. She answered his knock very quickly and invited him in, looking rested and fresh in a pleated yellow dress and matching shoes. Jade wondered how many dresses and pairs of shoes she'd squeezed into that suitcase.

"I take it black," he said. "How about you?"

"Cream and sugar, please," she said. He could feel her gaze on him as he got it ready. "What is it?" she asked him.

He gave her the coffee, then he gave her the news—and he watched her very closely, since a great deal could be learned at such moments, and there was a hell of a lot he needed to know, sooner rather than later.

He was quick enough to grab the cup and saucer just before she dropped them, but some still splashed onto the floor.

She sat on the edge of the bed a moment later, her eyes red and swollen. "I don't know why I'm crying," she said dully, looking through Jade as if he wasn't there. "I just can't believe it. It can't be."

"It is." He observed every movement of her fidgeting hands, every tic in her facial muscles, and measured them against the way she'd presented herself the day before, when she'd hired him—allegedly seeking protection from a man who, as it had turned out, only had twelve hours to live.

"How did it happen?" she asked.

Jade told her exactly what he'd seen. "Which is why I have to ask you again where you went last night."

Myrna gasped. "You don't think that I—"

"It's not so much what I'm going to think, although

you need to be worried about that too. It's what the cops are going to think, and they're going to want to have a word with you, that's for sure. They're going to want to know how your marriage was doing, if you two fought lately, that kind of thing. And you've got to admit, the truth about *that* won't look too good. But most of all, they're going to want to know where you were last night."

"I told you the truth."

"I want to trust you, Myrna. Hell, I *need* to trust you at this point, because I'm in as much trouble as you are. Maybe more. But you're not making it easy."

"I went for a walk," she said. "Down the beach, a long way that way." She waved vaguely southward, in the direction of Lummus Park. "I sat on a bench and looked at the water."

"Anybody see you? Anybody at all?"

She paused for a moment. "No. I don't think so."

Jade shook his head. "That's too bad."

There was a knock at the door. Claude stood in the hallway. "Cop car pulled up outside," he said. "Looks like the cap'n."

Jade threw Myrna a stare. "Right on time," he muttered.

Oscar Jade paused in the bathroom and looked at his reflection in the mirror over the lavatory. Well, he certainly *looked* bad enough. That, plus his reputation, might help sell the story. He wet his hands and rubbed them through his hair until he'd achieved the disheveled look he needed.

On the way downstairs he took a drink from his coffee and got into character as he came through the door behind the bar.

Billings had already taken a seat at the bar, his hat off and sitting to one side as Claude poured him a cup of coffee. He looked at Jade and said, "Jesus, you look like hammered shit. What the hell happened to you?"

"Late night," Jade said, and held his fingertips to his temples.

"That right? Business or pleasure?"

"Drinking."

"Fine line between the two," said Billings. "Especially the way *you* do it."

"Very funny," replied Jade. "But you know how it is."

The remark fell flat. "How's that?"

"Just kidding."

"Hell of a thing to kid about," Billings grumbled.

"Sorry about that." Jade sat down next to him. "No offense."

Billings hesitated, and then shrugged. "It's okay. I'm just a little tired, that's all. Up too early this morning. Business, don't you know."

"What brings you down here?"

"Why else?" the cop asked broadly, patting his narrow, flat stomach with both hands. "I'm hungry! And it's been way too long since I've had the best breakfast on the beach." He winked at Claude. "Three eggs, over easy, with toast and bacon and hash browns."

"Coming up, Cap'n."

They sipped their coffee in silence, and Jade waited for it. He didn't have to wait long.

"Say," said Billings casually, "You'll never guess who got himself killed last night."

"Killed?" Jade took a sip of coffee. He knew Billings' eyes were on him. "Who?"

"Horace Mallory. You know, that guy you told me about on the phone."

Jade turned sharply, met Billings' gaze, and put on his best mask of surprise. "You're kidding," he said.

"Nope. Dead as hell. Right at his desk."

"At the Caribbean?" asked Jade blithely, blinking in ostensible confusion.

"No," Billings answered quickly. "At home, in the middle of the night. Stabbed fifteen times, the coroner says. Nasty business. Real messy."

"God, that's awful. Who did it?"

"Well, I'm just getting started on that…which is why I thought I'd ask you."

"So it's not just breakfast after all," said Jade glumly. "By the way, Claude, I'll take what Al's having. Just *two* eggs, though." He grinned at Billings. "Where do you put it all?"

"What went on between you and Mallory, Oscar?"

"I told you last night," Jade said. "I was hired to find out if he might be in money trouble. And it turns out he is—was," he amended. "But I still don't know why. And now it's only going to be harder to find out."

"You told me you were working a matrimonial case."

"What can I tell you? Business is good all of a sudden. About time, too. Maybe it's the war. Brings out the worst in people."

"Huh," Billings grunted, and sipped at his coffee. "Who hired you to find out about Mallory?"

"I can't say right now."

"That right?"

"Yeah," Jade said.

"Well, if it was Mallory's wife, I sure would like to have a talk with her. Word is, she was on the outs with her husband. Maybe they were heading for a divorce."

"Where'd you hear that?"

"Oh, that kind of thing never stays a secret for long, does it?" Billings said with a wink, just as Claude slid a plate of breakfast in front of each of them. "Especially when somebody ends up dead, all of a sudden."

The cop sprinkled some pepper on his fried eggs. The two of them ate in silence for a couple of minutes. "My compliments to the chef," Billings said, and raised his coffee cup in a toast.

"Thanks, Cap'n." Claude smiled, but only with his mouth.

"So you're telling me you don't know anything about Myrna Mallory," the cop said.

Jade shrugged. "I'm working a few angles. I haven't covered them all yet."

Billings dipped a corner of his toast in the runny egg yolk. "You didn't really answer my question."

Jade shrugged again.

"But you can understand why I'm asking, right? I mean, one minute you tell me Mallory's running a racket, and the next minute he's dead."

"Did you check out the hotel?"

"Just came from there," Billings said. "They told me you showed up at Mallory's office yesterday evening. Matter of fact, somebody said *you* were the one talking about a divorce. How about that for strange?"

"Did you see the fourth floor?"

"Then they said Mallory kicked you out, and you beat the crap out of two hotel employees."

"Did you see the operation he had going on there?"

"They still haven't decided if they're going to press charges."

"Goddamn it, Al, did you see the operation?"

"I saw the fourth floor," Billings snorted. "There was nothing there, not a thing. It's all torn up."

"That's impossible," Jade said. "They had tables, they had girls—"

"They had a busted water pipe," Billings said. "The whole floor was cleared out, and part of the third floor, too. All kinds of water damage, people in their beds with water dripping from the ceiling, wanting their money back. Bad plumbing job, that's what the desk clerk said. He was in the middle of bawling out the plumber over the phone when I got there."

Jade couldn't believe it. How could they have cleared it all out so quickly? It would take a crew of guys, he figured, and even then they'd be doing it half the night. "That's bullshit," he managed weakly.

"Maybe," the cop conceded. "I thought it was a bit queer myself, being the same floor you gave me and all. But there's all kinds of funny business going on, looks like to me. I'm not used to having one of my best students playing footsies with me, neither."

"Oh, come on."

"No, I mean it, Oscar. You know the routine. Where were you last night—say around ten thirty, maybe eleven?"

Jade looked at Claude, who didn't hesitate. "Sitting right where he is now, Cap'n. Only then he was eatin' fried chicken, and drinkin' beer like Roosevelt just made it legal again. I poured him into bed at one in the mornin'."

Billings looked at Jade, then at Claude, and then back at Jade. "That right?"

"I've gotta take his word for it," Jade said, with feigned embarrassment. "That New Yorker got a piece of my bad foot yesterday, Al. Guess I had a few too many mugs of painkiller. Fell asleep at the bar. Don't remember much after that."

"Huh," the cop grunted, and they finished their breakfast in silence. Jade tapped out two smokes, gave one to Billings, and lit them both.

"By the way," said Jade as Claude cleared the plates away, "you ought to take a closer look at Nino Valletti. He ties in with Mallory somehow, you can bet your ass."

"How's that?"

"I'll tell you when I can," Jade said. "Believe me, Mallory had problems, and not just wife problems. He was expecting trouble, and I guess he got it. Bottom line is, I might have a line on who killed him, but you've gotta give me some room to work it."

"I got a couple of leads of my own," said the cop. "Mallory must've just planted fresh grass in his yard, and whoever killed him went out the back window. I've got two good sets of footprints to worth with."

Jade kept his face neutral. "*Two* sets? You figure somebody double-teamed him?"

"Could be." Billings shrugged. "Rusty was out there with a guy from the lab as soon as the sun came up. Besides the footprints, we got some clothing fibers from a hedge. He'll probably have something by lunchtime."

"Good," Jade said softly. "That's good."

"He really is a lot like you, when you first made detective. Smart, a go-getter, not afraid of anything—"

"And with two good feet," Jade finished.

"That's not what I meant."

"Sure it's not."

There was an awkward silence. "Well, then." Billings took out his wallet. "What do I owe you?"

"On the house, Cap'n," Claude said. "Your money's no good here."

"Nah, nah, I insist," said the cop, with exaggerated graciousness. "I'm buying Oscar's, too. How much altogether?"

"Dollar ten."

Billings gave him $1.50. "Keep the change," he said. He picked up his hat and put it on. "See ya around, boys."

"Much obliged," said Claude.

The cop got halfway to the door. He stopped, and turned around.

"Tell you what," he said apologetically. "Since I'm here and all, what say I take a quick look upstairs? No harm done, right?"

"Why?" Jade asked him.

"'Cause I've got a couple of bees buzzing around my bonnet, that's all. Once I take a quick look, I can relax about it. What do you say?"

"I don't think so," said Jade. "Not today."

A fresh set of lines appeared on Billings' brow. "Why's that?"

"Because I get the feeling you're trying to push me around. And it bugs me."

"Gee, I'm sorry you feel that way, Oscar. So the answer's no?"

"That's right."

"What if I insist?"

"Then I guess I have to ask to see your search warrant," Jade said.

"That's how it is?" Billings asked.

"That's how it has to be."

"Okay, then." He paused for a moment. "Tell you what: I'm going to go ahead and go upstairs, and have a quick look-see. If you guys stop me, we'll be playing a brand new ballgame, and then you'll *have* your search warrant. How about that?"

Claude gave Jade a look. Jade shrugged and said, "Suit yourself."

Upstairs, they checked Claude's room first, and then Jade's…and finally, Billings opened the door to the spare room.

The bed was made. The room was clean. There was no suitcase, and no Myrna Mallory. She was gone. Again.

Jade nearly laughed out loud. He wondered which of the three guys in the room was the most surprised.

Billings walked over to the nightstand, where half a cup of coffee with cream and sugar sat. Jade figured it would still be at least slightly warm. The cop swirled the coffee around in the cup, and set it back down. He gave Jade a hard stare.

"You're playing with fire, Oscar," he said, and left without another word.

8
The Furnace

Jade waited until he heard the door close at the foot of the stairs and said, “I hope Ben was here on time this morning.”

“Oh, yeah. Got here at the crack of dawn. Parked my truck across the street.” Claude looked out the window. “He ain’t there now, so the lady’s covered. I got a question, though.”

Jade noted the tone of his voice, which spoke volumes on issues for which there were no good words. “Okay,” he said, but he already knew what his old friend was about to say.

“We’re getting our chain pulled, here. How long are you going to back this dame if she keeps it up?”

It was a good question, Jade thought as he drove north along Collins Avenue a few minutes later, and the answer was obvious: not much longer, especially with the cops taking an undue interest in the Pelican, which neither of them could tolerate for any number of reasons. Myrna Mallory was very close to being handed to the Miami Beach P.D. on a silver platter with Jade's compliments and apologies, even though it seemed highly unlikely that she was the one who'd stabbed her husband fifteen times. Even if she'd managed to get all the way back to the house on Biarritz—which would have meant taking a taxi, borrowing or stealing a car, or at least having an accomplice—she'd surely have ended up wearing some of his blood. There had been no sign of it when she showed up at the Pelican. Sure, she'd acted distracted and detached. Maybe even suspicious…but it just didn't *feel* right. A gut feeling wouldn't stand up in court, and it sure wouldn't matter to the cops when the heat was turned up, but his intuition rarely let him down.

His original plan had been to pay another visit to the Marmalade Club and find out exactly when Greta Vincennes had said goodnight to Mr. Personality. Then he'd go to City Hall and use his connections there to do some digging on the ownership of the Caribbean Hotel. As it happened, however, Tinsel had telephoned the Pelican not long after Billings had left, and caused a change in plans.

"Jade, it's Danny. Can you meet me someplace?"

"What is it?"

"We gotta talk. Right now. I'll be at the Star Café in fifteen minutes."

"What's going on, Danny?"

"I ain't gonna get into it over the phone, but I think I got what you want," Tinsel said breathlessly, and hung up.

Jade found him hiding in a booth in the rearmost corner of the diner, his hat pulled down to cover his face, which was further concealed by a fidgety hand positioned, apparently, to convey the impression of deep thought. His beady eyes watched Jade's approach through splayed fingers, and Jade couldn't help but smile.

He sat down across from Tinsel. A waitress showed up, and Jade ordered a cup of black coffee. He'd had about four hours' sleep; today wasn't the day to skimp on the java.

Tinsel didn't speak until they were alone. "Mallory's dead," he said heavily. "The racket at the Caribbean's been scrubbed clean."

Jade sighed. "I hope that's not what you dragged me halfway across town for. A cop just gave the same news, and it didn't cost me sixty bucks to hear it."

"Okay, okay. I did some checking around yesterday. The hotel's owned by something called the Constance Holding Company, out of New York City. They've got a warehouse at the dockyard, a garbage pick-up business—"

"Sixty bucks, Danny."

"Okay, okay. You ever heard of The Furnace?"

Jade shook his head.

"Well, that's what they call him. His real name's La Forno, as far as anybody knows. Supposedly he's the guy behind the Constance Holding Company, which is why if you go to any of his businesses, they're lousy with 'made' guys, just kinda standin' around, watchin' people. You know what I mean."

Jade knew, all right. Freddie and the big goon from the Caribbean certainly fit the bill. So did Nino Valletti. All of them Italian, with sharp eyes, expensive suits and bulges in their armpits. Well dressed, well armed and not afraid of anything. "So the syndicate's expanding in South Florida," he said.

"Maybe…but they've been here forever, really, at least a few of 'em. And it's never been a big deal. Took their piece of the pie, but there's still plenty left for the rest of us, what with more and more people coming down for vacation, you know, even with times being tough. Business just keeps getting bigger.

"These guys are different, though. La Forno comes to town about a year, maybe a year and a half ago. Buys the Caribbean out from underneath whoever built it, still practically brand new, and sets up shop. Well, they took one hell of a bite out of the business on the beach. Know what I mean? So…you remember Dingo McTaggart, right?"

"Sure," Jade said. "The Mad Scotsman." He'd arrested McTaggart a couple of times on minor assault beefs, when the barrel-chested redhead had decided to wear his kilt and get keyed up on whisky in one of the local watering holes. Both times, he'd punched somebody for making fun of his 'skirt.' He was a bricklayer by trade, but most everybody knew he moonlighted as a collector for the bookies. He never had to get too tough with the locals, because they were always pretty good about paying up, but occasionally he laid into a tourist who got stupid. Still, nothing had ever stuck, and there was always money from somewhere to bail him out. Then, one day a few months ago, McTaggart had just vanished. "I'd heard he just left town."

"Yeah, that's what I heard too," Tinsel muttered. "Turns out the local boys start to notice how much of their business on the beach is going away. Word gets back to 'em about the Caribbean, so they send Dingo over to check the place out. The next day, somebody has a box left on his doorstep. Guess what's inside? A note that says: 'Leave the Caribbean alone.' Know what else is in the box? A piece of Dingo's arm, wrapped in wax paper. Remember that tattoo he had, the one that said 'Scotland Forever'?"

Jade nodded.

"Yeah, it was *that* piece of his arm," Tinsel said. "A chunk of meat. Sliced off the bone and wrapped up like a steak from the butcher's shop. And that's the last anybody ever saw of Dingo."

"Why didn't anybody call the cops?"

"You kidding? They cut their losses, and did just what the note said. They left the Caribbean alone, and things have been peaceful ever since."

"And the cops have kept away, too," Jade said.

"Sure as hell." Tinsel took out his filthy handkerchief and wiped the sweat off his face. "La Forno's got the fix in with the cops. Bet your life."

"I know cops high up who had no idea about the Caribbean."

"They tell you so? And you believe 'em, naturally."

"Don't be an idiot," Jade snapped. "I'd trust this one with my life."

"Billings?" Tinsel sneered. "Scuttlebutt is, he's on La Forno's payroll—"

Jade reached across the table, grabbed him by the collar of his shirt and twisted until it closed off the bookie's airway.

"Tell you what, Tinsel," Jade said softly. "Captain Billings is a friend of mine—a good friend. Do yourself a favor: don't just assume everybody else in the world is as crooked as you are, just because some other crooked asshole you know says so."

"*Eh*," was all Tinsel could manage in response. "Sorry, I'm sorry."

Jade eased up, but kept hold of him. "Who says Billings is on the take?"

"Just word on the street," Tinsel croaked. "Everybody."

"That's not good enough."

"Guy I know says he heard it from somebody who oughta know. Maybe another cop."

"What cop?"

"I dunno, Jade, I swear!"

"Better find out," Jade said. "I want a word with him."

"All right, already! I'll try!"

Jade let him go. A moment passed in silence. Jade sipped at his coffee. "So," he said conversationally, "Who is this La Forno?"

"All I know is a couple of stories, second- and third-hand," Tinsel said grudgingly, massaging his throat. "He came over from Sicily when he was a kid, like fifty years ago. Got in with the Terranza family as a soldier in Sal Gagliardo's crew, and worked his way up. Had a reputation for being loyal, and real scary. Made his bones burning stuff down—maybe that's where he got the name. Nobody knows for sure, but it's hard to believe they gave it to him at Ellis Island."

"What are you talking about?"

"La Forno's Italian for 'The Furnace,'" Tinsel said. "Anyway, somebody was stupid enough to start up a whorehouse in his Capo's territory, and he lit it up with a firebomb, all on his own. Didn't even ask Gagliardo for permission. Killed everybody inside—women, johns, everybody. Something like sixteen people altogether."

"Subtle," Jade said.

"Yeah. Well, it was too much, and everybody knew it. But it worked, and Gagliardo was afraid of him, so nothing happened—except he got promoted and put on a new 'protection' route. First they'd send somebody in to shake the place down, and set up weekly payments. If the mark didn't pay, next day they'd send La Forno. If they still said no, he'd come back that night and torch it. Well, pretty soon he had a reputation, so he didn't have to burn stuff down anymore, and then he had his own territory, and his own guys working for him, and his territory got bigger. Then Gagliardo had an accident, and La Forno was next in line for Caporegime. Then he married Terranza's daughter, and he was all set."

"What kind of accident?"

"Supposedly, he fell asleep in bed with a lit cigar." Tinsel smiled grimly. "Burned to death. Of course, the gasoline helped."

Jade shook his head, and drank his coffee.

"Then the war got started between the New York families," Tinsel went on. "La Forno was Terranza's senior Capo—he ran a crew out of Brooklyn—and they raised hell with the boys in Midtown. Once the war was over, Terranza was one of the big players in town, and naturally La Forno was his right hand man—head underboss. They made a lot of money."

"So what's La Forno doing in Miami Beach?"

"Well, he's supposed to be retired. That's the story. I had to dig pretty hard to find out about the Caribbean, call in a couple of favors. It's a surprise, 'cause everybody figured he'd be lying low, after what happened."

Jade finished his coffee and lit a smoke. "So what happened?"

"Well, this is the stuff *everybody* knows, but nobody talks about, 'cause it'll get you iced." Tinsel looked around nervously before he went on. "Don Terranza died of a heart attack three years ago. His son Gaetano—they call him 'Little Tom'—made a few moves and took over the family, and he pretty much froze La Forno out. He don't like La Forno much, they never got along all that well, so with the old man gone it just got worse. Tommy Terranza never got over La Forno marryin' into the family, an' he always figured La Forno was angling to take him out when he got the chance, so there wasn't any trust there, see what I'm sayin'?

"Now La Forno's wife—Little Tom's sister—had two sons for him right after they got married. Twins. By the time old man Terranza died, La Forno's boys were about twenty, and he was grooming 'em to follow in his footsteps. Well, get this: one day both of La Forno's boys get ambushed at a stoplight on Broadway, broad daylight. Car fulla wiseguys with tommy guns pulls up alongside 'em, and just tears 'em up—turns the car into Swiss cheese, and both boys are dead, just like that. Other car drives off. Nobody knows who did it, but it gets blamed on a leftover grudge from one of the other Five Families.

"Two weeks later, La Forno's wife washes down

a bunch of sleeping pills with a tall glass of gin and dies in bed." Tinsel gave Jade a meaningful look. "So…La Forno's in Miami Beach. Retired. He's got a big house over in Al Capone's neighborhood, if ya can believe it. Figures, don't it? Miami's where the bosses get put out to pasture. You know, they say Capone's gone crazy since he got out of the joint—his brain's gone rotten or something. I hear he throws a fishing line in his swimming pool. Sits out there for hours at a time, like he's gonna catch something."

"I don't care about Capone," Jade said.

"Yeah, sure," the bookie said. "'Course not. Anyway, La Forno's got a big house out there too, somewhere close to Big Al, with a big boat parked behind it—a forty-footer, maybe bigger. He throws parties on it, and sails around the bay like he's the governor or something."

Jade tapped the ash off his cigarette and mulled it over. "Does he still have connections with the Terranza family?"

"Not as far as anybody knows," Tinsel said. "He's all on his own down here—he's got his own machine. Constance Holding Company owns the businesses, and La Forno owns the Constance Holding Company—and guess what? Constance was his wife's name."

"Where can I find him?"

"*Find* him?" Tinsel blurted. "Why the hell would you want to?"

"I've got my reasons."

"Is this about Mallory? What do you care about *him* for, anyway?"

"I want to arrange a meeting, that's all."

"Yeah, well, finding him's no big trick. He goes to the track every day they have races. Has meetings there, everything—right out in the open. That's where he always did his business with Mallory."

"Hialeah?"

"Yeah, that's right, yeah. Loves to play the horses. Even owns a couple, and who knows what he's got fixed for the races? You wanna make some dough, forget about the odds and bet on one of La Forno's horses. He's got an owner's box in the grandstand. You wanna find him, that's where you'll find him. Just make sure you make out your will before you go. And keep my name out of it, for Chrissakes. I don't need any more trouble in my life than I got already."

Jade ground out his cigarette in the ashtray, and stood up. "I'll be in touch."

As he pushed open the door, Tinsel called after him: "If you run into ol' Dingo, say hello for me."

The Marmalade Club, like most establishments of its kind, looked vastly different in the stark light of day. Without the benefit of the multi-colored neon trimming and the busy in-and-out flow of merrymakers and drunks beneath its brightly lit marquee, it was just another seedy dive—ready for a fresh coat of paint, and every bit as hungover as its patrons from the night before.

There were only three cars parked nearby, and one of them was Oscar Jade's roadster convertible, which at the moment had its ragtop up in spite of the sunshine and 75-degree weather. He sat low in the driver's seat and checked his watch: 10:15. At this time of day, the only people in the Marmalade would be the manager, a barman for restocking, and somebody to clean the joint. All the same, Jade hoped that the phone call he'd made would pay off and another employee would soon arrive.

Just a few minutes later, she did. One of the big four-door '40 Chevrolets from the Kelly's Comfort Cab taxi fleet which Jade knew so well pulled up in front of the club's front door. Greta Vincennes, wearing a red and white flower-print dress and high heels, her platinum-blonde hair tied up in a red scarf, emerged from the back seat. She opened her purse and paid the driver, and the cab pulled away. As it drove past, Jade scribbled down the time and the car's number in a notebook he kept in the glove compartment. He put the notebook away, and got out of his car.

Her back was to him as he approached, and Jade took the fleeting opportunity to admire the finely-shaped legs, the way the high heels enhanced the curve of her calves, the way the dress—inexpensive and no doubt ordinary-looking on most anyone else—failed to disguise the long and magnificent body within it, and the sublime bend of her neck as she looked at her wristwatch.

"Good morning," Jade said, and she turned around.

"Good morn—" she began, and then she recognized him. "I guess you're supposed to be from the *Miami Herald*," she said frostily.

Post time at Hialeah was 1:15 PM, so Jade had

had plenty of time to follow up on the most obvious lead. He'd found a payphone and called the Marmalade's manager, claiming to be a reporter from the *Herald*. He was doing an article on the best of Miami Beach's nightclubs, and promised the guy plenty of free publicity for his club—in exchange for an exclusive interview with the star of his nightly show, the Exquisite Miss Greta Vincennes. Guys who ran joints like the Marmalade were easy marks when it came to the promise of more thirsty mouths, and ogling eyes, coming through their doors and paying the cover charge. But they had their limits, and were generally very protective of their talent: in the case of Greta's boss, he refused to give out her address—"Can't do that, Mac, she's got too many bums trying to make time with her"—but he promised to have her meet him for an interview at the club, and he was as good as his word. It had been less than an hour since Jade had made the call…and here she was.

"Well, I knew you wouldn't meet with *me*," Jade said. "And I told you I'd be in touch."

"It's not a very nice thing to do."

"Speaking of not nice things, you know your boyfriend Mallory's dead, right?"

A shadow crossed her beautiful face—an anxious look downward, a quick, darting flick of the tongue across those luscious, ruby-red lips—and then her eyes rose to meet his. Jade recognized the defiance in them.

"Good," she said.

"Really?"

"Yes. Really. I hated him. He was a miserable,

no-good bastard. But you knew that already, didn't you."

"And yet, you—?"

"A girl's got to do what she's got to do," Greta replied.

"That's exactly what I'm asking."

"It was just business, that's all. What did you say your name was?"

"Jade. Oscar Jade."

"Well, Oscar. You're a private dick, right? You understand business."

"When did you say good night?"

"Late."

"Can't have been *that* late."

She shrugged. "Before midnight, I guess. He left before I did my last show."

"Anybody with him?"

"Yeah," she said. "Nice looking guy, with an expensive suit."

"You know him?"

"No."

"They left together?"

"As far as I know," she said indifferently. "Got a smoke?"

Jade tapped out a couple of Luckies. He lit hers first, cupping the flame of his Ronson against the breeze with his other hand, and then lit his own. "Aren't you curious about what happened to him?"

"Not really. Why?"

"I'm putting together a list of people who might have wanted him dead. And you're on it."

She laughed. "Really? Gosh." There was something going on in those eyes, though, as Jade heard the front door of the Marmalade Club swing open, followed by the sound of brisk footsteps. Greta looked past him and exclaimed: “Watch out!”

He turned around, and jerked his head back just in time to avoid the haymaker—a fist the size of a ham—thrown at his chin.

As he stumbled backward away from his attacker, Jade saw that the huge fist was attached to an even bigger man—with bandages covering his nose and wrapped around his head, and eyes that burned red with rage—good old Freddie, from the loading dock of the Caribbean Hotel. His breaths huffed evenly through his mouth. He advanced, fists raised, with the sure confidence of a man bent on revenge.

“Whoa,” Jade said. “What the hell—”

Then came another swing, this time a fast moving left-handed rabbit punch that glanced off the side of Jade’s head, but now Jade had his feet beneath him and had seen it coming. He took another couple of steps back, and watched the guy move. Freddie was right-handed but led with his left, which told Jade he’d trained in the ring, a heavyweight who’d no doubt seen more than a few guys drop when he’d landed what would surely be a cinder-block of a right, but who hadn’t done enough fighting outside of the ropes to know that the rules of boxing didn’t always work out on the streets.

Jade found that spot on the outside edge of his bad foot which he knew—even though it hurt like a bitch—would give him all the foundation he’d need. “Listen, Freddie,” he said in a measured voice, as he worked his way to his right and gauged the ponderous, predictable rhythm of his opponent’s movements, "You don't want to do this."

"You're gonna pay," Freddie growled, and kept coming.

This time the left hand was a telegraphed jab, and it floated in toward Jade's chin. Jade deflected it with his left forearm and then brought a right hook, with every ounce of his 190 pounds behind it, that found the lower edge of Freddie's muscled ribcage and landed hard. It was like hitting a heavy bag, and for a moment Jade feared he'd broken something in his hand, but then Freddie bent over with a wheezing grunt and stopped his advance. Jade grabbed the offered head with both hands and pulled it sharply downward to meet his rising knee. Freddie rebounded from the impact and fell backward to the sidewalk, bleeding from the mouth, his two front teeth jaggedly poking through a flattened upper lip, the bandage askew from his already broken nose. He groaned and writhed on the sidewalk.

"Shit!" Jade rubbed his knuckles and turned to Greta. "What the hell is he doing here?"

"He works here sometimes," she replied, gaping at Freddie's ruined face. "Why did he come after you?"

Jade shrugged. "I guess he figures I got that coming."

"Are you the one who did that to him?"

He nodded.

She gave a reluctant smile. "You really do have a way with people."

Freddie rolled to one side, spat a tooth and a gob of blood onto the concrete, and burbled, "I guh kill ya, suh-bitch!"

"Shut up," Jade said, and kicked him hard, taking care to get him in the ribcage, right where his punch had landed. Freddie howled in agony.

"So let me guess," Jade continued, without missing a beat. "La Forno owns the Marmalade Club, too."

Jade took Greta to the Superb, a deli on the corner of 9th Street and Michigan Avenue, and bought her a sandwich. He'd noted the change in her demeanor when he said the name. It was like the flip of a light switch, the difference between night and day, and as they sat at the counter and Jade watched her eat, he told her what he intended to do.

"You really don't want to do that," she said. "If you were smart, you'd just walk away."

"Nobody's ever accused me of being too smart."

"If you're looking for trouble, you're going to find it. That's all I'm saying." She gave him a sideways glance. "If it's a paying job you want, I might have something for you."

Jade smiled. "Oh yeah? What do I have to do?"

"Nothing," she said. "That's the best kind of job there is."

"Mallory was in serious Dutch with La Forno, wasn't he? He owed him a lot of money. Why?"

"Because he was an idiot," Greta said. "He thought he could get away with…" She stopped, and sighed. "There's more going on here than you realize."

"I gotta be honest with you, lady," Jade growled, and stood up. "I'm getting pretty tired of hearing that crap. When I do find out what was going on between Mallory and La Forno—and you turn out to be messed up in it, which I know you are—then you better not be expecting anything from me except trouble. In spades."

"Wait a second."

"You better give me something to work with, or we don't have anything else to talk about."

"Mallory was stealing from the hotel," she said. "From the gambling business, too. And the boss found out."

"How much?" Jade asked.

"A lot."

"How much is 'a lot?'"

"Fifty grand," she said. "At least. Maybe more."

"How do you know?"

"I worked at the Caribbean. It wasn't hard to figure out what was going on."

"I'm guessing you didn't dance there," Jade said.

"No," she said. "I didn't."

"The fourth floor?"

She nodded. "That's how it started between me... and him."

"Who hired you? Mallory, or La Forno?"

"Well, I didn't work for Mallory," she said stiffly.

"You met with a cop last night before your first show."

"What in the world are you talking about?"

"Don't even try it," Jade snapped. "I know you did. Who was it?"

"It doesn't matter—"

"I think it does. Your boss has a cop on his payroll, right?"

"This has got nothing to do with that," she insisted. "It's personal. I want to keep it that way."

Jade offered to drive her home. "No, thanks," she said, and called for a taxi. She was waiting for it outside the deli as he took a moment to put his convertible top down, got into the roadster and pulled away. He watched her in his rearview mirror, and saw that she was watching him as well.

9
Hialeah

Jade drove west on 79th Street through the heart of Miami. Fifty large. The amount of the insurance policy Mallory had taken out on Myrna's life. At least *that* made sense. Mallory got caught with his hand in the cookie jar, and needed to pay back a big chunk of dough. But what about the money he'd stolen? Did he spend it all? Were the stories about gambling debts on the level? How else do you burn through fifty grand that fast, and have nothing to show for it? Maybe he caught his wife screwing around on him, and figured he could get some quick cash by arranging for something bad to happen to her. Maybe he hired Nino Valletti to make it happen, but Myrna made it to the Pelican before he could get the job done.

It made sense that La Forno did his business at the track whenever he could. He probably avoided telephones like the plague. The last thing he'd want would be to end up on a party line with the cops, or the FBI. Right out in the open, shoulder-to-shoulder with high society and small-timers alike, he was visible to everyone who counted in South Florida. It was like having thousands of impeccable alibis ready at a moment's notice. But that coin had two sides: with thousands of potential eyewitnesses, Jade hoped it would be equally advantageous to conduct his own business with him in public.

The main gates of Hialeah Park were a passage to another world; one that he rarely had the opportunity to visit. Money was a racetrack's lifeblood, and Jade never had any, so driving between the stone columns and their heavy black ironwork always felt like sneaking into the movies. The sounds of the city seemed to vanish. The clubhouse drive was lined with towering royal palms. The air smelled like a thousand different flowers. Magazines chattered about how many species of tropical plants and trees were on the grounds, but it didn't mean anything to him. Why not count the blades of grass on the first hole of the Bay Shore Golf Course? But it was all fancy enough, Jade thought as he wheeled the roadster down the lane between the perfectly manicured palm trees, toward the bend in the drive where a giant ficus tree stood guard near the clubhouse entrance. It was a perfect place for rich people to be rich.

Jade waved off the uniformed parking valet—no one touched his car if he could help it—and parked the roadster himself, in the cheapest space available, some distance from the clubhouse. He opened the glove compartment and chose a necktie from the three he kept there, finally settling on the maroon-colored one, and quickly tied it in the rearview mirror. This joint was big on dress code, and Jade hoped his suit would be good enough to get him where he needed to go. He put the suit coat on, straightened his fedora, and checked himself in the side mirror one last time. He was as respectable-looking as he could manage. A quick slug from the half-pint under the seat, and he was ready.

The clubhouse and grandstand rose like a giant mansion from the lush greenery, its Mediterranean architecture blending perfectly with the scattered red explosions of hibiscus blossoms against the bougainvillea vines that crawled across its sides and archways. On the front lawn was a stone water fountain that bubbled and sparkled in the noontime sun, and it was here that Jade joined the rest of the late arrivals as they filed toward the clubhouse entrance.

In the lobby, vendors sold programs and *Racing Forms*. Next to the entryway, framed photographs of winning horses and their jockeys hung on the wall next to their racing colors, and talk of the day's competitors was everywhere. Jade watched in amusement as middle-aged women checked their mink coats, in seventy-five degree weather, while their husbands busily studied their programs.

Jade's suit earned him a sneer from a clubhouse usher, but he successfully transacted his way into the prime real estate by disbursing some of Myrna's remaining expense funds. He lingered near the high-dollar betting windows for a while, and watched the traffic there. Eventually, he placed a bet for two dollars on a horse named Lucky Black to win in the first race, and tucked the ticket away in his suit-coat pocket. Then he went back to the veranda and studied the expensive box seats near the track's finish line. The first couple of rows were owned outright by some of the biggest names in American money: Vanderbilt, Guggenheim, Kennedy and Rockefeller. Behind them, the names would be only slightly less famous, many of them owners of horses, perhaps, and the occasional politician or movie star. Jade scanned the entire section for his man, and found two or three possibilities. Then he treated himself to an overpriced hot dog for lunch and washed it down with a cold beer while he stood on the clubhouse veranda and took in the view: hundreds of feet of flowerbeds, the wide expanse of perfectly cut green grass, the tall pine trees that lined the pathway back to the stables, and the shimmering lake in the track's infield with its tiny palm-dotted islands and a million birds.

Then he went to an usher, the same one who'd stared derisively down his nose at Jade's suit a few minutes earlier, and said, "I've got an appointment with Mr. La Forno. Can you show me where he's seated?"

To his surprise, the usher pointed toward the clubhouse veranda behind Jade, which sprawled beneath a mammoth odds board showing the status of horses in the upcoming race. The man who sat at the stone table, shielded from the sun with its own oversized umbrella, looked to be in his early sixties and wore an expensively tailored three-piece suit that admittedly put Jade's own to shame. But this man could have worn a Roman centurion's regalia without looking the least bit out of place. His full head of hair, and its low hairline, were salt-and-pepper. His ruggedly handsome, tanned ethnic face looked like it might have been chiseled from granite: a pronounced, hawk-like nose, a firm mouth with a permanent smile at one corner, and a straight and unlined brow beneath which a pair of razor-sharp, coal-black eyes—which had taken note of the usher's pointed finger—now gazed upon Oscar Jade in unblinking, watchful appraisal. Behind him stood four men in dark suits, and Jade already had their undivided attention as well.

"Right over there, sir," the usher said. "And you'd better have an appointment."

Jade smiled.

As he approached the table, the four soldiers behind La Forno split in half like a well-drilled military detachment and advanced to place themselves on either side of the table between Jade and their boss. Each of them had a twitchy hand (three righties and one lefty, Jade noted) that looked like it wanted to reach for something. La Forno gave a tiny wave, and they stood down.

"Good afternoon," Jade said. "Mister La Forno, right?"

The four muscle-heads glanced at each other. La Forno's expression didn't change. The tiny smile at one corner of his mouth remained fixed. He nodded slowly.

"I'm looking for a job," Jade ventured, "and I heard you're the guy to talk to."

"Is that a fact." La Forno's voice was like velvet. "Do I know you?"

"No." Jade winked at one of the muscle-heads,

who glared back at him. "Not yet."

"I don't employ people I don't know, son. And even if I did, what makes you think I'm hiring?"

"Well, you've got a vacancy at the Caribbean, don't you?" Jade asked casually. "In the manager's position."

La Forno looked out over the track, smiled with what seemed like genuine amusement, and shook his head. "Ah, I see," he said, as if to himself.

"I can do a better job of it than Mallory did." Jade reached in his suitcoat for his pack of smokes—he grinned at the way the movement caused La Forno's soldiers to flinch—tapped out a cigarette, and put it in his mouth. He took out his Ronson and lit up. "And," he said pointedly, as he flicked the lid closed and put it away, "I won't steal from you."

La Forno looked at him squarely. The man's eyes were jet black, and disconcertingly fathomless. Jade was suddenly reminded of being a young child, of a shark he'd seen caught, with a fishing rod, off a wooden pier not far from his home. The shark—all four feet of it—had still been alive, thrashing madly on the wooden planks, and an alert adult had kept the fascinated semicircle of children away from the gnashing, razor-sharp teeth and the whipping fins and tail with the abrasive skin that could cut as surely as those teeth could bite. But Jade had elbowed his way in, close enough to get a good look at those eyes—that deep, impenetrable blackness that somehow already looked dead—and it had been like looking into a bottomless pit. He could still hear the wet slap of that great fish against the dock, see the bright redness of its blood on the wood, and remember those black eyes. On that day, he'd had his first taste of real danger. It was like an electrical current in the air, a hum just beyond the range of hearing that changed the way people behaved. Now, as Jade looked into those eyes once again, the air around him carried that same unmistakable energy.

"Times are getting better," said La Forno smoothly. "Ambitious people are always going to find work. But I can't help you."

"Somebody's got to do it, don't they? Who are you gonna put in there, one of these guys?" Jade nodded scornfully toward the gunsels. "I don't think so. You need somebody you can trust. Somebody with a brain."

"You know, there's a war on now," La Forno went on, as if Jade hadn't spoken at all. "Maybe you should run away and join the service...oh, I guess you can't, what with the bum foot and all. They'd probably tell you no thanks."

"How many cops are you paying off, Mister La Forno? Between the overhead and Mallory's sticky fingers, I'd bet the profits aren't what you were expecting. Not a very good way to do business, if you ask me."

They stared at each other for a long, lingering moment.

"I didn't get your name, Mister—"

"Jade."

"All right then. How much do you know about Hialeah, Mister Jade?"

"Too rich for my blood. Besides that, not much."

"See all those flamingos in the infield? They were imported from Cuba about ten years ago. No expense was spared. Their wings were clipped to keep them from flying away. They were given as much food as they wanted, and guess what? They bred, and made more flamingos. The hatchlings have it so good that they're not even tempted to fly away. So they get to keep all their feathers." La Forno looked at him expectantly.

Jade looked back, half-smiling, and said nothing.

"What I'm saying is that loyalty is rewarded, son. But the reward has to be earned."

Jade took a drag on his smoke. "I've always thought *loyalty* was what had to be earned." He blew the smoke in the old Sicilian's general direction.

The four soldiers took a step toward Jade. La Forno stopped them with a raised hand, and smiled. "You got heart, kid," he said. "But I'm thinking maybe you need your wings clipped."

The bugler's call echoed across the grounds, and a wave of applause and excitement rose up from the stands.

"Got a horse in the race?" La Forno asked him.

"Two bucks on Lucky Black to win," Jade said.

La Forno glanced at the odds board, and back to Jade. "Forty-eight to one," he said, flashing a set of perfectly white teeth in a broad, charitable smile. "Good luck with that."

"How about you?" Jade asked him.

"In the next race," La Forno said. "Connie's North Star. You can take it to the bank."

"Your horse?"

"That's right."

Jade saw the opening, and was happy to exploit

it. “Named in honor of your wife, I suppose,” he offered conversationally. “Like the Constance Holding Company.”

La Forno’s smile faded. His mouth went thin. His lips and pearly-white teeth disappeared. Something flashed in those dark eyes for a moment, and then the smile was back. He shrugged.

Then, below and to the left of them, the starting gates flew open, and the horses were off. A flock of seagulls took to the sky in startled flight as the sound of hooves pounding dirt rose like thunder. As they galloped past, Jade gave La Forno a sideways glance.

La Forno wasn’t watching the race. Instead, he was staring at Jade with what seemed like a new appreciation.

Lucky Black finished dead last. The winner was a horse named Jolly Roger. La Forno handed a ticket to one of his boys and said, “Go collect for me, would you, Sammy?”

Sammy nodded dutifully and took the stub to the windows.

“Your money was on Jolly Roger?” asked Jade, impressed.

La Forno shrugged with exaggerated modesty. “Sure,” he said. “He hardly ever loses on dirt—and *never* when he runs five furlongs. He was at eight to one because people who think they’re smart figured Winsome Ways was a shoe-in just because he’s won his last four.” He snickered. “Didn’t even show.”

“Congratulations.”

“A guy’s got to think his moves out ahead of time,” La Forno said levelly. “He’s got to know what he's doing. Otherwise he can get in over his head, and get himself into trouble. That's when a guy does silly shit like poking a hornet's nest, or betting on a horse called Lucky Black. Guy can lose his money." He took a sip from a glass of iced tea. "Or worse."

"Thanks for the advice."

"No sweat, kid." La Forno waved a hand in dismissal. "We're done here for now. Good luck finding a job."

The Hialeah clubhouse had several very broad stone stairways, with wide granite railings and carved uprights, leading down from the second level to the courtyard and front lawn. Oscar Jade was halfway down one of them when he realized he was being followed by two of the soldiers who'd flanked La Forno at his table. They moved with energetic purpose as Jade made his way toward his roadster, walking as quickly as his limp would allow.

Greta's words came back to him: "If you're looking for trouble, you're going to find it."

10
Ninety Horses

The walk between the clubhouse and his car seemed much longer now than it had on the way in. Every step he took seemed too slow, every halting drag of his bad foot a gift of time to the guys coming up behind him. Jade took care not to give the appearance that he knew they were there, or that he was bothered in any way. It was a nice sunny day at the track, and he was strolling back to his car, that was all. He casually looked over his shoulder as he got into the roadster. One of the soldiers stood in the parking lot, about a hundred feet away, and stared at him. Where was the other one? Had he been flanked? Jade took a quick look around: the guy was nowhere to be found. The answer came a second later, when a brand-new black Cadillac Fleetwood pulled up in front of the gunsel, who climbed in and pointed in Jade's direction.

So that was the score. Jade started the engine. They weren't going to try anything on Hialeah's grounds—too many eyes. He let his car idle, and watched the Fleetwood. It didn't move. They were waiting for him. Well, screw them. He wasn't in the mood to make anything easy. Let them wait. He lit a fresh cigarette.

He calmly smoked the cigarette down to nothing, and tossed the butt out the window. The Fleetwood hadn't moved, but the two guys inside, who were just visible around the edge of a row of parked cars, were beginning to look agitated. Jade grinned, and lit another cigarette. Somewhere nearby, a tropical bird's mocking cackle echoed between the skyscraping pines.

When another car leaving the lot forced the Fleetwood to back up to let it pass, Jade made his move.

He shifted into reverse and hit the gas pedal. The roadster's tires chirped as it shot backward out of its parking spot. Jade kept the pedal down and cranked the steering wheel, then straightened out and continued to reverse, at speed, down the entire two-hundred-foot length of the parking lot. He braked to a stop, shifted into first, and turned onto an access road that led to Hialeah's main entrance drive. In his rearview mirror, Jade saw the big Fleetwood lurch from behind the parked cars and turn onto the access road. Rather than turning right, which would have taken him down the lane and straight out the main gate, he turned left toward the clubhouse.

The parking valet leapt out of the way as Jade howled around the circle drive, his tires squealing as the back end of the roadster tried to get away. Jade gave him an apologetic wave, and emerged from the driveway just as the Fleetwood arrived. As they passed each other, he caught a brief glimpse of the driver's surprised face. Jade tossed him a salute.

Jade turned back onto the access road, and took two more weaving laps between rows of parked cars. By the time he exited Hialeah's grounds through the front gate, he'd put several hundred feet between him and La Forno's men. He turned right on East 4th Avenue and ran at sixty miles per hour—blowing through stop signs and traffic signals, passing everyone else on the street—so it came as a surprise when he checked his mirror five minutes later as he raced alongside the Miami Canal beyond the Hialeah city limits and saw that the black Fleetwood was still with him. The two faces behind the windshield were implacable, and Jade was annoyed at the ease with which they had closed on him.

Okay. It was a new game. How bad did they want him? How far would they go to keep their boss happy? Okeechobee Road stretched on ahead, an enticing straightaway heading southeast. If there were any cops in the neighborhood, he'd know about it soon enough.

He jammed the gas pedal to the floor. The steady, hungry roar of the Flathead V-8's dual-exhaust took on a higher pitch as the custom-modified supercharger kicked in, and all ninety horses under the hood were whipped into full gallop. The speedometer needle edged past 70…80… The wind howled over the top of the windshield. Jade smiled. There was nothing like driving fast with the top down. He scanned the road ahead and planned his moves as he drifted from left to right and weaved his way through the slower traffic, which flashed by in a blur...90...100. Palm trees and intersections shot past. At the intersection of Le Jeune Road, Jade ran a red light and missed a milk truck by just a foot or two. A horn honked angrily and was gone. Then the road made a dangerously quick left-and-right jag, as Okeechobee turned into North River Drive. Jade threw his small car through it, braking sharply and shifting down and then back up in a quick racing change. He spared a glance in the mirror. The Fleetwood was about a block behind him, and made the sudden switch with difficulty, fishtailing wildly and losing some ground before it got itself straightened out. Must have been doing at least ninety when it got there, Jade figured, and suddenly he had an idea. Cadillac made a good machine, built for luxury and power—but it was a big, boxy chassis on a heavy frame, and it had its limits. Then again, so did his little '35 Ford: take a turn too fast in this light little bucket, Jade knew, and it would roll until there wasn't anything left that looked like a car. And the clumpy red stain on the street, a couple of hundred feet from where the twisted wreck would finally come to a stop, wouldn't look anything like a person. The trick was in knowing how far you could push it before the scales tipped against you. Jade hoped he knew his car better than La Forno's men knew theirs, and he was about to find out.

He gave his brakes a tap, shifted down and swerved to the left, where a filling station sat on a small, triangular curb-island at the five-way corner of North River Drive, NW 20th Street, and 27th Avenue. He shot through the narrow lane between the small building and its two gas pumps, doing over fifty, then yanked on the emergency brake, pulled the roadster through a controlled spin and somehow made the extra-sharp left turn, ending up on 27th Avenue heading north, and kept an eye in his mirror.

As he'd hoped, the Fleetwood didn't attempt to follow him through the filling station. Instead, it took the long way around the corner, but it was still going way too fast to make the oblique angle onto 27th—and so it folded its front end around a telephone pole in front of a drug store. The pole snapped off at its base and fell across the hood and roof of the Cadillac, pulling wires down with it. Other cars screeched to a halt. People screamed, and ran.

A block away, Oscar Jade smiled and pulled out a Lucky Strike. He lit it, took a luxuriant lungful, and blew the smoke into a blue sky. Then he spared a final glance at the chaos in his mirror, rounded a corner and drove discreetly away.

11
A Kind Face

Jade parked his car on the curb near the Pelican Bar & Grill at around three in the afternoon, having satisfied himself that there weren't any other tails behind him. Claude's battered old Dodge pick-up, a '31 that showed every mile in its faded, sun-baked red paint job and the rust eating away at its quarter panels, sat about half a block away on Ocean Drive, facing the Pelican. Ben Tuttle, the kid behind the wheel—eighteen years old, small-framed, blond-haired, blue-eyed and baby-faced—looked like he was sitting in the wrong vehicle. When Jade approached, he nodded and grinned. "Hey, Mister Jade."

"Hey, Ben," he said. "Thanks for doing this."

"No problem."

"When did she get back?"

"About noon…a little after, maybe."

"Okay, so what's the scoop?"

"She went out the back door this morning, just after Captain Billings showed up. Then she walked down Ocean for a couple of blocks and flagged down a Yellow Cab. It dropped her off over in the city, on Fourth Avenue...got the address here." Ben handed him a scrap of paper. "She was there for a couple of hours, maybe more. I got nervous for a while, I thought I lost her. Then finally she came out. Another Yellow Cab came and picked her up, and she went to a department store on Flagler. Stayed there for about a half hour, came out with a couple of shopping bags, and then just walked around downtown for the rest of the morning. Stopped and ate at Frank's around eleven. Took her time about it. Then she took another taxi back here. Hasn't left since."

Jade slipped him a ten. "You earned it, pal. Take the rest of the day off."

Ben tucked the bill into a pocket. "Sure. Claude's gonna be sore at me, though. He wants me to clean out the gutters."

"Leave him to me," Jade said with a wink.

"La Forno." Claude said the name slowly, measuring each syllable carefully. There was no mistaking the hint of reverence in his voice. "Are you sure?"

Jade gratefully took a drink from his beer and told Claude everything—from the piece of Dingo McTaggart's tattooed arm to the meeting at Hialeah, and the wrecked Fleetwood. The big man listened attentively, his ruggedly angular face darkening as the story went along. Then, when Jade had finished,

Claude gave a sullen nod and made a pass around the bar, refilling regulars' drinks and taking orders for the grill. Claude drew himself a beer from the tap—unheard of during business hours—drank half of it down, and then refilled it.

"That ain't good, Oscar," he said finally, when he came back to Jade's perch in the middle of the bar. "Ain't good at all. It's just what we don't need, that kinda trouble, I'm tellin' ya. A guy like that ain't gonna stop, not until he gets what he wants." Claude topped off Jade's beer, and took another swallow of his own. "What *does* he want?"

"Good question," Jade said. "Right now, I guess he wants me. He's gonna want to know why I know what I do, and who I've talked to."

"You need to talk to the cap'n, that's who you need to talk to." Claude was emphatic. "It's no good us bein' on the outs with the cops, boss. Not when we got a bunch of made guys from New York crawling around, and La Forno callin' the shots. He's got a way of makin' things happen. Bad things." He shook his head. "Nothin' good can come of it. Nothin' good at all."

Jade studied his friend. There weren't many things in the world that rated more than a few words from the big man from Chicago. This was a man who'd grown up dirt-poor on the South Side, gone to the Great War in 1917, seen and done things in the trenches of France that he still wouldn't talk about to this day. He'd also never told Jade why he'd made the move to Florida—or where he'd gotten the money to buy a place on the beach and an antique bar fixture—but then he really didn't have to. His skills extended far beyond what he now did for a quiet living, and the practical knowledge he'd shared over the years had answered more questions that Jade would have ever asked. Claude Applegate wasn't a man to run his mouth, but when he felt the need to say something, you were a fool not to listen.

"Couple of my cousins were working for themselves in Midtown, way back when," Claude said. "Ran a card game every Saturday night behind a tavern on 42nd Street. Really small-time stuff, not enough to make a living—just a little something on the side, to get by. In come the Terranzas, looking for a piece of the action, more than my cousin Joe could afford to pay. He told them to go take a flying leap—that's just how he was. Nobody pushed him around in his own place. You just didn't do it." Claude shook his head. "Sonofabitch La Forno burned the place down a couple days later. Joe's little brother, Gene... well, they found some of his bones when they finished hosing off what was left. Joe...he just went nuts. Nobody could talk to him. He drove over to the barbershop where La Forno's guys always hung out. Nobody ever saw him again. Or his car. He was just gone, and that was it." Claude stared at Jade. "That's the way this guy works. He either burns you out, or he *disappears* you. That's it. And if he's here on the beach..." His words trailed off, and his eyes looked like the windows of a haunted house. "He can sure as hell do it to us."

Jade took a drink of his beer. "Yeah," he said slowly. "I suppose he can."

"You can bet your ass on it." Claude jerked a thumb toward the doorway leading upstairs. "I'm tellin' ya, boss, something smells funny, and it ain't the fish."

"She say anything when she came in?"

"Not at first. Doin' a whole lotta not talking. Acting real strange."

"Like last night?"

"Kinda. Like her mind was somewhere else, but the rest of her was here. She went upstairs without sayin' anything to anybody, stayed there 'bout an hour. Then she came back down and did the lunchtime dishes for me, even though I said she didn't have to. Wiped off the tables, too. Somewhere in the middle, she started talkin' again."

"About what?"

Claude shrugged. "Just stuff. The weather, the Japs bombing Pearl. And baseball. She knows the game real good for a dame. Says the Dodgers are gonna get back at the Yanks next year." He grinned sagely. "Asked a lot of questions about you, that's for sure."

"Swell," Jade grumbled.

Upstairs, he found the door to his room ajar. He pushed it the rest of the way open. Myrna Mallory stood at his bookcase, her back to him, arranging items on the top shelf that hadn't been there when he'd left that morning.

"Make yourself at home," he said, and she jumped.

"Oh, my God," she said, a hand to her mouth. "You frightened me." She wore a light blue skirt, and a sleeveless white blouse with a plunging neckline that showed more of her assets than Jade had thought she possessed—he noted that the freckles didn't stop at her face—and still another pair of matching shoes. "I'm sorry, the door was unlocked… I found these things yesterday when I cleaned. Why did you have them put away?"

"I'm not too fond of the notion that somebody's pawing through my stuff when I'm not around," Jade said. "It's nobody's business but mine."

She picked up a framed photograph of Jade and another man, both wearing baseball uniforms, with a few words and a signature scrawled in one corner. "Is that really Dizzy Dean, from the Gashouse Gang?"

"That's right."

"Mr. Applegate told me you tried out for the Cardinals," Myrna gushed, and Jade shifted uncomfortably. "But I had no idea…he said you threw the hardest fastball they'd ever seen."

Jade took a drink of his beer. "Spring training, '34," he said.

"They won the Series that year!"

"Uh huh."

She read the writing. "'To Oscar. All the best… Jay.'" She looked up from the picture, and then—hesitantly, perhaps ashamedly—at his foot.

"If it was easy, everybody'd be doing it," Jade said. "They needed somebody who could get down the line."

Myrna put down the picture, and then pointed at one of two trophies. "And you were a middleweight boxing champion, too."

"Regional amateur. It was no big deal."

"Mr. Applegate said you were undefeated when you quit—"

"So you decided to run around town and buy some new clothes," he said.

"I—yes. I had to. I can't be walking around wearing the same thing day after day, can I?"

Jade just stared at her.

Finally she sighed. "I know I shouldn't have run out this morning."

"I thought we understood each other."

"I suppose I panicked when the police showed up."

"Maybe it's just as well. If you had been here, we'd have both had one hell of a lot of explaining to do—you especially."

"I didn't kill my husband, Oscar!"

"I believe you," Jade said evenly. "Maybe the cops will, too. Pretty soon you're going to have to take a chance on that. When the music stops, you're going to need to find a chair, Myrna, and I'm damned if I know why I ought to grab one for you. Run out on me one more time—"

"I'm sorry."

"—and I'll slap some cuffs on you and drag you down to the station myself. That's a promise."

"I'm sorry."

"You hired me because you needed protection from your husband. Well, your husband's dead, so there's really no reason for you to retain my services any longer. I'd be within my rights to kick you to the curb right now." Jade stared at her in silence, letting that sink in for a good long moment. "Unless," he said, "There's something else going on."

"There is," she said softly.

"Of *course* there is."

She sighed. "I just need some more time. A few days, that's all."

Jade took a step toward her. "If the cops turn up anything—anything at all—that puts you in your house last night, we could end up going to jail. Both of us. And when you start talking about doing time, three hundred bucks isn't going to cut it."

Myrna reached quickly for her purse, and produced a small roll of bills. "How about another seven hundred?" She counted it off and thrust it at him. "Make it an even thousand, altogether."

Jade reached out, without hesitating, and took the cash. "Why should I trust you?"

"Because I've never lied to you," she said simply. "And I think you know it." She hesitated. "Don't you?"

He re-counted the money, and tucked it away. "You're not telling me everything, either. Ever hear of a man named La Forno?"

"Who?"

"La Forno." He said it very slowly.

She frowned and shook her head. "Who is he?"

"He owns the Caribbean Hotel...and a few other things. He's from New York City. Word is, your husband stole from him, and got caught. La Forno was putting the squeeze on him for payback."

"How much money?"

"Your life insurance policy would have covered it."

"Did he kill Horace?"

"I don't know," Jade said. "Maybe, but he wouldn't have done it himself. He'd hire it out; that'd figure. This guy's bad news, Myrna—the worst."

She went to the window and gazed down at Ocean Drive. "And that man who followed me here yesterday?"

"Nino Valletti. He's from New York, too. My guess is he works for La Forno."

She was silent for a long moment. "But it shouldn't matter anymore, should it?" she asked, her voice tiny. "Surely they don't think I've got any of that money?"

"Do you?"

She turned around and gazed at Jade with those huge brown eyes. "I wish I did," she said. "I'd spend every penny of it."

"Like going shopping for some new clothes? How about slipping some extra cash to the hired help when they start to get twitchy?"

Myrna frowned. "I suppose I deserve that."

"Sure as hell."

"I have money of my own, Oscar. Money my husband wasn't able to get his hands on…and God knows he tried. Not a lot of money, though—I promise you that."

"You don't have to promise me anything," Jade said. "Just tell me where this seven hundred bucks came from."

She shrugged. "It's not like it's anything illegal. I won it at the racetrack."

The simple statement just hung there in the air for a moment, like a mist hangs over warm water in chilly weather. In the stillness, Jade could hear his own heartbeat thumping in his ears. "You won it at the racetrack," he echoed stupidly.

"That's right. Peter and I went to the track a few

times. He's got his own box seats down front."

"Uh huh. This guy Peter...he probably does real well with the horses."

"I won almost two thousand dollars once!" she said, with a little-girl excitement that turned Jade's stomach inside out. "I was nervous, but Peter told me to relax. He said, 'You can take this one to the bank.' I'll never forget it. The horse's name was—"

"Connie's North Star," Jade said.

She looked at him, astonished. "How did you know that?"

Jade searched her face for a moment, looking for a sign that he was being played—any hint at all—and could find none. He shrugged, drained what was left of his beer, and motioned downstairs. "Come on. I'm buying drinks."

"I'm not drinking," she protested.

"That makes one of us," Jade said. "Follow me. We need to talk."

The Pelican, like many of the drinking establishments on the beach, did a lot of its business outdoors. Once the shutters were opened up and the striped awning rolled out, most customers sat at the tables out on the wooden deck beneath big red, yellow and blue umbrellas. Inside, there was just enough room for the old wooden bar, a jukebox, two tables and one booth on each wall.

Jade and Myrna sat at one of the booths, just inside the building. At least, Jade reasoned, he had the Pelican behind him and would be able to see if anyone approached. The .38 was a welcome presence at the small of his back. He'd taken his suit-coat off to make sure he could get to it in a hurry, and had whispered a few words, in shorthand, to Claude as they took their seats. The big man would be ready for anything, but Myrna was a different story, and Jade knew he had to be careful in how he laid it out for her. Claude brought the drinks. Jade had ordered a Jim Beam on the rocks, Myrna a bottle of Coca-Cola, no glass. "You know, we can go ahead and spice that up if you want," Jade said as Claude retreated.

"Any other time I might take you up on that," she said, and took a sip. "But not right now."

Jade grunted, and lit himself a Lucky Strike. "Seems like a perfect time to me."

He offered her a cigarette; she declined. He asked her for a complete physical description of her erstwhile mystery man. She gave him one, and it matched up picture-perfectly.

"All right, then," he said. "I want you to tell me more about him."

"What do you want to know?"

"His last name, for starters."

"He didn't—he never—I don't know."

"Oh, come *on*," Jade snapped. "When I asked you yesterday, you told me you'd rather not say. Which is it?"

"I was embarrassed, Oscar! He never told me. Once we'd spent some time together, it never came up. And once we'd—it never occurred to me to stop and ask him what his last name was."

"How long did you see each other, altogether?"

"A couple of months, maybe."

"Where did you go besides the racetrack?"

"We went everywhere. We ate lunch all over town, anywhere I wanted to go. We went for long drives. We went to the pier and watched the ships come in. He took me to the movies a few times, the matinee. He's a big fan of Jimmy Cagney and Edward G. Robinson. He said gangster movies made him laugh."

"Sure they did," Jade muttered. "What kind of things did you talk about?"

"I guess I did most of the talking," she said with a down-turned smile. "He listened. He was a good listener. I used to try to get him to tell me more about himself. He'd always talk about the future—he said he wanted a quiet life. He said he wanted to be able to sleep with his back to the door. I never understood what he meant."

"Did you ever see other guys hanging around him? Guys in suits, like the one who followed you here yesterday morning?"

Myrna frowned. "No. But I do remember thinking we were being followed, more than once. I told him so, and he just laughed. He told me I was imagining things."

"Well, you weren't." Jade took a swallow of bourbon.

"What do you mean?"

"He never told you what he did for a living, did he?"

"He said he was retired. A retired businessman."

"Yeah, well…he's a businessman, all right," Jade said. "Not exactly retired."

She stared at him.

"Remember what I told you about the man who owned the Caribbean Hotel? The man your husband stole money from?"

He watched her face as realization began to dawn. "No," she said softly.

"I don't know if Peter's his real first name," Jade said. "But I can tell you what his last name is—"

"No! You don't know what the hell you're talking about!"

"Listen to me Myrna. This is what you hired me to find out, even if you didn't know it at the time. This guy had your husband over a barrel. It can't be a coincidence."

"Well, you're just wrong," she snapped, and got up from the table. She turned and walked past the outdoor tables to the edge of the wooden deck and stared out at the ocean, exposed to God and everybody else, her arms tightly folded across her chest.

Jade gave her half a minute, which seemed to last forever, and then he followed. He put his arm around her and casually rested his free hand on the butt of his gun, his eyes expertly sweeping all around them.

She turned her head, and rested it against his chest. A sob caught in her throat. "Oh, my God. I don't believe it," she said. "It can't be true. It just *can't*."

"Come back inside," he said, and firmly led her back to their booth.

She sat down and stared at her bottle of Coke. Her eyes welled up with silent tears that ran down those freckled cheeks and dropped on the checkered tablecloth.

"We can't keep you here after tonight," Jade said. "It's not safe. Tomorrow we've got to find someplace to put you until I have a chance to sort things out—"

"What did he mean?" she suddenly asked.

"What?"

"The last time I talked to him on the phone." She dabbed her eyes with a napkin, and then threw it down with disdain, as though angry at herself for the emotional display. "When I told him it was over. He kept saying, 'You can't do this.'" She looked at Jade. "What did he mean by that?"

"That's what I'm going to find out. But in the meantime, we've got to tuck you away."

"But...what if—"

"Do you trust me, Myrna?"

"Yes, Oscar."

Jade took a drag on his smoke, and a slug of whisky. "Then drink your soda pop," he said, "and let me worry about the details."

Nightfall came early, as it did this time of year, the December sun sliding away somewhere far behind the Pelican. Gulls circled over the beach, looking for scraps left behind by the day's visitors, and squawked irritatedly at the occasional passerby. The blue sea darkened in the twilight, beneath a sky that went from amber to pink, then to black, as the last light of the day passed from sight. Tiny pinpoints appeared in the black sky, winking like diamonds. The night grew cool. Oscar Jade drank five Jim Beams to Myrna's single bottle of Coke.

Claude brought each of them a platter with a huge hamburger—with pickle, lettuce, sliced tomato and onion—and a heap of French fries. Myrna devoured everything on her plate, and asked Jade if he was going to eat all his fries. He pushed his plate across, and she ate the rest. They talked baseball—National League versus American, Brooklyn versus St. Louis, the Negro Leagues versus the Majors—and he finally got her to laugh once or twice. Their eyes met across the table.

"You have a kind face," she said. "Has anyone ever told you that?"

"No," Jade said, which was a lie. In truth, it was nearly always the first thing a woman told him.

"Well, you do."

"Thanks."

"Oscar…how long do you think a person should have to pay for a mistake?"

Jade said, "I guess it depends on the person. And the mistake."

"That's fair," Myrna said. "What if I'm the person?"

"Then it depends on you."

"That isn't very helpful."

"It's your life, not somebody else's. You just need to get on with it."

She nodded. "I don't know if you've noticed," she said quietly, "but I've had terrible luck with men."

"You're just on a bad streak. They don't last forever."

"How about you?" she asked, a hint of mischief in those big brown eyes. "What kind of a streak are *you* on?"

Jade made the obvious gesture of checking his watch. "On advice of counsel, I'm asserting my rights under the Fifth Amendment."

At nine o'clock, he announced that he was tired and was going to bed early. They had a big day tomorrow. Myrna agreed, and followed him upstairs. Outside his door, she lingered. "I just wanted to thank you," she said.

"No need to. You're paying me."

"That's not what I mean, and you know it."

"Well—" Jade began, and she threw her arms around him and hugged him tight. He hugged back, and was suddenly aware of her warmth, the yielding softness of those breasts pressing against him, the whispering implication of that sigh, so near his ear, and—even more dangerously—how good it felt.

He gently pulled back. Their faces were an inch apart; her eyes were glassy. "Myrna..."

"I know."

"If you're on a bad luck streak with men, I'm not the guy who's going to break it."

"I know," she said, and moved away. At her door, she turned and said, "Good night, Oscar." She quickly closed the door behind her.

Sleep didn't come easily.

The next morning, they ate a breakfast of pancakes and sausage links at the bar. Myrna was in good spirits, and complimented Claude on his cooking. Claude grunted monosyllabic thanks, but Jade caught the ghost of a smile on his friend's face as Claude busied himself with the cleanup.

Jade and Myrna left through the Pelican's side door, passing an empty Pontiac sedan—a brand-new, maroon-colored Super Streamliner with no license plates—parked nearby, where the short stretch of 15th Street essentially came to a dead end alongside the Pelican. Its presence there gnawed at the back of Jade's mind, like an itch he couldn't scratch. Maybe somebody parked it here and then went for an early morning stroll in the surf?

They walked along the south wall toward the parked roadster, with Myrna a step ahead. It was an unusually quiet morning, with sparse traffic along Ocean Drive, which is why Jade noticed the sound of the empty Pontiac's engine turning over. When he heard the sound of chirping tires and rapid acceleration coming up behind them, he instinctively put a hand up between Myrna's shoulder blades and shoved hard—she gasped in surprise and sprawled forward onto the sidewalk—just as the Pontiac drew alongside them, the unmistakable snout of a .45 Thompson submachine gun angling from the backseat window.

12
The Chicago Typewriter

"Stay down!" Jade shouted. His .38 cleared gunleather as he dropped to the concrete and flattened himself out to present as small a target as possible. He fired his first shot just as the Thompson's barrel flashed and roared in the Pontiac's window. Jade was aware of thudding impacts on the wall just above and behind him, and chips of stucco raining down onto the back of his neck. He fired his second and third shots into that car window, aiming just above the barrel of the machine gun, but by then the car was past them and gaining speed.

Jade got to one knee and steadied his Smith & Wesson with both hands. He fired his last three shots with deliberate purpose, putting all three rounds through the Pontiac's rear window, which shattered just as the car slid into a squealing right turn onto Ocean Drive. Behind the wheel, a head turned to look in Jade's direction, and Jade recognized the face as their eyes met across the distance.

In the next second the car was gone.

Myrna lay on the sidewalk, her arms and legs splayed, her skirt riding up the back of her thighs in a most unladylike manner, one of her high-heel shoes lying in the gutter next to the curb. She didn't move.

He knelt beside her, and frantically rolled her over. "Myrna! Myrna!"

Her eyes opened.

"Are you hit?" he asked, quickly patting her down. "Did they get you?"

"I…don't think so," she said, her voice very soft between deep panic-breaths.

"Jesus Christ," he said. "I'm sorry."

Jade lifted her into a sitting position and gently brushed her dark hair away from her freckled cheeks and those big brown eyes. She grabbed him by the collar and kissed him hard, her mouth open and earnest, her lips soft, her breath still faintly sweet with pancakes and maple syrup, her other hand behind his head, pulling him in. He surrendered to it, for a moment. Then he was vaguely aware of Claude standing next to them, and the sound of police sirens.

Finally he untangled himself. "Yeah," he muttered as he stood up, holstered his still-smoking piece and put his hat back on.

Allen Billings bent over and gazed closely at the line of bullet holes—twenty-four of them in all, one every three inches or so—that had chewed into the stucco of the Pelican's south wall in a jagged line, starting about two feet above the sidewalk and moving from right to left, finally curving sharply upward to about six feet high at the impact of the last round. He gave Jade a grim smile. "Chicago typewriter," he said. "With a drum."

Jade nodded. Myrna stood next to him, nervously fidgeting under the collective gaze of Miami Beach's Finest. Four uniformed cops, the first to arrive on the scene, had set up a perimeter. One of them scribbled on a notepad while Claude gave a statement. And Billings' earnest young protégé, Detective Rusty Connor, was giving Myrna his undivided attention.

"Right here," Billings said, pointing at the first bullet hole, "he had you bulls-eyed. You returned fire—"

"About the same time he started shooting," Jade said.

"Which must'a surprised him," Billings went on, moving his fingertip along the crooked line of holes in the stucco, "'cause it threw off his aim for a second, here, then he brought it back down toward where she was, on the sidewalk in front of you. And I'm guessing that here," he pointed to where the holes tracked downward, and then sharply curved upward to the final hole, high off the sidewalk, "is where you fired the next couple, and they must've been good ones, 'cause it looks like he gave up on you, and scrammed." Billings gave Myrna a knowing smile. "It's a good thing you had the South Atlantic pistol shooting champion with you this morning, Mrs. Mallory."

Myrna looked at Jade with new respect. "The

other trophy," she said. Jade shrugged dismissively.

"So who was it, Oscar?" Billings asked him.

"I'll give you three guesses, and the first two don't count," Jade said. "Nino Valletti."

"You sure about that?"

"He was the wheelman."

"Who was the shooter?"

"The only thing I saw in the back seat was the tommy," Jade said apologetically.

"So we know you have a history with this Valletti guy," Connor interjected, "because of the complaint you filed on Tuesday. But what does any of this have to do with Mrs. Mallory, or her husband?"

Jade gave him a thin smile. "That's a good question, detective. I'm working on that."

"Why was Valletti here on Tuesday?" Connor pressed.

"Maybe you should ask him that question," Jade said, and saw Billings' eyes narrow. "At the time, I figured he was following her—probably working for Mallory."

Billings motioned toward the Pelican's front door. "All right," he said amiably. "Let's all go inside and have a talk."

As they walked in, Jade noticed that Rusty Connor stared at his limp, with the turned-in left foot, and gave Billings a meaningful nod.

They sat at the bar, four in a row. Jade put himself between Myrna and the cops. Claude poured coffee for everyone in watchful silence. Connor spooned enough sugar into his cup to bake a cake. Jade lit himself a Lucky, and spoke up first. "So you know I was at Mallory's house the night he was killed."

"Uh huh," Billings said.

"But that was around one in the morning, and he was already dead. At least a couple hours dead. Claude was telling you the truth yesterday. I was here when it must've happened."

"So what were you doing there?" asked Connor.

"I was there on behalf of my client," Jade said. "She hired me on Tuesday morning because she'd been threatened by her husband. She asked me to go and retrieve some of her personal belongings, because she was afraid to go back there."

Myrna, to his immense relief, didn't hesitate. "That's right," she said. "I gave him my key."

"But first you were at the Caribbean, causing a fuss," Connor said.

"The lady wanted me to make contact with Mallory and inform him that she wanted a divorce, which I did."

"Mrs. Mallory, I'm sure you realize this is serious business," Connor said, in between sips of his coffee. "Your marriage wasn't too good, was it?"

"You don't have to answer that, Myrna," Jade cut in.

"But she'd be doing herself a favor if she was honest with us," Billings said.

"Sure, swell," Jade said. "Let's be honest. What about Greta Vincennes?"

He watched as the cops exchanged a quick look. Billings spilled a dribble of coffee down his chin, and dabbed at it with a napkin. "What about her?" Connor asked.

"Seems like *somebody* ought to bring her up, especially since Mallory was making time with her at the Marmalade Club. I saw him there Tuesday night, around nine o'clock. He always hung around to catch her last two shows. And he usually had a little snack in between."

Beside him, Myrna blanched, and stared at her own hands as they fiddled with her coffee cup.

"My understanding is that Miss Vincennes has an alibi for the time of the murder," said Connor. "So you just gave your client a motive. Your husband was having an affair with a stripper, Mrs. Mallory. How did that make you feel?"

"Jeez," Jade said. "Gimme a break, here."

"For all we know, she hired you to bump off her husband."

"Come on, Rusty," Billings barked. "Nobody's saying that."

"Captain, we've got footprints in the victim's back yard with a club left foot, plus by his own admission he was at the scene of the murder—"

"You've got two sets of footprints in the backyard, right?" Jade shot back. "Who's the other set belong to?"

"Funny you should ask," Connor said. "They belong to a woman. What size shoe do you wear, Mrs. Mallory?"

"You've gotta be kidding," Jade said.

"I'm just telling you what the evidence is."

Jade looked Billings in the eye. "Al, could I have a word with you? In private?"

Billings gave him a long, appraising look. "Sure," he said.

As he and Jade stood up, Connor asked Myrna: "So, Mrs. Mallory, where were you on Tuesday night, say around ten or eleven o'clock?"

"Don't say another word, Myrna," Jade said quickly, and turned to face Connor. "Is she under arrest?"

Connor looked at Billings, who shook his head. "Not yet," the young detective grudgingly replied.

"Well, when she is, you can talk to her lawyer," Jade said. "His name is Saul Rothstein. Until then, she doesn't have to tell you a goddamned thing. She was with me, right here, all night…wasn't she, Claude?"

Claude looked back at him, and didn't blink. "That's right," he said. "She was here all night."

Myrna looked at Jade and Claude in surprise, but kept her mouth shut.

Jade and Billings walked out the front of the Pelican and stood on the wooden deck beneath a bright blue sky. Waves crashed on the beach.

Jade offered his pack of Luckies. "Smoke?"

"Yeah, sure." Billings took one, and Jade lit it for him. The cop took a drag and asked, "Does Saul know he's her lawyer?"

"Not yet. But he will."

"Oscar, what the hell are you up to?"

"She didn't kill her husband, Al. You have my word on that. She's got a Guinea from New York trying to shoot her dead for Christ's sake. There's something else going on here."

Billings shook his head, and looked at the horizon. "I'm listening," he said.

"The Caribbean's owned by a guy straight out of the Terranzas in New York, a guy named La Forno—Peter La Forno, I guess. He owns the Marmalade Club, too, plus a bunch of other stuff. Uses an outfit called the Constance Holding Company as cover. Bottom line is, Mallory was stealing from him, and he got caught. When I showed up at the hotel he thought I was one of La Forno's guys and that I was gonna put the squeeze on him—or worse. When he found out I was there because of Myrna, that's when it got rough. Mallory took out a life insurance policy on his wife for fifty grand. My guess is, he planned to use that cash to get himself out of trouble with his boss, and Valletti was supposed to be his button man."

The cop shook his head. "Son of a bitch. This stinks to high heaven. And you're in it up to your neck. Right now I could arrest her on suspicion of murder, and take fingerprints. What if they match up with what's on the knife?"

"It was her kitchen," Jade said. "Why wouldn't her prints be on the knife? Like I said, she didn't kill her husband. She was with me."

"Which makes you an accessory, if you're lying," Billings said. "Claude's word is the only thing keeping that from happening."

Jade looked him squarely in the eye. "Is it? Really?"

Billings sighed. "Goddamn it, Oscar. You were one of my best men, and I'm sorry about how things worked out. But there's a limit to how much slack I can play out here, especially since you haven't been a hundred percent square with me. Look, I don't think you killed Horace Mallory. But I can sure see why his wife might've. The guy was stabbed fifteen times. That ain't a mob hit, and you know it. It means somebody was mad at him. And if it turns out to be her—"

"Meantime," Jade said, "You've got a wop goon driving around Miami Beach with a tommy gun in the back seat of his car. You need to check La Forno out, Al. And see if Valletti's on his payroll."

"Duly noted," Billings said. "But right now, you're a heartbeat away from getting your P.I. license pulled, Oscar. Don't try to push me any farther, 'cause I'm gonna start pushing back."

"That's not all of it," Jade said carefully.

"Oh yeah? What else?"

"Word on the street is that *you're* taking payoff from La Forno."

Billings glared at him. "Who says?"

"Tinsel Pettone."

"That little weasel?"

"He just passed it along. It's gossip. Didn't start with him, he doesn't have those kind of guts. But it's out there. I figured you ought to know."

Billings turned away from him, walked to the edge of the deck and stared out at the ocean, his arms folded. He turned back toward Jade. "Do you believe it?" he asked finally, his voice quavering.

"No," said Jade. "I don't. But somebody's looking to hurt your reputation, and there's got to be a reason why. La Forno's got an in with the cops for sure, and so does this Vincennes girl at the Marmalade club."

"Well, then." Billings leveled him a long look. "We're just going to have to trust each other, aren't we?"

Jade and Myrna gave written statements. He promised Billings that Myrna would remain available to the cops in case anything broke. Rusty Connor stared at the bad foot in silence. A police photographer took pictures of the bullet holes in the south wall.

Once the cops were gone, Oscar Jade sat down at the cluttered desk in the Pelican's tiny office just off the bottom of the stairwell, and placed a call to Saul Rothstein, Attorney-At-Law.

Rothstein had an office over in Miami, on northwest 9th Street. He'd started out as a contract lawyer for a real estate company during the city's boom time in the early '20s, but had quickly learned that the money was better in private practice—and criminal law—especially if he catered to a clientele who tended to get in trouble on a regular basis. Saul Rothstein had kept a lot of bootleggers out of jail during Prohibition, keeping the booze flowing for South Florida during the toughest of times. He had a reputation as a tough defender with a few tricks up his sleeve, and he won more cases than he lost. Jade had helped him out with a problem a few months back, so he owed him a favor.

"Oscar!" exclaimed Rothstein, his good-natured, deep baritone carrying a smile over the phone line. "Long time, no hear from. Been quiet, I guess?"

"Yeah, but not anymore. Got a live one for you, Saul. I suppose you've read about the Mallory murder."

"Sure I did. Made the paper. Looks like a nasty business."

"Well, the dead guy's wife is my client."

There was a silence. "I suppose she's my client too, then. Right?"

"I'd appreciate it. The cops are all over her."

"Are they pressing charges?"

"Not yet, they're not. They're dying to fingerprint her, though."

"Not until they arrest her, they won't," his lawyer said. "If they do, give me a call and I'll be there."

"I appreciate that. But actually, I was hoping you could come out anyway...you know, talk to her about it. I want to hear what you think. She's gonna need help with her husband's funeral arrangements, wrapping up his affairs, that kind of thing. Plus you're going to want to take a look at his will, if he's got one. That'll tell us a lot."

"Yeah, I can do that. Just one thing, Oscar. Not that it really matters, you know me, but I'm always curious..."

"She didn't do it, Saul."

"Are you *sure*?"

"As sure as I can be," Jade said.

Rothstein hesitated. "Oh, *boy*," he said.

Claude was refilling Myrna's coffee cup when Jade came out of the office. She looked at him warily. "What now?" she asked.

"My lawyer's going to come out and meet with you in a couple of hours. He's a good guy; you can trust him. I want you to be square with him. Tell him everything you've told me...and I mean everything. Understand?"

She nodded.

Jade pulled Claude aside, and spoke to him quietly. "Listen, she can't stay around here anymore. It's getting too hot. When Saul's done with her, I want you to find a place to put her for a couple of days, just to buy me some time. Make goddamned sure you don't have a tail."

The big man considered for a moment. "Where you thinkin'?"

"Try to stay off Collins and Ocean, for sure. One of the older joints that aren't as busy. Someplace like the Shelby, or the Carlotta. Set her up so she doesn't have to go out for food. I want her off the street, and out of sight. Okay?"

Claude frowned. "I'll see what I can do. Where you goin'?"

"I got some legwork to do," Jade said, "and a hunch to follow up on."

13
Helluva Job

Oscar Jade paid extra close attention to his rearview mirror as he motored down Fourth Avenue. His head swiveled from side to side at every intersection. He made a mental note of how long certain cars remained behind him before they turned, and tried to determine whether or not another one took their place. Sometimes he thought so, other times he couldn't be sure. How much of a machine did La Forno have in South Florida, and just what it was capable of?

He drove past the Gavin Theatre. The marquee proclaimed: *'SUSPICION' – starring Cary Grant and Joan Fontaine.* Jade shook his head and smiled ironically.

The address Ben had given him, 1015 Northwest Fourth Street, was just three doors down from the theatre. Jade parked the car and stood at the front door of the modest three-story office building. He looked at the directory. On the first floor there was an advertising agency, a psychiatrist's office and a mail-order catalog company. The second floor housed two lawyers and an M.D. Another doctor, another lawyer and a jeweler occupied the third. Jade decided to start at the top and work his way down.

The elderly jeweler looked up at him patiently over a pair of illuminated magnifying glasses. "Can I help you, son?" Jade introduced himself, and opened his wallet to show his P.I. license. The light mounted on the jeweler's glasses shone on the credentials as the old man examined them. "I haven't done anything wrong," he said.

"Actually, I'm trying to find out about a woman who came to this address, sometime yesterday morning. Her name is Myrna Mallory. Ring a bell?"

The jeweler shook his head. Jade showed him a picture—Myrna and Horace Mallory's wedding photo—and again, the old man shook his head. "Sorry, son," he said. "Business is slow. I get maybe two or three customers a day, sometimes not even that. She's a nice-looking gal. I'm sure I'd remember."

Jade visited each business, refining his story as he went. Nobody had seen her. In the doctor's office on the second floor, the uniformed nurse-receptionist shook her head at the name—but when he showed her the picture it was a different story, and her face told it without a word.

"You recognize her, don't you?"

"But her name wasn't Mallory," she said. "It was…" She referenced the appointment book, and paged back to the previous day. "Jones. Elizabeth Jones."

"What was she here for?"

"Oh, I'm not allowed to talk about things like that," she said.

"I understand, ma'am, believe me." Jade leaned forward on the counter and gave her his best aw-shucks smile, lowering his voice in the patented manner of the chatty conspirator. "And I'd never want you to break any rules, or get yourself in trouble. But this is a special situation. Truth is, I'm a friend of the family, and I'm supposed to be watching out for her. I promised her mother I would."

"Her mother?" The nurse leaned in toward him, ever so slightly.

"Yeah. Sweet little thing lives up in Tallahassee. She's been a wreck since her little girl married this guy from, well, the wrong side of the tracks, if you get my meaning."

"Oh, yes," she said, gobbling up his words like buttered popcorn.

"Her momma's terrified that he's going to lay his hands on her. And if she finds out Elizabeth's had to see a doctor, she'll be fit to be tied. Is she all right? Has she been hurt?"

She considered for a moment, and Jade knew he had her. Just as she opened her mouth, a stern voice came from behind her.

"We don't have anything to say to you."

A hard-faced middle-aged man stood in the doorway to an examination room. He wore rolled-up shirtsleeves, a loosened necktie and a scowl. The nurse looked down, and suddenly appeared to be contemplating the quality of her manicure. "Doctor Angelo?" Jade asked.

"That's right," the doctor said. "Miss Jones is my

patient. And I'm not in the habit of violating doctor-patient confidentiality. What did you say your name was?"

"I didn't. But it's Jade. Oscar Jade. I'm a private detective."

The doctor's eyes narrowed. "Did I hear you right? You're supposed to be watching out for her?"

"That's right."

The doctor shook his head. The corners of his mouth curled nastily into something halfway between a smile and a sneer. "Helluva job you're making of it, Mr. Jade."

His next stop was the back room of Brumly's Grocery, where the phones rang constantly as Tinsel's boys busily took bets for the upcoming weekend's football games. When Jade came through the door, Tinsel regarded him with undisguised dread.

"I'm kinda busy here, Jade."

"Yeah, me too." Jade took him by the arm and led him to a corner of the tiny room. "I need a favor."

"I don't know what I'm gonna do," Tinsel sputtered. He dabbed at the beady sweat on his brow, and itched nervously at his toupee. It slid around on his head like a throw rug on a hardwood floor. "Two of my guys volunteered for the army today. The *army*! Can you believe it?"

"Sure," Jade said. "There's a war on now, Danny. Things are gonna change for everybody."

"Yeah, yeah, but they could've waited until they

got drafted, for Chrissake! Gimme some time to get some fresh help. I'm gonna have to maybe find some high school kids, or something. You know any?"

"Listen," Jade said impatiently. "You said Al Billings is on the take."

Tinsel flinched as though Jade had drawn a fist back. "It's just something I heard. I don't know nothing else, I swear!"

"I need to know where that story's coming from."

"What? You believe it now?"

"Not necessarily. But there has to be a reason it's out there."

"It's a rumor, Jade. That's all. The guy who told me heard it from somebody else."

"Fine. I want to know who started the rumor. And I need to know pretty quick."

"How quick?"

"An hour ago. By tonight, at the latest."

"Jesus," Tinsel mumbled. "I don't know…"

Jade plucked out a fifty-dollar bill and stuffed it into the breast pocket of Tinsel's sweat-stained shirt. "Here's a U.S. Grant. Spread it around if you need to. If you get me the straight dope, there'll be another one. And you can keep that one all for yourself."

"All right, Jade." Tinsel grinned nervously. "If it turns out to be on the level, you can apologize to me later."

"Maybe I will," Jade said. "One more thing. I need to talk to your boy Marty for a second."

Tinsel wasn't happy about pulling his boy off the telephones. "Okay, okay. But make it quick. I'm trying to earn a living, here." He scurried over to Marty, who was working two different phones at the same time and scribbling on a notepad. Tinsel pointed at Jade. Marty nodded.

Five minutes later, Jade stood in the alley behind Brumly's with the part-time bartender from the Marmalade Club. He handed him a smoke and lit it for him. "Marty, I want to ask you about Tuesday night," he said.

"Yeah, okay."

"I left after the first show, about the time Mallory showed up. What happened after that?"

"Pretty much the same as usual," Marty said. "At least at first. Mr. Mallory had a reserved table, right up front by the stage. That's where he always sat, so he could keep an eye on Miss Vincennes. And he always had one of his strong-arm boys with him. In case somebody tried something funny with her, know what I mean? Every once in a while, somebody'd get the crap beaten out of him, just for looking at her too close. Anyhow, it was like that Tuesday night, except Mr. Mallory had somebody new with him—I'd never seen this guy before. Wore a real nice suit, but he looked like a tough guy. I don't think he worked for Mr. Mallory."

"How do you mean?"

"I dunno. It's hard to explain, but Mr. Mallory didn't treat this guy like hired help. It was almost like it was the other way around. When the guy with the fancy suit talked, Mr. Mallory listened. But they started to argue with each other during the second show, and it got pretty loud. The band got tripped up—Miss Vincennes even stopped dancing for a second—and then they calmed down, but both guys looked mad. I mean, *real* mad, like..."

"Like what?"

"Like they wanted to kill each other," Marty said. "Then the guy started pointing at Miss Vincennes, and Mr. Mallory yelled at him to get the hell out. The guy left after that. Mr. Mallory watched the rest of the show with nobody else at his table, and nobody wanted to talk to him. It ended up I took him his drinks because the waitresses were afraid to go near him. After the show, Mr. Mallory went back to Miss Vincennes' room, and there was some yelling back there, too. Then they both left around 11:30, and she didn't get back until after midnight, so the last show started a half-hour late."

"Is that so," Jade said.

"That's right," Marty said glumly. "The manager was pretty sore about it, too. People come to see Miss Vincennes, and the midnight show's the biggest one. He almost had to pay back a room full of cover charges. As it is, he had to buy a round of drinks on the house until she finally showed up."

Jade took a moment to light a cigarette of his own. "What about the cop who came to see Greta before the show?"

Marty shrugged and spread his hands. "I dunno any cops. Like I said, a flatfoot's a flatfoot."

"Yeah, sure. But what did he look like? Give me everything you can remember."

The kid thought for a second. "Little guy," he said. "Short. Skinny, too. He coulda been a jockey—you know, ride horses. Can't weigh much more than a hundred pounds."

Back at the Pelican, Jade sat at the bar and had Claude pour him two shots of Jim Beam, back to back. He chased them with a draft beer and stared at the bubbles in the glass. "Myrna tucked away?" he finally asked.

Claude nodded. "At the Carlotta, up north. She's not going anywhere." He shook his head. "It's no good for very long, though. Too many ways in and out of the place...and I don't have anybody there I can count on. A lot of new faces on their payroll. But at least it ain't *here*."

"No tails on the way?"

"None I could see," Claude said.

"Good. We can't keep her there for too long." Jade took another drink. "Hell, we can't keep her anywhere for too long. Not until we know who we can trust."

"I don't buy it, boss," Claude said. "Don't feel right. The cap'n's a tough nut, sure. Always was. But he's always been square."

"I know." Jade had another swallow. "He saved my life once, back when I was still in uniform. I ever tell you? It was before...the other thing."

The big man shook his head.

"Three guys who thought they were the next Dillinger gang tried to knock over the Bank & Trust back in '36. The alarm must have gone off quicker than they expected. My partner and I were only a couple of blocks away when it happened, so we were the first ones there. Pulled up right in front, and they got hung up in the front door of the bank. They had tommies. Shot up our car pretty good, so we were pinned behind it, but they couldn't go anywhere either. I took one of 'em down, waited for them to reload, then I made a move. I came out from behind the car and had a bead on another one, but I didn't know the third guy had gotten around behind a row of parked cars by the front door. Somebody fired on my left, and the robber went down. That's when I saw Al Billings, along the front of the bank. He was having a cup of coffee around the corner when the alarm went off. The guy he killed would've had me dead to rights. Later on, after the paperwork, he bought me lunch and told me, 'Always watch your flank, kid.'"

Claude nodded thoughtfully, and frowned as he went back to his work.

The sun went down. Besides the regulars, business traffic was slow. Jade had three more beers and a pastrami sandwich, and went upstairs to lie down at nine o'clock. He read a few pages from his dog-eared copy of Ed McGivern's book on revolver shooting, and was beginning to drift toward a welcoming sleep when Claude knocked on the door. "Phone call for you, boss."

He took the call at the foot of the stairs. "This is Jade."

"Jade, this is Russ Connor," said the voice on the other end. "Meet me at the corner of 79th Street and Harding, right away. There's been a shooting."

14
Sideshow

There was a phone booth on the corner of 79th Street and Harding Avenue, next to a drug store and across the street from a gas station, where flashing red police lights danced across the brickwork in the darkness and men in uniforms kept an expanding semicircle of gawkers at a distance. Sudden death has a way of drawing an audience, like a traveling sideshow. Nobody wants to be the dog-faced boy, but everybody wants a look at one. It was the same way with dead bodies.

Jade parked about fifty feet away, next to the medical examiner's meatwagon, and was met by Connor, whose detective shield hung proudly in its leather wallet from the handkerchief pocket of his suitcoat. "Happened about an hour ago," the young copper said in a clipped, professional cadence.

"Witnesses?" Jade asked.

Connor shook his head. "Guy who works at the gas station heard the shots, and a car peeling out.

Said he was in the can at the time, 'cause business was slow. So he didn't see anything."

"That's it?"

"That's it," Connor said. "It's a quiet corner. Everything else was closed up for the evening. Did he call you tonight?"

"No," said Jade. "He didn't."

"Any reason he might have?"

Jade shrugged.

"'Cause it looks like he was about to." Connor looked at him pointedly. "He had a scrap of paper in his hand with a phone number on it. I called the number. It was yours."

They stood at the booth's door, which was open now but had been closed when the killer had fired through the narrow pane of glass. Tinsel Pettone must have seen who pulled the trigger, but that was one secret the snitch would be keeping for good. He had a bullet hole squarely in the middle of his forehead, another beneath his right eye, and a third in his chest. Blood and bits were sprayed against the shattered glass behind where his head had been. He'd slid into a sitting position, his legs oddly folded up Indian-style beneath him, his toupee askew on his head, his eyes and mouth gaping in droll astonishment. He looked like a vaudevillian comic who'd been interrupted in the middle of his best joke.

"Thirty-eight," Jade observed.

"That's my guess," Connor said. "At least one of them went all the way through. That one'll be across the street somewhere. But I'll bet we find one of the others still in him, or in the booth somewhere. It'll keep the lab busy." He squinted at Jade. "Any ideas?"

"If I were you, I'd sweat the gas station jerk for a while," Jade said. "Run him in, scare him a little. Put a light in his face. I wouldn't be surprised if somebody slipped him a sawbuck to go take a leak at the right time."

"I got a couple ideas of my own."

"Good for you," Jade said. He looked at Tinsel's face again. The dead bookie stared him straight in the eye, his punch line undelivered. "Then I guess you don't need me."

"But you need to be here," Connor countered. "Am I right? This guy was one of your sources, that much I know. I hear you used him a lot, and he had something to tell you, so you've got a piece of this action, wherever it goes. What I want to know is, what does this have to do with your client?"

"I don't know."

"You had him chasing something down, though. What was it?"

For a moment, Jade considered holding back. He decided against it. "There's a rumor on the beach about La Forno paying cops to leave the Caribbean alone. Danny was trying to get me some particulars."

"Looks like he got 'em, unless I miss my guess," Connor said heavily.

"Yeah." Jade took a breath, and let it go. "Where's Al, Rusty?"

"Hold on a second." Connor turned toward the guy from the M. E.'s office. "Let me know when you're done," he said. "I'm looking for a couple of pieces of lead, here and across the way." The guy from the meatwagon nodded gravely, and went to his work.

"Let's take a walk," Connor told Jade, and the two of them moved beyond the fringe of ghouls and looky-loos, many of whom had begun to drift away as the body was covered up and laid on a gurney. The young cop watched as the lab boys went to work. Despite himself, Jade was impressed with the way the kid conducted his business. No doubt about it, he was a pro.

"Al left the station at five o'clock, straight up," Connor said. "Didn't say anything to anybody. And that's not normal."

"No it's not," Jade reluctantly agreed.

"My first day in plainclothes, Al told me 'Perps don't take coffee breaks, so a cop shouldn't ever give a damn what time it is.'"

Jade had to smile. "He's got a million of 'em. He always told me, 'When your shift's over, make sure the next guy in line knows what the score is. *Then* you can go home to Sally.'"

Connor grinned. "Yeah. He still says every cop's married to a girl named Sally."

"That's his wife's name," Jade said.

The grin faded. Connor nodded. "Uh, yeah. They've been having some trouble. I don't know if you knew."

Jade shook his head.

"I called his house. There's no answer." Connor lowered his voice. "Listen, Jade. I don't know you except what I hear from the old-timers, and even some of them aren't sure. This business with the Mallory woman and her husband is bad, and I know you're in it pretty deep. But Al thinks the world of you, and you've got a reputation for being a square dealer.

Sorry if I came on too strong earlier today, but I'm just trying to do the right thing, I hope you know that."

"You don't have to apologize for being a good cop, Rusty."

"Maybe not, but I shouldn't let myself get carried away, either." Connor nodded toward the phone booth. "Somebody's playing for keeps here, Jade. I hope you've got your client bundled up tight."

"Not as tight as I want. She's gonna need police protection, at least until I can get her off the beach."

"Damn right she does," Connor said. "I can do that. When are you going to move her?"

"Probably tomorrow morning."

"Then she ought to have a detail on her right now. Where is she?"

Jade hesitated. "No offense, Rusty, but—"

"What, you don't trust me?" Connor gave an ironic smile. "I guess I got that coming after this morning, don't I? Okay, Jade, here's the deal. You need the cops on your side right now. You know that. Who else you got?"

"I'd like to talk to Al."

"Yeah, well, that makes two of us." Connor paused. "How much do you know about what's going on with him?"

"We don't talk so much these days."

"Well, I know more than I ought to. He's started drinking again."

"When?" asked Jade quickly, his voice taut.

"Last week or so. All of a sudden." Connor cleared his throat. "I've heard something went on between you two about five years ago, when you were working a case together. They say you spent a couple of weeks in the hospital when he—"

"That was five years ago," Jade said. "It's ancient history. Any clue what got him going again?"

"Sure," Connor said. "What else? A broad. Not his wife."

"Greta Vincennes."

"That's right."

Jade tiredly rubbed his eyes. "Son of a bitch. Something's not right here, Rusty. This doesn't make any sense. It's not like him."

"I wouldn't have thought so either." Connor shook out a Chesterfield and lit up. "But things change. People change. Ever since he got tangled up with the dancer…"

"How'd it happen?"

"No idea. But I got a call from his wife one morning a few days ago, about four o'clock. He wasn't home yet. That day, he was three hours late to work. Hadn't changed his clothes. Smelled like a distillery." Connor frowned. "Different guy than the one I thought I knew, that's for sure. Later on we're in the car driving around, and he just starts crying. He tells me he's made the biggest mistake of his life. Said he woke up in bed with the dancer, and can't remember how he got there. Bottom line is, I'm not so sure you want him babysitting Myrna Mallory right now."

"I guess not," Jade said.

The cop held out his hand. "You can trust me, Jade. I give you my word. I won't let you down."

Jade reached out and shook the hand. It was

firm and solid. "She's at the Carlotta," he said. "Up in Surfside."

"Okay, good," said the cop. "I know the place. I'll put a cruiser out in front, and have another one watching the alley. Nobody gets in or out. Okay?"

"All right," Jade said. "About Greta…this morning, you told me she had an alibi for the time of Mallory's murder. But her midnight show started a half hour late. That gives her plenty of time, more than enough to do what she needed to do. Where'd you get your information?"

Connor threw Jade a meaningful look as two guys rolled Tinsel's covered body past them toward the meatwagon, the wheels of the gurney clattering noisily on the street.

"Al told me," Connor said.

15
Temptation

It was a modest living room in a small one-bedroom apartment, with a miniature kitchen off to one side. The only light in the place came from a streetlamp, a dim shaft of yellow straining in between breeze-tugged lace curtains. An occasional car passed by on the street outside. A palm tree gently brushed against the side of the building just beyond the screened window. The place smelled clean, like a freshly laundered bedsheet hung out to dry in the sunshine of a spring day. It smelled like her.

Oscar Jade checked his watch. It wouldn't be long now. He used the time to unload, clean and reload his Smith & Wesson, and then he dropped it into the side pocket of his suit coat. From there it could be fired without the wasted time of a draw, and he didn't kid himself that it might be necessary.

At 1:15 in the morning, a key turned in the lock of the front door. The light came on; Jade squinted against the sudden brightness. Greta Vincennes, wearing a silky-silver low-cut evening dress, stood in the doorway. When she saw Jade sitting on her sofa, she jumped and gasped, a hand to her mouth—but to her credit, she didn't scream. He should have known better. This broad was tougher than she looked—a lot tougher—and he needed to remember that.

"What the hell are you doing here?" she demanded. "And how did you find out where I live?"

"That was the easiest thing I've done all week," Jade said, which was true enough. He'd scribbled down the number of the cab that dropped her off at the Marmalade Club, and the time of day. From there it was a simple matter of calling Kelly's Comfort Cab and checking the logbook to see where the driver had gone to pick up his fare. "I've got a question for you," he said. "What in the world made you think you could get away with killing Horace Mallory?"

She kept her armor up. She closed the door behind her, laid her purse on a small table, and slowly crossed to the kitchen, where she opened a cabinet and took out a bottle of Four Roses whisky. When she spoke again, her voice wasn't quite as steady as before. "Drink?"

"Absolutely," Jade said.

She took out two glasses, and poured a generous measure into each. Jade noted that she poured more for herself. She brought him the other. "How do you know I did it?"

"For starters, you're not denying it."

"He was alive the last time I saw him."

"I don't think so. Thanks for the drink." Jade raised his glass in a quick toast, and tossed it back in a single swallow. He savored the burn at the back of his throat, and the welcome heat when it hit bottom. "Mind if I have another?"

"Help yourself," she said. Her crystal-blue eyes didn't blink.

Jade went to the bottle and poured himself a refill. "You told me that Mallory left before your last show. That was true enough, except you left with him, around 11:30, after having an argument with him backstage. And the last show started late. Isn't that right?"

She took a drink, crossed her arms, and stared at the glass in her hand.

"You went back to his house with him," Jade went on, "and after you killed him, you took his car. How am I doing so far?"

She looked up from her glass and stared at him, her ruby-red lips thinning until they all but disappeared. She quickly turned away from him, without saying a word, and slinked over to where she'd laid down her purse.

As she opened it and fished around for something inside, Jade casually transferred his drink to his left hand and placed his right into his pocket, where it curled in readiness around the butt of the .38. If her hand came out of that purse with a rod, he'd be ready. From here, ten or twelve feet away, it would be the easiest shot in the world, even from the hip, and Jade was reasonably sure he could drop her without killing her. If he screwed it up and caught an artery, with any luck an ambulance could get there before she bled out. But even if it didn't, all it would mean was an uncomfortable stretch with the cops, an inquest with a few tough questions, and one hell of a lot of paperwork. He might even be able to get the blown-out pocket of his cheap suit fixed, and the powder burns removed. Then would come the living with it—but that was for later. Now was all about now.

But when the hand came out of the purse, it held nothing more sinister than a single key, with a small brass tag attached. Greta dangled it in front of him. "Do you know what this is, Oscar?"

Jade let go of his gun, slowly withdrew his hand from his pocket, and took a drink of Four Roses. "I'm more happy about what it *isn't*," he said.

"It opens a locker at the train station," she said. "And what's in that locker is yours…if you let this go."

He gave a tight smile. "What's in the locker?"

She took another drink. "Five thousand dollars," she said.

"What a surprise," he dryly replied. "And I bet I know whose five grand."

"This money belongs to nobody," she said. "It's been lost, and stolen, and stolen again. It's anybody's money. And you can have it."

"And you'll just give it all away, right? If I keep my mouth shut."

"Don't be silly," she said. "There are more keys."

"I see. So you're flush."

"I'm leaving town," Greta said. "And I'm never coming back."

"Do you realize that Mallory took out a life insurance policy on his wife to pay that money back to La Forno, and that somebody tried to kill her this morning? Does that bother you at all?"

She turned away from him, and walked to the window.

"But it's not your problem, right? You take the money and run. And an innocent lady takes the fall for killing her husband. But maybe that doesn't matter, because she could get rubbed out before it even gets to trial."

"Stop it," she said, without turning around. "Just…stop it."

"Money doesn't fix everything, Greta. Sometimes, it's the reason things break. It changes people, especially if it's blood money. And the problem with blood money is that you can never get the blood off. Even if you run away, it's going to follow you. You need to think about that."

She turned away from the window, and came toward him. "I didn't have any choice," she said, and looked at him with a strange light in those eyes. Once again Jade had a sense of her heat, the fragrant intoxication of warm invitation, as she reached out and grasped his arm. Standing in front of her was like standing in front of a blast furnace, except that when you stood in front of a furnace, you never wanted to jump in. "He didn't give me a choice. You have to believe me."

Jade pulled his arm away. "You're wrong about that, you know. I don't have to believe you." He took a drink. "You *need* me to believe you. There's a big difference."

Greta gazed at him for a moment, and pushed away a lock of golden blonde hair that had fallen away from the shiny nest of carefully done-up showgirl-curls. She took a seat on the couch. He gave her a Lucky and lit it for her.

"Have a seat," she said.

"I'll stand for now, thanks."

She took a long pull at the cigarette, and blew a lungful of smoke into the center of the room. When she finished her drink, Jade took her glass to the table and refilled it. She thanked him.

"My father was an accountant," she began. "In New York. He worked for Wyeth and Jackson, on Fifth Avenue, for fifteen years. I'm very good at mathematics, and that's probably why. He used to help me with my schoolwork…he showed me how to read a ledger book when other girls were still playing with dolls. I got the best grades in my class." Greta frowned. "He always treated me like an adult, though, or a junior business partner. Never like a child, and certainly not like his daughter. He was very…distant. So was my mother. She was a singer for the Metropolitan Opera, and was gone most nights. They were both almost forty when I was born, so I suppose I was a surprise to them. Or an afterthought, at the very least. I don't remember either of them ever telling me they loved me, and I learned very early that I shouldn't worry about pleasing them, because it was just impossible."

"That's tough," Jade said.

Greta shrugged. "I was nine years old when the stock market crashed, and he lost his job. He sat me down in our living room and told me that things were going to get tough for a while. It was the first time I ever saw him cry—the only time he actually seemed like a human being. He told me that we might have to move out of our house, but the family was going to stay together, no matter what. He told me I was going to have to be brave, and help my mother. When I went to bed that night, I remember thinking that the world was coming to an end. And it seemed that way, with people lining up for food at the soup kitchens, and sleeping in the alley—whole families, sleeping in the alley! In the rain and snow. As the days went by, I kept wondering when it was going hit us—you know, like some terrible illness, like consumption or polio—and you couldn't do anything about it, except pray and hope it didn't happen to you, even though it was happening everywhere.

"But it never happened to us. It was like we were living a charmed life. We did move out of the house. But we got a bigger one in a better neighborhood. There was always food on the table, and lots of new clothes at Christmas-time. I was put into a private girls' school, and took ballet lessons." She smiled ironically. "It was easy to forget what was happening to other people, even though I saw it every day of my life. Probably too easy. I asked my father about it once, and he told me that we were just lucky. He said he'd found another job. I couldn't figure out why he wouldn't have told us, but my mother told me not to worry about it, even though she looked plenty worried to me. I always had the feeling she knew more than she let on. I guess I should have asked more questions.

"My father hired a driver, a very nice older man named Mr. Kelso, who always drove me to and from school. He would always smile and ask me how my day had been, if I had a boyfriend yet, that kind of thing. He'd say, 'Make sure Mr. Right treats you right, Greta, 'cause if he doesn't, he'll have to answer to me.'" She smiled. "And the boys did pay a lot of attention to me. Their school was right across the street from ours. One time a boy from their football team, his name was Ted, waited for me after school. He said he wanted to give me a kiss, and took me around the corner of the building. Well, he wanted a lot more than a kiss. I told him no. He pushed me up against the wall and was trying to reach up my skirt when Mr. Kelso showed up. I'd never seen him mad before, and it was frightening. He had a crowbar in his hand. He told him: 'If you touch her again, I'll kill you.' When Ted ran away, he said, 'That wasn't Mr. Right, Greta. You can do better than that.' After that, it was different between us. I always felt safe with Mr. Kelso.

"It was towards the end of my senior year in high school—I was seventeen—when Mr. Kelso came and picked me up for the last time. He didn't ask me about school...he didn't say hello. He wouldn't even look at me when he opened the car door. I tried to talk to him, and he didn't answer. When we passed the street I lived on, I asked him where we were going. He wouldn't tell me...but pretty soon we were in Brooklyn.

"I'll never forget it, as long as I live. He told me, 'You can't go home, Greta. You can't ever go home again. It's over.' I asked him what he meant, because I was scared. All of a sudden, you know what I mean? I knew something was wrong—*really* wrong—but I just couldn't imagine how bad it was. You probably don't understand what I'm talking about."

Jade knew very well what she was talking about.

"I asked him what had happened," she continued, "and of course he wouldn't tell me. I asked him if something had happened to my father. He just nodded, and I started to cry. 'Don't cry,' he said. 'You're going to be all right.'

"We pulled up in front of a townhouse. Two men in suits were standing outside the front door. They stared at me through the car window. Mr. Kelso turned around and told me he knew I was a strong girl the second he met me, and now I was going to have to be, because things were going to get tough for a while. He told me to go along with them, and do what I was told, no matter what. He said, 'Remember, at first, he's going to be able to do whatever he wants with you. Just don't give him any reason to do something bad. When the time comes, maybe you'll be able to get even...and I hope you do, because he deserves it.'

"He waved at the men standing outside. One of them opened the car door, and the other one yanked me out. Mr. Kelso drove away.

"They took me inside and led me down a long hallway. One of them knocked on a door, and I could hear somebody say, 'Come in.' They opened the door, and pushed me inside. An older man in a smoking jacket was sitting there by himself, at one end of a long table. He stared at me for a long time, and then told the two men to leave us alone. After they were gone, he pointed at a chair and told me to sit down. I did.

"'My name is Pietro La Forno,' he said. 'Your father worked for me. Did you know that?'

"Of course I didn't. My father never talked about

his job, but I was afraid to say anything. I just shook my head.

"He said that my father had stolen money from him. He spoke in a soft voice—he actually sounded like a nice man, that's a laugh—but there was something about his face. I don't know how to describe it. It was like a mask. I could tell there was something terribly ugly behind it. I shook my head again. He said my father thought he could get away with stealing from him, but he thought wrong. Then he told me my father was dead. He said, 'I'm going to take care of you from now on.'

"I asked him where my mother was. He told me there had been a 'tragedy,' and that my mother was in the hospital. The doctors didn't expect her to recover. Then he said that my parents had both agreed, in writing, that he would become my guardian if anything ever happened to them. I didn't believe him—I didn't want to. He said, 'When the newspaper comes tomorrow morning, you can read it for yourself.' He was very calm. He almost smiled—almost. I couldn't stand it. I got up and ran for the door. When I opened it, the two men who'd taken me out of the car were waiting right outside, and they grabbed me. Peter came to the door and told them: 'Take her to her room. Give her some dinner...and lock her in.' He looked at me, and then he *did* smile...and it seemed real. 'We'll talk soon. In the meantime, make yourself comfortable. You've got a bathroom of your own and a nice soft bed. You won't be going to school tomorrow. Believe me, they'll understand.' He patted my cheek and said, 'Goodnight, dear.'

"I think that first night was the worst night of my

life—not knowing what had happened, or what was going to happen to me. I cried until I didn't have any tears left. When I was nine, I'd thought the world was coming to an end, but I was wrong. Now it was really happening. The strange thing was that I didn't cry for my parents. I couldn't, and I felt guilty that I couldn't. In a way, I'd been alone all along. So I only cried for myself.

"The next morning, one of his men came in with a tray of breakfast and a newspaper. It had made the front page. My mother was always in the society pages, so everyone in town knew her. It said my father had just gone crazy. He shot my mother first, and then killed himself. My mother was alive when they found them, but she died a few hours later. Then the article said that a 'family friend' was looking after me!"

"Didn't you have any other family?" Jade asked. "Anybody who'd ask questions?"

She shook her head. "My grandparents were long gone. And my parents' friends were never what you'd call real friends. They were people who came to cocktail parties, gossiped about each other and wanted free tickets to the opera. I'm sure it made for some entertaining conversation at the next party… they probably loved talking about how shocking it all was. I never heard from any of them.

"The rest of that day was a blur. The same man brought me lunch, and then dinner. He didn't speak to me. It got dark outside, and I went to bed…but I couldn't sleep. Sometime in the middle of the night, the door opened, and then closed. A man sat on the edge of the bed, and put his hand on my leg. It was *him*. The room was dark; I couldn't see his face, but I could hear his breathing, and I could smell his after-shave. And I knew why he was there.

"'My dear,' he said. 'You don't have to worry about anything. I'm going to take care of you from now on. You're a part of my family now.' Then he started to... touch me. I was afraid to say or do anything. He got into bed with me...I don't have to tell you what happened next. It was my first time...I just let it happen. All I could think about was Mr. Kelso, that day after school, telling me that the boy from the football team wasn't 'Mr. Right'...and then he brought me to this man's front door, and drove away.

"He came in like that, every night for three weeks, and it was always the same. When he was done, he kissed me on the forehead, got out of bed, put his robe back on and left the room. Then it stopped. A few days later, his men brought in a doctor, who examined me..." Greta paused, and glanced down her body. "Down there. He drew some blood from my arm, and made me give him a sample of my urine. I asked him why, and he told me he was supposed to find out if I had any 'diseases.' Then he left. Of all the nerve. I was furious! I'd never been with another man before! How would I? Then I began to wonder if the old man had caught something and given it to me. But nothing came of it. I didn't see him for another month.

"I never went back to school. Three times a week after that, during the day, a very nice older woman named Miss Darby came in and gave me dance lessons—not ballet, but showgirl style—like what the Radio City girls do. Compared to what I was used to, it was easy. She said I was a natural, and that I could be a star some day, if I worked hard enough." Greta smiled. "A star. That's what she told me. She said I could be the next Ginger Rogers.

"They started to let me out of my room. Pretty soon I had the run of the house, and I found out it wasn't Peter's house at all, it was just one of the places he used. And he had them everywhere. I got to be friends with Bobo and Joey, the two guys who kept an eye on me. I figured out pretty quick that if I gave them what they wanted—what I knew they wanted—I could get what I wanted. They let me go outside...but they always had somebody watching me. Like a babysitter. One day they took me downtown and bought me a bunch of expensive dresses, shoes. Even jewelry. I couldn't believe how much money they spent. When we got back, Peter was there, sitting at the table just like the first night. He told me to sit down.

"He told Bobo and Joey to take everything upstairs. He asked me if I'd gotten myself some pretty things. I said yes. He said that was good, because it was time for me to start earning my keep. He said, 'You're going to get some freedom, and some privileges, to see if I can trust you. If you do good—and I know you can—you can make yourself a nice living. If you *don't* do good...well, we don't want to think about that.'

"After that, I took dancing lessons six days a week. Bobo and Joey drove me downtown, to Miss Darby's studio, and I learned choreography. I started working in nightclubs all over New York, from the Catskills to Midtown, and Atlantic City. For the first six months I was one of the background girls. Then one night the headliner had the flu, so I got to take center stage." Greta looked at Jade, and could not hide her pride. "And I've been there ever since. The money was pretty good...but I made more after the shows.

"He was always bringing other men in to watch me dance. They were all just like him: expensive suits, shiny shoes, big gold rings on their pinky fingers, oily hair and too much after-shave. After the show, my job was to be an 'escort' for the one he pointed out to me."

"An 'escort,'" Jade echoed knowingly.

"That's right. I got close to them, and gave them what they wanted. Then I would get whatever I could, and bring it back to Peter."

"Such as?"

"Information," she said. "Names, numbers, maybe an address. Rumors. Could be anything. Sometimes I was told to take the guy's wallet. It was easy. All I had to do was use what I have. Pretty soon I had my own apartment. I almost had my own life...but Bobo or Joey was always there."

"Did you ever meet La Forno's sons?"

"No. They died just before my..." She stopped herself. "Anyway, I read about the shooting in the newspapers. Horrible pictures. It wasn't until a lot later that I realized he was their father."

"How about his wife?"

She shook her head. "He never talked about her. But I knew when she died."

"How's that?"

"Well, that's when we all packed up and moved

down here," Greta said. "All of a sudden. Men showed up at my apartment one morning with a truck, and had the place emptied in an hour. I rode with Bobo and Joey. They took turns driving, and we never stopped except for gas and food. When we got here, Peter already had this place rented for me. He never talks about his wife. Never."

"How'd you end up with Mallory?"

Greta hesitated. She ground out what was left of her cigarette in an ashtray. "Maybe I've already told you too much."

"Not nearly," Jade said. "I need all of it."

"Five thousand dollars, Oscar. Please—"

"You're not gonna buy me off with cash, so give it up," he snapped. "From everything I've heard, the world's a better place without Mallory in it, so I don't give a damn if anybody sits in the chair for it or not—except I'm not about to let my client rot on death row for something she didn't do. But *somebody's* going up the river. You need to be thinking real hard about how you can convince me it shouldn't be you, and the best way is to tell me everything. Right now. If you've got a better patsy to hand over, I'll consider it."

She sighed. "Got another smoke?" Jade gave her one, and lit it for her. "You're a bastard," she said.

"My parents were married."

"It's funny. You don't look like a son of a bitch. You look like somebody who ought to have a good heart."

"I can't help that. It's the way God put my face together."

She laughed. It was short and harsh. "I like you,"

she said.

"Finish it."

She rolled her eyes, smoked some more and went on. "Peter hired Horace to run the hotel—I think there must have been a connection from New York. After a while, he came to me and told me he thought Horace was sifting some money off on the side. He told me to find out." Her expression grew steely. "Can you imagine that? He must have sent somebody after my father the same way, and now it was my turn to do it to somebody else. That's the kind of person Peter is. He uses them up and throws them away. That's when I knew what I needed to do…

"I got myself hired on as one of the girls on the fourth floor." She made a face. "But I didn't have to work there very long. I made a move on Mallory, and he took the bait. Probably the easiest thing I've ever done. It's funny…Mallory thought *he* was the one who got me the job at the Marmalade Club, because he knew Peter.

"When I finally got a look at the books, it was easy to see what he was doing. For one thing, he had a second ledger. He kept it hidden in his office. He took a percentage from everything for himself—almost ten percent—and not just from the tables and slots. He took from the girls, from every transaction…even from the straight hotel business. He must have thought Peter wouldn't see it because he hadn't owned anything in Miami before. He just told Peter that business was slower than he thought.

"As soon as I found out what Horace was doing, I knew I could take some for myself. I convinced him I was falling in love with him and I needed to see him every day. Of course he believed it. Horace had a bank account under a dummy name. Every day, I took what I could after the money had been counted, and bundled up. As long as I changed the entries in the second ledger, and convinced him to let me take the deposit to the bank, I figured he'd never miss what I took. I started off at twenty percent, and then I took more, and I knew I was right. He didn't have any idea. Before long I was taking more than half of what he stole from Peter...even more."

"Okay, so Mallory didn't know he was being played. I can buy that." Jade took another swig of Four Roses. "But La Forno must have wondered what was taking you so long."

"Peter kept asking me what I'd found out. I told him I needed more time." Greta smiled. "I made Horace out to be a lot smarter than he really was. I said I'd need at least two more weeks to figure out what he was doing with the ledger books."

"Then what?"

She hesitated, took another pull on her smoke. "Then I had to give him something. I told him I thought Ricky was stealing from him."

"Who's Ricky?"

"Horace's accountant. He handled both sides—the straight hotel business and the fourth floor—but he didn't know Horace was skimming. He only knew about the first ledger, not the second one. He counted and bundled the cash for the deposits."

"Before you took your cut."

"That's right."

"I'll bet that didn't mean anything good for Ricky."

"He never showed up for work again," she said, smiling with what looked like genuine amusement. "He just…went away, for keeps."

"So you threw this Ricky over."

"He was just as dirty as anyone else who works for Peter," she said, a casual, honey-flavored venom dripping from each word. "They all deserve what they get."

Jade took another drink. *Maybe they do.*

"I knew I didn't have much more time. I took less than before, but I kept taking. I wanted enough to get away for good. About that time, Bobo and Joey told me Peter was seeing someone, and he wasn't around so much during the day. He just wasn't paying as much attention. It wasn't like him. Then I found out it was Horace's wife." Greta's face darkened. "I followed them once, on one of their little lunch dates, just so I could get a look at her. I kept thinking about how Peter had sent a doctor up to look at me. Did he send a doctor over to look at her? To see if *she* had anything he might catch?"

She lapsed into silence for a long moment, and finished her drink. Jade refilled it.

"But when I saw them together, they both looked so…happy." She frowned. The frown became a scowl. "I guess I should feel sorry for her—she has no idea what kind of man he really is, no idea at all—but I hate her, with her Sunday school dresses and the way she always held his hand and laughed with him, like they were actually a *couple*."

"Tell me about Tuesday night," he pressed.

"All right." She sighed. "When you showed up at the club, I knew something had changed. If somebody was sending a shamus, it had to mean trouble. Then, that man who was with Horace...they made a big scene. After the show, Horace came backstage, and told me to come with him. I said I still had another show to do, and he said he didn't care. He told me I was a 'no good bitch' who was going to get what was coming to me. On the way to his house Mallory said that he knew that I'd been stealing from him, and that I was going to give him back every penny or he'd tell Peter that I was the one who'd been stealing from him all along. I started to cry, and told him I was sorry, that of course I'd give him everything back. I begged him for mercy. But at the same time, I knew what I had to do.

"When we got to his house, and got inside, he hit me. Not in the face where it would leave any marks, but in the stomach. I couldn't breathe. When I was on the floor, he kicked me. I just lay there, and took it. Finally he went and made himself a drink, and then went into his office. I got up, and went into the kitchen. I found the biggest knife in the knife rack, hid it behind my back, and followed him." She gave a thin smile. "He was surprised. You should have seen the look on his face." She took another drink. "I put on a pair of *her* shoes. They were two sizes too small. I made some tracks in the back yard."

"And now what?"

"I'm leaving for California tomorrow morning," she said. "Hollywood. I'm going to make something of myself, no matter what it takes. I can do whatever I set my mind to do. I know that. But I can't go on like this." She stood up, and took the few steps to where Jade stood. She reached out and took one of his hands. "Please," she said softly and leaned in close, her breath sweet and warm as she spoke into Jade's ear. "Take the money. I promise, you'll never hear from me again."

"It's not that simple," Jade said. "Unless you've got one hell of a lot of faith in your mysterious cop friend to keep things covered."

"I've bought myself some insurance," she said, her cheek touching his. She ran her hand along Jade's upper arm. "Mmm," she cooed approvingly. "Strong…and tall."

"I thought you said it was 'personal' with him."

She smiled coyly, and kissed the side of his neck, her voice scarcely above a whisper. "It's always personal," she said. "We can make our own arrangement."

"Listen—" he began, and she moved in. Her mouth—hungry, skillful and knowing—was on his, gentle but insistent. She took his hand and placed it squarely on her breast, which was soft and warmly inviting, its summit rigid beneath his touch. He returned the kiss with equal force. She shuddered and sighed, and melted against him. Then, a long moment later, just as Jade's breathing deepened into a rhythm that matched her own, she drew away from him with a sureness that must have come from endless rehearsal and practice, like one of her dance numbers, and deftly undid the catch at the back of her neck. The silvery dress dropped away, and landed in a silky heap around her ankles. Another quick movement, and her brassiere hit the floor next to it. Her flawless body received his gaze with unflinching immodesty.

Jade took in the view. Here he was, with this deadly dangerous animal, who had learned to survive in her own personal jungle—so accustomed to having her way, especially with anyone who might otherwise wield influence over her, that she probably couldn't imagine anyone saying no, simply because it had never happened. Well, there was a first time for everything. Once you knew a magician's secrets, it was harder to enjoy the trick.

"You know," he said with a smile, "since you like tall guys so much, I wouldn't think little Al Billings would be your type."

She stiffened, and Jade enjoyed the surprise on her face. "What the hell—"

"Don't take it personally, sweetheart," he said. "You're a real looker, for sure, and it'd be fun to roll around with you, but I don't want to be on the receiving end of the next butcher knife. Besides, I've never been one for picking a number and waiting in line, like I have to do at the barber shop."

"Go to hell."

Jade laughed. "I'll race you there," he said, and left through the front door.

Like every apartment in the building, it opened directly to the outside, one of a row of modernist-style doorways facing another row of them across a narrow courtyard divided by a concrete walkway garnished with flower beds, short ferns and palm trees, sparsely lit at either end by an ornamental lamp over a wrought-iron gate. Without the darkness of the courtyard, they might not have gotten the drop on him. At the very least, he might've gotten his hand on the .38 still in his jacket pocket, but they had his hands before he knew they were there.

A big, heavy fist came in hard just below his breastbone, and his breath was gone. Jade doubled over and found himself on his knees, gasping for air that wouldn't come. A foot came down on the back of his head, and the side of his face found the concrete. He bit into his tongue, and a tooth broke off at its base. His mouth filled with the salty taste of his own blood. Kicks rained down on him like anvils falling out of the night sky. It might have lasted forever, or five seconds. Jade had no idea.

"That'th good," a voice said. "Get 'im up."

Jade was hoisted back up. In the dim light, he could make out the bandaged face of Freddie, from the Caribbean and the Marmalade Club. Good old Freddie, of the broken nose and smashed lip and ham-sized right hand. Jade fleetingly wondered if Bobo and Joey were the guys who had him by the arms.

Freddie nodded at someone. It was the last thing Oscar Jade saw.

Something exploded against the back of his head. The world flashed bright white, and then went dark.

16
La Forno

He was asleep, and he was dreaming. The sleep was good, but the dream was bad—warmth and comfort, the cushioned safety and darkness of his childhood bed, intermittently broken by flashes of angry light, barked words and pain from nowhere, or everywhere at once. For a long time it seemed that he might never wake up. When it was good, that was just fine with him…but when it was bad, the notion was huge and terrifying. He had to wake up. He had to wake up. He had to—

A sharp slap across his face jerked him once and for all out of that dark and warm bed, and summoned back a vague, dull sense that something was very wrong.

"Wake up!"

He became aware, very gradually, of being upright. He was sitting in a chair. His head throbbed. A tidal wave of nausea came from nowhere, and suddenly overtook him. Reflexively, he vomited until he had nothing left, his stomach muscles squeezing vainly upon themselves. Someone nearby cursed viciously. Very slowly, Oscar Jade opened his eyes.

The only light in the room came from a small brass lamp on the corner of a very expensive-looking desk made of what looked like varnished cherry wood, some five feet away. Behind the desk, his hands folded across the red felt blotter as if in thoughtful prayer, sat La Forno. His lined hawkish face wore an expression of relaxed amusement, a Mona Lisa smile playing at the corners of his mouth. His black shark's eyes, as dead and bottomless as those of a porcelain doll, might as well have been looking at a squashed bug on the ground. "Sorry about the rough stuff, Mister Jade," he said. "But I needed to make sure I have your undivided attention...and besides, you're getting to be a real pain in my ass."

Jade tried to raise a hand to his face to wipe off the moistness he felt on his chin, and only then did he finally realize that his arms were tied behind the chair. He tried to move his legs; they were tied to the legs of the chair. Nothing budged.

"Pretty good licking the boys gave you." La Forno was matter-of-fact. "You puked on yourself."

Jade looked down. It was true. Vomit was splashed down his shirt and suit jacket, and his trousers. It was on the floor, too, except that it wasn't the floor. The chair he sat on was in the center of a large, brown sheet of tarpaulin laid down in the center of the room. Around the edges could be seen a very shiny and immaculately polished hardwood floor.

"S'okay, though," La Forno continued in that same peculiarly conversational monotone. "We're not worried about a mess, as you can see. You need to keep that in mind while we have our little talk. A lot of really messy and unpleasant things can happen to you, right here, and all we have to do is roll you up and throw the whole thing away. You can be feeding the fish by sunup. But you're a pretty smart kid. You get the picture already. What do you bet Freddie back there wants another shot at you while you're all trussed up like this? Would you like that, Freddie?"

"Yeah, bawth." The voice came from over Jade's left shoulder. He tried to look back, but the hurt at the back of his neck wouldn't let him. "I'd like that juth fine."

"I bet you would." La Forno was scornful. "Because if he wasn't tied up, I bet the guy with the funny foot could take you."

"No thir," Freddie said quietly.

La Forno laughed. It was genuine and hearty, like he'd just been told a good joke over dinner. "No *thir*!" he mocked, and looked squarely at Jade. "You messed him up pretty good, Jade. I gotta hand it to you. The boy's a champion heavyweight. Almost went to the Olympics, if you can believe it. Now he can't even talk right anymore. When I told him to bring you in, he took four guys with him. Four guys. That says something." He held up Jade's .38 snubnose, swung out the cylinder and emptied it. The six bullets dropped onto the desktop. All but two of them rolled off and fell to the floor. "You're a guy who does serious business, aren't you?"

Jade hesitated. He ran his swollen and lacerated tongue along the inside of his mouth. There was a jagged void there where a tooth had been. His lip felt grapefruit-sized. He shrugged, and nodded.

"I can understand that. And I can respect it," La Forno said, "because we're here to do some serious business, you better believe it. You've kept me up past my bedtime, here. I don't like that. Old men like me appreciate their rest." He paused, and took a drink of what looked like coffee from a white cup. "I didn't know what to make of you when you showed up at the track yesterday. I thought to myself: Who is this kid, come out to poke me in the eye, in public? What the hell is he thinking? Doesn't he know who I am? Then I thought, maybe you don't. How could you? Otherwise, you wouldn't have gone and wrecked my new Cadillac like you did. A guy like that must be tired of walking around. Or, at least, he doesn't give a damn. I don't know. Either way, I got to deal with him. I can't have a guy like this just walking around. Getting into my business."

"I can't help it if your boys can't drive," Jade croaked. "I didn't make 'em chase me."

La Forno leaned forward, his elbows on the desktop, and looked him in the eye. After what seemed like a very long time, he smiled. "Okay," he said. "That's fair enough. So what can I tell you? Good help is hard to find."

"I offered my services." Jade tested the ropes restraining his arms and hands. They were expertly tight. "You said no."

"Maybe I was too hasty." La Forno took another tiny sip of coffee. "Maybe I've got some work for you after all."

"Hell of a way of offering."

"It's not what you think. First of all, there's something we need to settle. I'm very protective of my stepdaughter, as I'm sure you can understand, so I need to know something. What were you doing at her place at two-thirty in the morning?"

"Your stepdaughter?"

"That's right."

It figured. If Greta had been telling the truth, La Forno had the paperwork that made it legal. Outwardly, it would have been the easiest way of passing her off in social circles (if he even worried about that kind of thing), or with any authorities whose palms couldn't be greased. When she was working, none of the marks who saw her shows—and got her 'special attention' afterward—were the type to ask questions…and by the time she had finished with them, the only option would be for them to slink away, and shut the hell up.

"I'm looking into the murder of Horace Mallory," Jade said, choosing his words carefully. "I have reason to think she was the last person to see him alive."

La Forno smiled. "But that's not the whole story, is it?"

Jade took a breath, and slowly let it out. "I don't know what you mean."

"Aw, come on. You're clever enough, but you're not *that* clever. You know exactly what I mean, and I know who you're working for. But first things first: stay away from Greta. Leave her out of this. Or else."

Jade didn't say anything.

La Forno got out of his chair and walked around

the edge of the desk. It was the first time Jade had seen him standing; he guessed he was about six feet tall—average build, but very fit for a man in his early sixties—and there was a calmness in his posture. He obviously knew he'd always be the best man in the room, if push came to shove…and if he weren't, he'd have plenty of backup. "After you wrecked my car, I asked around town about you. Turns out you've got a reputation."

"So do you," Jade said evenly.

"Ex-cop," La Forno went on. "Made detective—youngest one ever in Miami. Hell of a shot with a pistol. Chip on your shoulder. Wouldn't take money on the side…then you quit, just like that." He snapped his fingers. "Something to do with that foot of yours, maybe, but nobody seems to know for sure. Maybe it was something else. Either way, everybody knows you're flat broke. Behind in your rent with the big dope who runs that bar on the beach. You got a private dick's license, but you don't take any jobs, and you're not making any money at it. Most people figure you for a loser who's gonna suck on the booze bottle until it's too late for you to do anything else. Pretty sad…what are you, even thirty yet?"

Jade stared at him.

"I'm going to give you a chance," La Forno said. "Fair and square. Stay away from Greta. That's the first part of the deal I've got for you. And it's non-negotiable." The black eyes didn't blink. "Agreed?"

Jade shrugged, then nodded.

"Good," La Forno said. He walked back around the edge of his desk and took his seat. "Serious, and reasonable. We can do business together after all.

That makes me feel good. I'd hate to think I'm just wasting my time here. It's almost four in the morning, after all." He finished his coffee, and put the cup down next to Jade's emptied revolver. "The second part of the deal is this: I want Myrna Mallory."

"I'll bet you do," Jade said. "But she's not the one who stole from you." His voice still sounded thick and muddled to his own ears. "It was her husband. You know that. And since somebody clipped him, you won't be getting it back from *him*. Myrna doesn't have it, so killing her isn't going to put anything right."

La Forno shook his head. He opened his desk drawer, and withdrew a pipe and a bag of tobacco. "There's a lot you still don't get," he said as he packed the pipe, put it to his lips and lit it. He puffed several times; smoke swirled gently upward in the stillness of the room. "She's stealing from me, all right. Or she's trying to. For some reason she thinks she's going to get away with it. But she won't. They never do. One thing I've found, over the years, is that there are always a few who think they can skim a little off the top for themselves. And then there are others—not many—who think they can actually pull off a heist. Make off with the big prize. Myrna's one of those, and I'm going to set her straight, that's for sure. But I promise you, Jade, I don't want to hurt her. Not at all. I want her safe and sound."

"Sending Valletti around with a tommy gun is a funny way of showing it," Jade said.

"What the hell are you talking about?"

"One of your hired hands. He came by yesterday morning and took a few shots at Myrna. He missed…

but it was close. Real close."

"What was the name?" the old man's voice was razor-sharp.

"Valletti," Jade said. "Nino Valletti. From Brooklyn, unless I miss my guess."

La Forno looked away, and his face underwent a brief but profound change, much like the one Jade had seen at Hialeah. The black eyes narrowed into slits, and his mouth drew into a lipless straight line that looked more like a knife wound just before it begins to bleed than anything that belonged on a human face. He stared at the wall. "Valletti," he whispered. Finally, he turned to meet Jade's fascinated gaze. "He doesn't work for me, son," he said softly.

"Who the hell does he work for?"

"Never mind about him; he's not your problem. Leave him to me."

"If he's shooting at my client, he's my problem," Jade said.

"He won't be doing that anymore," La Forno said. "You have my word on that."

"If he doesn't work for you, how can you—"

"I said I'd deal with him!" The words cracked like a whip. Then he shook his head, and calmly took a pull on his pipe. "A man in my position has enemies, son. And believe me, you don't want to be one of 'em. The sooner you hand Myrna over, the better. If anything happens to her before then, anything at all, I'm going to hold you personally responsible."

"She hired me to protect her."

"Not from me, she didn't. I promise you that."

"Doesn't Myrna have a say in this?"

La Forno's eyes twinkled. "Women don't always

know what's best for them. It's a man's job to know that. It's the way it's always been—it's the price we pay. This might surprise you, Jade, but I'm a sentimental man. Some things are worth a hell of a lot more than money. Any idiot can get a job...earn money, print money, steal money. The same with broads. They're a dime a dozen, and most of 'em aren't worth half that much—so when you find one that is worth a damn, she's worth a hell of a lot more than *that*."

Jade didn't take the bait. He sat there, tied to his chair, and stared at La Forno with raised eyebrows. The old man nodded to the men standing behind Jade. Jade heard them leave the room.

When they had closed the door behind them, La Forno continued. "I'm sure you know that Myrna and I have a relationship."

Jade nodded.

"That idiot Mallory didn't know what he had. What can I say? I care about her. It's no more complicated than that. And you want to know something else? She cares about *me*."

"Good for you," Jade said dryly.

"You don't believe it?" The old man chuckled. "Don't bet against it, son, I'm telling you. Don't put your money on Lucky Black again. This is bigger than you think it is—and you don't know her like I do."

They looked across the desk at one another, and Jade felt the first hint of doubt creep in, like a thief through a window in the dead of night.

"The last conversation I had with her on the telephone wasn't a good one, and I regret that," La Forno continued. "She was having a bad time of it, wasn't thinking straight. It happens. I didn't fully appreciate the difficulties she and her husband were having. Obviously"—he shook his head—"she's a stronger woman than she seems to be. And a woman like that has her limits. That's why I think she killed him."

"You think so?" asked Jade. "Really?"

"Yes, I do. And that's why I'm the one who can actually protect her, son. I can make sure that nobody bothers her with any of this business. God knows she doesn't need that, not now. He had it coming. That's all there is to it, and that's all there needs to be. Sometimes things happen for a reason."

"So here we sit," Jade said. "Talking about what happens to somebody's life."

La Forno grinned coldly. "No, son. We're talking about what happens to *your* life. Now, I've got a couple of ways I can do this. One of them is that things can get messy, like we talked about earlier. And you better believe it, my boys are pros, and they enjoy their work. Eventually, you're gonna tell me where you've got her. And then you're dead, and that's that." The black eyes didn't blink. "The other way is this: you're going to give me Myrna. I'm going to give you ten thousand dollars in cash, as a token of my goodwill. You're going to take that money, walk away and forget about the whole thing. Just consider it a good week for your lousy little detective business."

"Ten grand," Jade said. "That's the price for something that's worth a hell of a lot more than money?"

"It is what it is."

"People keep offering me money. And the number

keeps going up. I wonder why."

La Forno was impassive. "If you don't take my offer, you'll have to get the answer from God." He raised his voice. "We're finished."

The door opened again. There were footsteps, and La Forno motioned someone to come forward. Freddie came to the desk. La Forno scribbled something on a small sheet of paper, and handed it to him. "You've got until six o'clock tonight," he said. "That's about...thirteen hours from now. Call this phone number when you're ready to hand her over." He motioned toward Jade. Freddie, his face dark with hatred, stuffed the sheet of paper in the front pocket of Jade's jacket. "And don't get the cops involved," La Forno said. "I'll know if you do, believe me."

"*That* I believe," Jade muttered.

"If you do, the deal's off, and then things get unpleasant." La Forno nodded again, and someone pulled a black hood over Jade's head.

They kept his hands bound as they untied him from the chair. He couldn't see anything, except scattered pinpoints of dim light through the weave of what felt and smelled like heavy canvas. The hood was cinched tight around his neck; his own breath felt cloying and hot against his face. He was unceremoniously kicked off the chair by a foot impacting squarely on his chest. His head cracked hard against the floor.

"Boys, boys." La Forno laughed. "You've rattled his head enough for one night. We need him to be able to think. Jade, I'm going to hang onto your piece for safekeeping. I'll just consider it a token of your goodwill, until you hold up your end of the deal. I don't have to tell you what I might do with it later. To you, or maybe someone else. You know how these things work, right? I'll be waiting to hear from you. Okay, guys. That'll do."

Jade was dragged along the floor for a pretty good distance—across the room, down a hall and around a couple of corners, he figured—then he heard the sound of a doorknob being turned. He was pulled across a threshold, and heard the ocean, and the indifferent squawk of a distant seabird. He felt a hint of cool early morning air on his hands and at the base of his neck. The toes of his shoes dragged through gravel as strong hands lifted him up, then there was the metallic sound of a key being inserted in a lock, and a heavy click as it was released. Jade realized it was the sound of a car's trunk being opened, and then he was quickly hoisted up and dropped inside. A ham-sized fist thudded into his gut with brutal, heavy precision. Jade groaned—or tried to—but all that came out was a thin wheeze as he vainly gasped for air. He tugged in fury at the knots that kept his arms behind his back.

"I think I owe you another one," he heard Freddie say. "Try thith one." The ham clubbed up against the side of his head; Jade nearly blacked out again.

"Better watch it, Freddie," someone said. "If you kill him, it's your ass, not mine."

"Shut up," Freddie said, and the trunk lid was slammed shut.

Jade counted out the seconds into minutes, kept track of the minutes with his fingers, and tried to estimate how fast the car was traveling, how often it stopped, and where it made left and right turns. At one point there was a long straightaway, where he guessed they were going across one of the causeways that separated Miami Beach from the mainland. Anything beyond that was pointless.

The car stopped. The trunk lid popped open. Jade was pulled out of the trunk, and dropped onto concrete. He took one last kick to the gut while they cut the ropes from around his wrists and pulled the hood off his head. The others got into the car, a black Studebaker, but Freddie lingered, just out of Jade's reach.

Jade got to his hands and knees, and looked him in the eye. "See you around, Freddie."

Freddie grinned. "Better hope not, gimp," he said, then spat onto the ground in front of Jade and got into the car. The tires squealed as it pulled away.

Jade looked around, took a deep breath and slowly let it go as he painfully stood up. The sun wasn't up yet; it might as well have been midnight. He was on Collins Avenue, not far from home. The street was deserted. It was quiet, the kind of quiet you only get at five in the morning, when everyone with a normal life—a wife, kids, a nine to five job, a pension and chronic headaches—is at home, still in bed, dreaming about a new lawn mower, or maybe his neighbor's wife.

Oscar Jade limped painfully in the direction of the Pelican.

17
The Carlotta

Jade finally lurched through the back door at 5:15 in the morning.

"Jesus *Christ*," Claude exclaimed, and helped him to the bar, where Jade gratefully took a seat. A moment passed in silence as his old friend made a quick and professional appraisal of the damage. Finally he said, "Good to see you, boss."

Jade grinned crookedly, and ran his tongue across a split upper lip that felt as big as a tractor tire's inner tube. "Good to be seen."

"Who was it?"

"La Forno."

"Fuck," Claude said.

"But that's not all of it. Tinsel's dead, and nobody's heard from Al since it happened."

"You don't think—"

"I don't know," Jade said. "I really don't know, anymore. How about a drink?"

Claude went behind the bar. "Coffee?"

"Make it Irish."

"I'll make it two." The big man put out two cups, put a shot of bourbon in each, topped them with black coffee and pushed one across the bar. "Bring it with you."

"Where we going?"

"Upstairs," Claude said. "You need some work done…and you stink."

Jade got his first look at himself in the bathroom mirror, and it wasn't a face he immediately recognized. Crusted with dried blood and bile, and misshapen at random points, it looked as if an eccentric sculptor had finished work on a portrait bust in clay—using a halfway decent-looking guy as his subject—then gotten raging drunk and mauled it, mercilessly, with his fists. The left eye was swollen nearly shut. Jade gently probed at the cheekbone underneath, and wondered if it had been broken. Above the right, a deep gash ran horizontally through the eyebrow and had bled liberally down the side of his face and neck. He guessed that Freddie must have worn a ring on his right hand, probably one of those 'fighting rings,' the ones with sharp edges that you could buy in the joint. His lips were fat, the upper worse than the lower. He pulled it back to get a look at the broken tooth—on the top left side, fourth from the back—which throbbed with a deep-down hurt. That would mean some time in a dentist's chair pretty damned soon. He reached behind his head. There was a knot the size of a golf ball at the base of his skull. He gingerly turned his head from side to side. Concussion, he guessed, taking a generous sip of the spiked coffee.

Behind him, Claude filled the bathroom doorway.

"Get those clothes off," he said, and Jade obeyed, wincing as he removed his shirt. He found he could barely raise his arms. His lean torso, especially around the ribcage, was blotted with angry, purplish bruising. He felt his ribs. "Might've busted a couple," he grunted.

Claude reached in and quickly probed with a pair of expert fingers.

"Sonofabitch!" Jade said. "Take it easy, for Christ's sake!"

The big man shook his head. "Nah. Cracked, maybe, but they're still together. Pretty close, though. They knew what they were doing. You were lucky—it coulda been worse. They coulda busted off and poked a hole in your lungs." He took Jade's clothes, and made a face. "Gonna burn these," he said as he tossed Jade a towel.

"Before you do, there's a phone number in the breast pocket. I'll be needing it."

Claude nodded, and fished it out. "Get yourself cleaned up," he said, and put the scrap of paper on the edge of the sink. "I'll get the kit."

Jade stood in a shower, as hot as he could stand it, for several minutes. Claude was right. It could have been worse—a lot worse. He wondered what would have happened if La Forno had decided to push it to the limit. What then? Would he have had him screaming for mercy, ready to hand Myrna over, anything to make him stop? Probably. He had no idiotic illusions otherwise. Jade knew, because he'd been told by Claude, and others—and he'd read dozens of police reports—what the New York mob did to make people talk. What was left behind, if it still had a pulse, usually didn't want to go on living. Often it begged to be killed, for any number of reasons. Pieces were often removed, pieces that identified who and what a person was, pieces that made a person a person, and without them you could never go home again, not really. And that was the point. He remembered the story of Dingo McTaggart: a hunk of the Mad Scotsman's arm, wrapped up like a New York strip steak, and sent back as a message. And Mallory, telling his men to take Jade to "the Place." Had he been to "the Place" and back? If so, La Forno had stopped well short of what might have been. The only question was: why?

Wearing only a fresh set of boxers, sitting on the closed toilet seat and pressing a washcloth-wrapped ice cube to his swollen left eye, he watched Claude open his small leather satchel and thread a curved needle with what looked like black silk thread. "Gotta close up that eyebrow," Claude said. He dabbed at the cut with an alcohol-soaked cotton ball. Jade gritted his teeth. "Gets your attention, don't it?" Claude chuckled. "Well, if you're havin' fun now, just wait." He got to work with the needle. "So," he said, "What's the score?"

Jade gave him the short version. He finished with Myrna, then added: "La Forno says he cares about Myrna, that he doesn't want her hurt. He says he'll give me ten grand to hand her over…ow, goddamn it! That hurts."

"Quit belly-aching…you believe him?"

Jade thought about it, and tried to ignore the sharp sting, the insistent tugging sensation of the thread being drawn through the soft flesh of his eyebrow. "At least that part of it makes sense. He says Valletti doesn't work for him, and I sure as hell believe that. You should have seen his face when I said the name. It looked like he was gonna come out of his skin. Valletti wants Myrna dead. That's the wild card, and I don't know what it means."

"How much time we got?"

"Until six o'clock tonight—uhhh! Goddamn it!"

"Sorry," Claude said.

"S'okay…and La Forno says no cops. That's gonna be tricky with our girl sitting right under their noses up in Surfside, so we're going to have to move her again, and fast. I mean, in the next couple of hours."

Claude paused, holding the needle, and took a drink of Irish coffee. He gave Jade a measuring stare with narrow eyes. "What'cha thinking?"

Jade stared back at him, the thread hanging from his half-stitched eyebrow, and didn't reply.

"Ain't thinkin' about the ten grand, are you?"

"A couple of days ago you would have thrown her over for a hell of a lot less," Jade said.

"That was before I found out who wants to put his greasy paws on her, and you know it," Claude grumbled. "You ain't gonna sell her for cash. Who you kiddin'?"

"As far as La Forno knows, maybe I am. So that's the way I've got to play it. But I'm gonna have to get a lot smarter. I'm tired of being behind the eight ball." Jade sighed, and slumped where he sat as the last few hours caught up with him. He looked up at his friend. "I need your help," he said. "This could get pretty goddamned bad in a hurry, and I don't think I can do it without you."

Claude flashed a hard smile. "I got a family beef with this guy, Oscar. So you know where I stand. Thing is, La Forno's got a machine, for sure, an' he means business with it, but it ain't nothin' like what he had up north. See, if I were him, and I figured to haul you in and give you a good slapping around like he did, I'd've had guys making a move here, too. That would'a been the smart play. But it's been quiet. La Forno ain't got *that* much muscle. I say we make a stand, right here. I ain't afraid of the son of a bitch, not anymore. If that New York wop wants to play in Miami, he's gonna know he's been in a fight."

A few minutes later, wearing a fresh set of clothes and nine thickly knotted stitches in his eyebrow, Jade followed Claude into the Pelican's cramped office. Claude manipulated a lever behind the desk, and opened a hidden double-door in the wall above it. Inside was a deep chamber, three feet wide and four feet high, lined on three sides with racks and shelves of weapons of various types. He reached in and grabbed one Jade recognized—a big, heavy hunk of artfully shaped metal with a wooden shoulder stock and a long barrel. Claude hefted it expertly, and slammed a loaded magazine home. "Browning automatic rifle," he said. "Puts out thirty-ought-sixes, 'bout five hundred rounds a minute, and they'll punch through pretty much anything." Next, he selected a double-barreled shotgun, with the stock completely removed and the barrels sawn off to a length of about eight inches. Claude loaded it with a pair of twelve-gauge shells, snapped the breech closed and tucked the gun into the waistband of his trousers.

He dropped several spare shells into the waist pockets of his frayed old suit-coat.

Jade reached in and grabbed a replacement from a row of three Smith & Wesson .38s lined up on a notched shelf inside a panel door, loaded it, spun the cylinder and flipped it shut. With some fresh iron in his holster, he began to feel better about things.

Back up front, Claude cleared the pilsner beer glasses from a shelf beneath the bar, and carefully slid the Browning and a half-dozen spare clips in their place for quick access. He turned to Jade. "You know, you really oughta get some rest."

"What about you?"

Claude shrugged. "I took a nap," he said. "Where's your car?"

"Over on Meridian. And it can stay there, for now. They're watching Greta's place, and the last thing I need is to have them spot me there again today. Let's go get Myrna."

The sun was just breaching the horizon, turning the sky orange-red and striking a brilliant flare path across the ocean, as Claude's tired old Dodge pickup turned left onto 93rd Street in Surfside. The streets were still mostly deserted, except for the occasional passing car. The Carlotta, a modest old two-story hotel painted salmon pink and trimmed in pale cream yellow, was on 93rd and Abbott, just two blocks from the public beach. Right now, like everything else, it looked as if it were still asleep.

Claude pulled up to the curb in front, and looked around. "I thought you said the cops were watching the place."

"That's what Connor told me," Jade said. "What room's she in?"

"Two-A. First one at the top of the stairs."

Jade got out of the truck. "This doesn't smell right," he said. "Circle around, and keep an eye out. We'll meet you right here in five minutes."

Claude nodded, and pulled away.

The Carlotta's lobby was painted the opposite of its exterior—cream yellow, with the baseboards and ceiling trim done in pink—with a mural of dark-haired and dark-skinned Spanish women bearing baskets of fruit dominating the wall on the right side. Directly ahead was a check-in desk, currently unoccupied, with a stairway to the left. Jade quickly crossed the room and went up the stairs, slowly removing the .38 from its holster and letting his gun arm hang naturally at his side, slightly behind his back and out of sight from anyone who might approach him from the opposite direction. It was totally quiet; his footsteps seemed to echo as he drew near the door to room 2A.

Jade stood to one side of the door, and knocked with the butt of the .38. The sound was abrupt and sharp in the silence. He waited about ten seconds, and knocked again. Then he gave it another few seconds, and knocked a third time. He was reaching into a pocket for his lock-pick set when he heard Myrna's voice, tight and hushed: "Who is it?"

"Oscar Jade," he said. "Open up."

There was the soft clatter of a door chain being

removed, and the door opened. Myrna, pale and drawn-looking, wore a pink and blue nightgown. When she saw Jade's face, she gasped. "Oh my God! What happened?"

Jade stepped inside, and put his gun away. "Why didn't you answer the door?"

"I was—" she hesitated. "Never mind. Your face—"

"I had a talk with your boyfriend," he said coolly. "Actually, he did most of the talking."

"Peter?"

"Yeah, that's right. Peter. I gotta be honest with you, lady. I don't know what you see in the guy."

"Oscar, this isn't a good time—"

"No kidding," he barked. "You need to get dressed. We're getting the hell out of here."

"Peter didn't do that to you," she said. "He couldn't have."

"Not personally, no. He doesn't get his hands dirty anymore. Not for a long time, I'll bet. But other people do, and he watched. If he had any moral objections, he kept quiet about it."

"But why, Oscar? Why?"

"Get dressed," Jade said. "Now."

"Not until you tell me what's going on."

"Myrna...he's given me until six o'clock tonight to hand you over to him. Or else. Do you understand what I'm saying?"

"Hand me over," she slowly repeated.

"That's right. And he wants you pretty bad."

She tilted her head slightly, and arched an eyebrow. "How bad?"

"Ten grand worth of bad. In cash."

Her eyes widened. A smile slowly spread across her face.

"What the hell is *that* about?" Jade demanded.

"I'm sorry, Oscar," she said. "Honestly, I am. But it's better than somebody wanting fifty thousand dollars if I end up dead."

"That could still happen, you know." Jade took her by the arm. "If you don't get your ass moving right away—"

"Did you take the deal?" she asked, pulling out of his reach.

"Did I—well, no. Not yet, anyway. Should I?"

"I'd probably hand me over, if I were you," she said quietly. "I wouldn't blame you if you did."

"Is that what you want?"

"I…don't know."

"Well, that's just great," Jade said. "So exactly what do you want me to do while you piddle around here and make up your mind?"

She stood there for another moment with an infuriatingly wide-eyed look of stupid surprise on her face, her mouth forming soundless o's like a fish out of water, and then she scrambled to the bathroom. Jade followed. When he got there, he found her on her knees in front of the toilet, heaving violently. Finally she leaned back on her haunches and wiped her mouth with a towel. "I'm sorry," she said.

"What's wrong with you?"

She took another long, ragged breath. "Morning sickness," she said hoarsely.

"Morning sick…" Jade began, and then found himself at a loss for words, as facts from the past couple of days began to reluctantly, stubbornly, finally, line up in his mind. What an idiot he'd been. What an idiot he was.

Myrna rolled her eyes. "I'm pregnant," she said as she got back to her feet. "I wasn't sure before. But now I am."

They stared at each other for a long moment, an arm's length apart, her lower lip quivering, her hair disheveled, a narrow dribble of vomit still on the tip of her chin.

"Pregnant," Jade said.

She nodded.

"Marvelous." He shrugged. "Congratulations?"

"I don't know what to say, Oscar. It's just…one of those things."

"It sure as hell is."

"What do you want from me?" Anger brought fresh color to her face. "An apology?"

"An answer to a simple question," Jade said. "What now?"

"Here's what now," said a familiar voice. Jade remembered with sick certainty that the door to the hotel room had been left wide open. His right hand made a move, and the voice said, "Uh uh! Put your hands up and turn around, nice and easy."

Jade did as he was told. Nino Valetti stood inside the open doorway. He held a Colt .45 in an outstretched hand and sighted along its barrel—which was squared up on Jade's head from a sure killing distance of about ten feet.

"Okay," Valetti said. "I'm going to shoot you first," he told Jade. "*Then* her."

18
Aviation Avenue

It was one of those moments where neither the past nor the future mean anything, since one is gone forever, and the other might not come at all. Oscar Jade had every expectation that he would be dead before he knew it, that he'd never hear the shot that killed him. There was barely enough time to be angry that it came at the hands of this man, Nino Valletti, with the rakish forward tilt to his fedora and the smug, self-satisfied, punchable smile—the Guinea jerk who'd stomped on Jade's bad foot in front of the Pelican's bar, the same man who had shot the side of the place up with a tommy gun just a couple of days later...all for what? To kill a woman?

Anybody but this guy, he thought desperately, in this moment that would end without notice, and when he was gone—stupidly dead, without another thought, on the floor of a cheap hotel room in Surfside—Myrna Mallory would be alone. And his failure would be complete. He slowly raised his hands, showing empty palms to Valletti. His holstered .38 might as well have been a million miles away.

"You don't want to do that," Jade said. "She's worth big money to La Forno. Cash money." He spoke quickly, conversationally, and without pause. What he needed was time, as much of it as he could get, anything to stretch this moment out as far as he could. "You knew Mallory. You knew he was skimming off the Caribbean's operation. I'm talking fifty grand, here—plus what La Forno will pay you to get the dame back." Jade motioned to Myrna, who gaped at him in disbelief.

"He ain't getting nothing," Valletti snapped, "Except what's coming to him." He steadied his aim at Jade's head, and grinned. "This ain't about money. It's about payback."

"Payback for who?"

"It won't matter to you." His knuckle whitened as the finger tightened on the trigger.

"Goddamn it, wait a second!" Jade said. "Think about this! What do you have to lose by making some green on the side? You don't have to worry about me. That's a promise."

Valletti gave a short laugh. "No," he hissed. "I don't."

"Yes, you do," said a gravelly voice behind him.

The mobster's posture suddenly shifted.

"If you shoot him," Claude said, his voice a low rumble, "I will *absolutely* spray your brains across the ceiling, and you'll be explainin' yourself in hell. Get your hands up."

Valletti complied. He stared daggers at Jade.

"Now, real slow, step into the room."

Valletti did, and Claude moved with him, the stubby twin barrels of the .12 gauge jammed against the base of the mobster's skull, which was still bandaged from where the beer bottle had struck it not so long ago. "Give your piece to the man."

Jade took the gun. He looked at Claude. "Took your time," he said.

"Sorry 'bout that, boss. I got busy. Listen, we can't be stickin' around here. We need to get moving, and be quick about it."

Myrna had herself dressed, and her suitcase packed, in five minutes that seemed to take forever. Claude used curtain cord to tie Valletti's hands behind his back, and held the shotgun to the base of his spine as they took the lead down the hallway toward the service stairs at the back of the hotel. Jade brought up the rear, keeping the .45 ready. They left through the back door, which emptied onto a narrow alley. Claude's pickup waited there, parked behind a maroon-colored Pontiac Super Streamliner that Jade recognized immediately. He noted, with some satisfaction, the missing rear window—and the bullet holes in the trunk lid and right rear door. Then he saw the large, darkly pooled stain on the back seat, and got that familiar old heavy knot in the pit of his stomach.

Claude opened the Pontiac's trunk. Inside, dressed as nicely as Valletti, trussed up by hands and feet like a Christmas turkey, was Valletti's backup. He looked desperately up at them, squinting in the early morning light, his protestations limited to futile monosyllabic grunts through a professionally tied gag.

"I guess you *were* busy," Jade said.

"Stupid son of a bitch. Didn't even see me coming." Claude grabbed Valletti by his bound wrists, and pushed him into the trunk on top of the other guy.

Valletti cracked his head against the edge of the car as he went in. "Ow! Goddamn jerk!"

"Aw, golly gee," Claude said. "That looked like it smarted." He picked Valletti back up, and slammed his head against the car again. "Damn. So did that. You oughta be more careful." The two men completely filled the cramped space of the trunk; Claude had to bend one of Valletti's legs at the knee, and wedge it in on top of the other guy. "You two girls behave yourselves," he said, and slammed the trunk lid shut. "You drive this one," he told Jade. "I'll take the truck."

"You thinking Charlie's?" asked Jade.

Claude nodded. "Meet you there."

Yet another exile from Capone's Chicago, Charlie Bechelli had been Claude Applegate's friend since childhood. They'd joined the army in 1917, did their time in the same division on the Western Front, and had returned to Chicago when the war ended; that much Jade knew. The precise reason they'd both left Chicago in February of 1929 remained a mystery. They never reminisced about the 'old days.'

Charlie ran Kelly's Comfort Cabs from a gigantic garage complex on Alton Road, with a large fleet of

Chevrolet sedans. On most days, he was clearly visible from dawn until dusk, manning his post at the dispatch desk behind a large window at the front of the garage. Today was no exception. Jade wheeled the Pontiac into the large concrete lot, and saw the recognition on Charlie's face when Claude's truck pulled up alongside. The old cabbie emerged from his office immediately.

He was short and bow-legged, with skinny legs and a slight frame that looked somewhat out of place with the rounded belly it supported, as though he was smuggling a basketball inside his shirt. His olive skin was sun-aged, like a newspaper left outdoors, adding years to his prematurely wrinkled face. The lenses of his spectacles were as thick as magnifying glasses. A graying fringe of dark hair ringed a copper-colored bald dome of a head.

Charlie grinned, displaying teeth that reflected a lifetime's lack of attention. "Hey, Jade!" he said, and pumped his hand in a very firm, dry handshake. "Whaddaya say?"

"Good to see you, Chaz. This is Myrna."

Charlie turned his gaze to the girl. "Well, hellooo." His eyes twinkled. He nodded courteously, and shook her hand. "My pleasure, Miss." He glanced at Claude, and gave the Pontiac—with its bullet holes and missing rear window glass—a quick but thorough once over. "What're ya up to today, ya old bandit? No good, I'll betcha."

Valletti's muffled voice came from the trunk. "Let us out, goddamn it!"

Charlie's eyes narrowed to a squint. He grinned at the three of them, then laughed, which always came out like 'Hee, hee.' "Oh, sure…I gotcha."

"Doin' some business, Charlie," Claude said. "Need a favor."

Charlie's grin was undiminished. "The old spot?"

"If that's okay," Jade said. "Buster still there?"

"Hee, hee! Oh, hell yeah. Just talked to 'im yesterday, matter of fact. He runs the place when my guys aren't around. Hee, hee!"

"Perfect." Jade reached into a pocket and produced some bills. He shook Charlie's hand again, and this time pressed $200 into the leathery palm. "Anytime I can do something for *you*—"

"Oh, I know," Charlie said. "I know. Hee, hee!" He went back to the office, nimbly tucking the cash away, and came out with a key. He tossed it, and Claude caught it. He gave them a final buoyant grin. "You kids have fun," he said. "Hee, hee!"

"Thanks, Chaz," Jade said. Charlie raised a hand without looking back at them.

Jade motioned to the Pontiac. "You drive 'em over," he told Claude. "I'll meet you there."

It was several minutes later, as the sun moved higher into a clear blue sky and Claude's pickup bounced along Biscayne Boulevard, when Myrna finally broke the silence. Jade had firmly resolved not to say anything until she did, but he could feel her eyes on him from the old Dodge's passenger seat. "Where are we going?"

"Coral Gables," he said. "I've got a place there.

Things are going to get bad, and I need you out of the way." He glanced over at her; she looked the other way and watched the buildings go by, her dark hair waving in the breeze, her hands folded low across her belly, which at this point gave no hint of the secret it was carrying. Jade wondered if the protective gesture was deliberate.

"What are you going to do with…them?" she asked, without looking at him.

"Don't worry about it," he said.

"Surely you're not going to—"

"Nothing's for sure, Myrna. These aren't nice guys, and I need some answers. It's a little late to start getting squeamish."

"I know."

"You need to think about what they want to do to you." He glanced down at her belly. "Both of you," he lamely amended. "How long have you known?"

"Tuesday night. I went to a payphone and called my doctor."

"That was when you snuck out on Claude."

She nodded. "I had the test done a week and a half ago, because I was…late, with my…"

"I understand how the plumbing works." Jade was impatient. "You must have had some idea on Tuesday, when you showed up at the Pelican."

"Of course. But I didn't know, then. Not for sure. I hoped not. I felt like enough of a fool as it was, without making it worse for myself. You don't understand, Oscar. I guess I shouldn't expect you to. I was *ashamed*. I'd been unfaithful to my husband. Never mind that our marriage was a wreck. I guess I was getting back at Horace for the way he treated me.

It's the most selfish and stupid thing I've ever done, and now I've got to pay the price for it. With a baby, everything changes. Everything. I was afraid...and desperate. I called Peter the next morning, the day the police came to the bar, and told him about the baby. He asked me where I was staying—"

"Did you tell him?"

"No! Of course not. I told him I'd call him back."

Jade shook his head as he made a right-hand turn onto Flagler Street, keeping an eye on the rearview mirror.

"I called my friend Betty, from the bank. She gave me the phone number of a...different doctor. He told me he could...get rid of it, if that's what I wanted."

"Doctor Angelo, right?"

"Yes." She shuddered, and wiped her swollen eyes. "I went to his office. And I almost did it. God forgive me. But I ran out at the last minute. I couldn't go through with it—even if it means the baby might not have a father. Something good's got to come out of all this. And it will. I swear to God, it will."

"What about La Forno?"

"What about him?"

"Well, I assume he's the lucky father-to-be."

"Of course he is." Myrna met his glance. "I hope you don't think I was out sleeping with everyone in town. That's not what I'm talking about. I'm going to keep this baby...but I'm afraid of doing it alone."

Jade pulled over, and parked the truck in front of the broad white stucco façade of Eldridge's Supermarket. He switched off the engine. "I'm listening," he said.

"When I was waiting in Dr. Angelo's office, I

kept thinking about Peter, the way he sounded on the telephone. It was the tone of his voice. He didn't even sound surprised when I told him. He just kept asking me if I was all right, and he wanted to know where I was. He must have asked me half a dozen times. He kept saying, 'Tell me where you are and I'll come and get you.' When I didn't tell him, he got angry. He told me he loved me, and that he wants us to be together...but he was shouting at me when I hung up, Oscar." Her freckled cheeks were flushed, her eyes wide as they welled with tears. Her tremendous natural beauty struck Jade anew, quite unexpectedly. "I don't know what to do," she said simply. "I just don't know."

He put a hand on her arm. "It's time to figure it out, Myrna," he said. "Does my opinion count for anything?"

She put her hand on his. "Yes, it does."

"Then let me help you decide. You and your baby'll get by, one way or another—that's the easy part. We'll figure it out down the road. I'll help you any way I can. All right?"

She nodded.

"Everything this guy touches ends up dead. You paid me good money to keep you alive, and that's what I'm going to do. The first part of that is, you need to stay the hell away from him. For good—no matter what. Otherwise, nothing else matters. We got a deal?"

She nodded again.

"Promise me, Myrna."

She smiled, and wiped a tear from her cheek. "I promise."

"Good. That answers the next question."

"What question?"

"Whether or not I'm still working for you." He climbed out of the truck, limped around to the passenger door, and opened it for her. "Come on. There isn't any food where you're going. Let's get you some provisions."

Eldridge's was a much bigger grocery store than Brumly's, with its own meat counter, bakery, dairy and fresh produce departments, and it already had a few scattered customers at just after eight in the morning. Jade picked up a wire basket just inside the doorway, and stayed close to Myrna, keeping his hat low over his face as they shopped the canned vegetables. He was uncomfortably aware of the stares they drew, mostly from old ladies. Jade wondered what they made of these two: the pretty, dark-haired woman who looked slightly pale, with puffy eyes (probably from crying not all that long ago, they'd no doubt speculate), and the tall, thin man with the crooked left foot, who kept a watchful gaze on their surroundings; whose face looked like it had been repeatedly struck with a meat tenderizer. *He's probably up to no good, that one! Shifty-looking, if you ask me! They look like they might be in trouble, and he'd be the cause of it!*

Myrna was distracted and distant while they picked up a basket full of food. She asked Jade if he liked beef stew. He said he did.

The middle-aged woman at the cash register, resplendent in a blue and white checkered apron and wearing enough pancake makeup for a Broadway musical, seemed as if she lived in a different world.

It was a world where people weren't fighting and dying across two different oceans, and trussed-up New York gunsels weren't riding around Miami in the trunks of shot-up Pontiacs. She was as bright and cheerful as the morning sunshine. "Good mornin', sweetie," she said to Myrna in a lilting, distinct Alabama twang. "How are you today?"

"Fine, thanks," Myrna said softly.

"Find everything you was lookin' for?"

Myrna nodded and glanced self-consciously over at Jade, who noticed the way the cashier winced when she got a good look at his face. "Oh, dear! Honey, are you all right?"

Jade winked at her, and flashed his best fake smile. "Tough night, ma'am, that's all. Everything's fine. We've got everything we need. Thanks for asking."

"Well...all righty, then." She smiled uncertainly and totaled up their purchase while a pimpled young man packed everything in two paper sacks. "Comes to four dollars and eighty-nine cents, altogether."

Jade paid her.

"Thanks, honey...and if you don't mind my saying so, y'all make a real nice couple. I'm sure everything's gonna work out just fine. God bless ya both."

Jade glanced at Myrna, whose smile wasn't convincing. He tipped his hat. "Thank you, ma'am. We'll take all of that we can get."

Aviation Avenue crossed South Bay Shore Drive

and met the Gulf of Mexico at Dinner Key, where a coast guard air station stood watch over the beach and the distant horizon. It was a quiet, tree-lined street in a neighborhood that seemed much farther from downtown Miami than it actually was. Sparsely located older houses shared the street with empty lots that were still waiting, after a twelve-year money drought, for something to be built there. There was little hint of the sprawling city just out of sight beyond the treetops. The sound of birds, the gently rustling tree branches, and the sigh of the ocean drowned out everything else.

The old Dodge pulled into a driveway alongside #3062, one of the oldest houses on the street. It was a modest white bungalow with windows shuttered closed and an untended lawn. In the center of the front yard was a coconut palm, now more than ten feet tall, sprouted from a coconut planted there, by much smaller hands, in another lifetime.

"Whose house is this?" Myrna asked as Jade opened her door.

"It's mine." Jade reached in and took the two bags of groceries from the floor in front of the passenger seat. "C'mon. Let's get you inside."

The place smelled of disuse. White sheets covered the furniture in the living room. The floors were hardwood; a maroon and dark green area rug was rolled up along the baseboard. Myrna looked around. "It's nice," she gently offered. "Needs some fresh air, though. How long has it been sitting empty?" She flipped a switch on the wall. The overhead light came on. "Can't have been too long."

"I'll get the windows open." Jade nodded to the

bags in his arms. "Let me get these to the kitchen and get the water going first."

"If you've got this place, why do you live in a room over a bar?"

"There's a bedroom through that door and to the right," he said. "There are sheets for the bed in the linen closet in the hallway. It's going to take me a few minutes to light the pilot for the water heater."

In the kitchen, he set the bags on the counter. Then he opened the cabinet doors beneath the sink, found the water main shutoff valve and opened it. He heard the gurgles and thumps through the pipe as water began to move. As he stood up, he glanced around the room, which managed to be both strange and familiar at the same time. He allowed himself the indulgence of a memory—a baby's high chair sitting in the corner—then pushed the image out of his mind. Turning around, he found Myrna standing in the doorway. "Oscar? What's the matter?"

Jade turned the tap in the kitchen sink. "Nothing," he said.

"The look on your face just now…"

"It's nothing," he repeated nonchalantly, wanting her to believe him and stop asking. The water out of the faucet looked like black coffee at first, and then gradually began to look more like iced tea. "Let it run," he said. "I'll go get your suitcase."

She looked him squarely in the eye. "Whose house *is* this?"

"I told you," he said. "It's mine. I'll be right back. You might want to flush the toilet a couple of times, to make sure it works."

"You're not going to talk about it, are you?"

"Nope," he said, and left the room.

"You're a very stubborn man," he heard her say behind him.

He retrieved Myrna's luggage from the truckbed and took a good, long look around the neighborhood, thinking about how much smaller everything looked.

Back inside, he got the water heater lit and pulled the sheets off the furniture. The last sheet revealed a Motorola console radio with a built-in phonograph.

"Thank God, you've got a radio!" Myrna hurried over and switched it on. A Glenn Miller tune was playing. "I've missed my shows."

"Okay, I think you're all set." Jade spoke matter-of-factly. "Keep the curtains closed. No sense advertising that you're staying here. Everything in the kitchen works. You might want to give it all a good cleaning, since everything's going to be a little dusty. The refrigerator will be cold pretty soon, so the milk will be fine."

"Are you coming for dinner?"

"Am I what?"

"Dinner," she said. "Let's say five o'clock this evening. Casual attire."

"Listen to me, Myrna. I'm not joking around. I've got some things I have to do, and you can't be with me when I do them, so you've got to keep yourself under wraps. Can you do that?"

She nodded.

"Stay inside. Keep the doors locked. Don't answer the door for anyone but Claude or me. We'll knock three times, wait five seconds, and then knock four times. Got it?"

She repeated it back to him.

"Good," he said. "Ever use a gun before?"

"What? Of course not!"

"All right." Jade took out his .38 and showed it to her. "You've got six shots here. If anybody comes through that door who's *not* me or Claude, point it at 'em and squeeze the trigger. Don't jerk it. Squeeze it. And try to use these sights, here." He pointed at the front blade and rear notch on the weapon. "Line 'em up on 'em. But don't let that slow you down. If you have to, just point and shoot. Don't try to be fancy and hit 'em in the head or anything like that. Aim for the biggest part of the body—their chest. If anything, shoot low instead of high, because she's gonna buck on you when you shoot, and that's gonna bring the barrel up. Keep it low, and keep squeezing until they go down. And when the gun stops shooting, drop it and *run*. If they come in through the front door, go out the back. The coast guard station is three blocks away, by the water. You saw it when we turned, right?"

She nodded.

"Okay, then. That's where you go. Find someone in a uniform, and tell him what happened. You got that?"

She nodded again. He put the Smith & Wesson in her hand. "It's heavy," she said with a gasp.

"Don't be afraid of it. It's a tool, that's all. It'll do what you tell it to do, and it won't go off until you pull the trigger. Just make sure you're behind it when it goes off, and you'll be fine."

"All right, Oscar." Her voice was small. "What about dinner?"

"Oh, I'll be here, all right, and it'll be way before sundown, so don't worry about that. Just remember what I told you."

Five minutes later, as Jade backed the wheezy old Dodge out of the driveway, he saw Myrna watching him through the open front door. She smiled and waved, but he could see the smile go away as she closed the door.

19
Buster

Jade used the first payphone he found, a booth outside a gas station on the corner of Elizabeth Street and Blue Road, and placed a call to Allen Billings' home. The voice that answered was a woman's, and it was frantic. "Allen?" she said.

"Sally, it's Oscar."

"Oscar! Thank God! Have you seen Allen?"

Jade sighed. "Actually, I was hoping you had."

"He hasn't been home since he left for work yesterday morning! It's not like him to not call. Something's wrong, Oscar. Something's happened to him, I just know it."

"Well, hold on, now. We don't know that for sure—"

"When was the last time you saw him?"

"Yesterday morning," he said. "At the Pelican."

"Is everything all right?"

He hesitated, for a moment too long. "Sally—"

"Is he on a case?"

An image of Greta flashed through Jade's mind—toned, statuesque, and stark naked in the light of the lamp next to her sofa. "I think so," he said miserably.

"He's in trouble, isn't he?"

"Sally, I've got to ask you a question. It's about the drinking."

She sobbed, convulsively.

"Is it true?" he gently prodded.

"Y-yes."

"When?"

"Just a few days ago…I couldn't believe it. I didn't want to."

Jade said, "I'm sorry, Sally. If there's anything I can do—"

"You can find him," she said. "Bring him back to me."

"Of course I will."

"I'll hire you," she said, her voice laced with desperation. "I'll pay you."

"Come on, Sally, we're not at that point yet. You don't have to—"

"I mean it, Oscar. Bring him back home, no matter what. Please."

Out beyond the extreme southwestern edge of the Miami sprawl, past Florida City, where the buildings got more scattered, the sky got bigger and things got a lot greener, the city began to give way to the everglades. Every time he came out this way, it seemed that the city had pushed itself a little farther out. The grey, dilapidated two-story warehouse, with its corrugated steel roof, sat on the edge of a huge, glistening sawgrass marsh at the end of an unkempt gravel road. Not so long ago, it had been the only structure in sight. Now, newer versions of it dotted the horizon in all directions. Nature was yielding, but only grudgingly. Out here on the perimeter, there was an uneasy truce with the upright, two-legged interlopers…but it couldn't last. The two-leggers were clearly winning. Before long, as civilization got within earshot, Charlie Bechelli's old outpost would have outlived its usefulness.

The maroon Pontiac sat near a flight of exterior stairs. As he parked the old pickup alongside it and climbed out, a half-dozen spoonbills flew gracefully overhead and disappeared behind a line of sawpines and Cyprus trees. Closer than that, something splashed in the water near the spindly, exposed roots of an ancient black mangrove.

Oscar Jade suddenly realized that he was tired. He lightly fingered the doughy-feeling cheekbone beneath his left eye, poked at his broken tooth with his tongue, and winced at the lancing pain in his ribs as he drew a deep breath and let it go. How long since he'd put his head on a pillow, or had a bite to eat? He couldn't remember, but he smiled to himself as he realized that he hadn't thought about his bad foot in several hours. Then he pushed everything else out of his mind except for the task at hand. It was time to do some business.

He knocked on the door, using the code he'd given Myrna, a long-standing custom known only to

Claude and him: three times, wait five seconds, then four more.

The door opened and the big man said, "They're ready for you."

The place smelled like mud and rotten wood. After the bright day and blue sky, it took a couple of minutes for Jade's eyes to adjust to the relative darkness. Slivers of daylight peeked through tiny gaps between the boards of the walls. Jade and Claude stood on an elevated floor, some eight feet off the ground, and leaned on a wooden railing as they looked down and surveyed the job at hand.

Sitting back-to-back on the bare ground in the center of the room, their legs splayed out in front of them, were Nino Valletti and the guy with whom he'd shared a trunk ride from Miami Beach. With their expensive suits and silk ties, they looked very much out of place, like two hapless bankers who'd taken a wrong turn in a bad neighborhood. Their arms were raised over their heads, their wrists cuffed with heavy iron manacles. The four chains met at a steel ring and a swivel, suspended about six feet over their heads. A thicker single chain attached to the top of the ring disappeared into the darkness above the rafters.

Valletti glowered up at Jade. "You're a dead man, Junior. A dead man."

"Maybe if your trigger man was a little better at his job. But right now, I'd say I'm doing a little better than you are, Nino."

"You're gonna pay. Believe me, you're gonna pay. You don't know what you've done. You got no idea the shit you started."

"Well, that's why you're here," Jade replied affably. "You're going to tell me all about it."

"I ain't gonna tell you shit."

"Is that so."

Valletti angled his head in Jade's general direction, and spat contemptuously. "You're already out of time," he said.

"Okay, then. Have it your way." Jade used a ladder fashioned with wooden two-by-fours to descend to the ground level, where the men were sitting. He slowly circled around them. Valletti wouldn't meet his gaze. Instead, he stared at the wall, wearing the same cocksure smile. But the other guy, at least ten years younger than Valletti, was breathing so hard and fast that his nostrils flared. He couldn't take his eyes off Jade. "What's your name?" Jade asked him.

"Don't you say a goddamned thing," Valletti snarled.

Jade didn't hesitate. He formed a cup-shape with his right hand, stepped in and cuffed Valletti smartly over the opening of his right ear, making contact with a sound similar to that of a champagne bottle being uncorked. If done properly, it could cause a fair amount of lingering pain. If done exactly right, it could rupture an eardrum. Valletti shouted out a vicious obscenity, and crooked his head to one side, his jaw gone slack. A line of drool ran down onto his suitfront.

Oscar Jade looked at the guy chained to Valletti again. "I don't want to hurt you," he said simply. "But I will, if you make me. Now, I asked you a question."

"C-Carbone," the kid said. "Vincent Carbone."

"Mind if I call you Vince?"

The kid looked confused, but nodded his head.

"Okay, Vince, here's the deal. You guys are gonna to tell me who you work for, and why you're in Miami with such a hard-on for Myrna Mallory...and you're gonna do it real soon. If I ask you about your favorite color, who's buried in Grant's tomb, or what your momma liked for breakfast, you're gonna tell me—and you're gonna be goddamned glad to do it. You need to get all these stupid ideas out of your heads about how you're gonna be tough guys and not give anything up, 'cause we're not having a picnic, and I'm not gonna be playing shuffleboard with you here. You're out in the middle of nowhere. Nobody's gonna hear you screaming, or crying, or praying to God. The cops aren't coming to rescue you. This is old country. Things have been dying out here for a long, long time, and there's no funerals, or write-ups in the paper. It just gets covered up, and forgotten. You'll be gone, just like the dinosaurs."

Vincent Carbone's Adam's apple jumped as he swallowed hard.

"But it doesn't have to be that way. If you give me what I need, I'll cut you both loose on the edge of town and forget about you—as long as you agree to stay out of Miami, and out of my business. If you ever show up on my turf again, I'll *kill* you—and I'll leave your carcasses on your boss's doorstep. That's the deal. And there won't be any others." He paused. "Anybody got anything to tell me?"

Neither guy said anything. Valletti, a trickle of blood running from his ear, stared at Jade without fear—in fact, it was more like disgust; the casual disgust of someone who's seen a neighbor's dog take a crap in his front yard. Carbone's lip quivered. He looked like he was about to cry.

Jade looked up at Claude. The big guy shrugged, and gave a nod.

On one wall, beneath the elevated walkway, there was a tall rectangular cabinet painted red. Jade made sure that both Valletti and Carbone were watching, and then he opened the cabinet. "Nino, you've been a made guy for quite a while now, right? So you know what a 'turkey' is. Hell, you've probably even done a couple of turkey jobs in your day."

Valletti kept his mouth shut, but there was no mistaking the shadow that had flickered behind his eyes. Behind him, Carbone's eyes were like saucers.

"So," Jade went on, "you know that the whole point is to keep the person alive, no matter what. You just take pieces off, a little bit at a time, and be sure the guy you're working on stays awake for it. We've got everything from smelling salts to Benzedrine to help with that. Now Claude up there," Jade motioned with a thumb, "has forgotten more about first aid and medical stuff than I'll ever know, so he'll make sure you don't bleed to death, or check out too early just because you go into shock." Jade took something out of the cabinet that looked like an elongated leather wallet. He opened it, and displayed a dozen surgical scalpels, of various sizes and blade curvatures. Next came surgical clamps, dental tools, three different sizes of bone saws, a boat hook, an iron fireplace poker, and ice-block tongs. "After a day or two with this stuff, you'll just be a big piece of hamburger on a table, with a head attached to it."

Jade showed them a mirror. "You'll get to watch the whole thing happening, because I'll cut your eyelids off and feed 'em to you. You won't even be able to blink. Isn't that right, Nino? That how they taught you to do it up in Brooklyn?"

Valletti's voice was a thickened, constrained croak. "You don't have the guts."

"You sure about that?" asked Jade with a leering grin. "Are you really sure? You don't know me." He looked up at Claude. "He doesn't know me, does he, Claude?"

"No boss," Claude gravely replied. "He don't know you."

"See, I'm kinda funny about wiseguys who think they can muscle me around whenever they want, like they do to everyone else. You come onto my home ground and attack me? Twice? What in the world made you think I'd sit still for something like that? What do your *paisans* do to guys who pull that shit up north…and then get caught?"

"Over a dame?" Valletti bellowed angrily. "A lousy dame?"

"Crazier stuff than this has happened because of a lady," Jade said. "You need to ask yourself: what's crazier? Me piecing you off…or you letting it happen when you've got a choice?"

Carbone blubbered, "Nino, I c-can't—"

"Shut up!"

"T-Terranza," Carbone stammered. "W-we work for Terranza."

"Goddamn it." Valletti's voice was a whisper.

"Well, no kidding," Jade said. "That wasn't so hard, was it? Bad news for you two is, that's the easy part. I need more. What's so important about Myrna Mallory?"

"I don't know," Carbone said. "I swear to God, I don't know."

"Right now you're probably asking yourself: does he believe my bullshit? And you know what? The answer's no."

"Sweet Jesus, mister! I don't know nothing! I'm not a boss! I do what they tell me to do!"

Jade stared at him. "They told you to do the wrong thing, Vince." He walked around and stood in front of Valletti. "I think I'm gonna do the kid first, Nino—"

"Ah, Jesus, no," Carbone blubbered. "No, please mister, no—"

"And that way, you can tell me if my technique is any good. Then, if he doesn't give anything up, I guess he was telling the truth, and I'll be good and warmed up for you."

"Okay," Valletti said. "Go ahead."

"Nino, goddamn you! You *know* I don't know what's going on here!"

"He's bluffing." Valletti's eyes didn't quite seem to reflect the conviction in his voice.

Jade stood there for a moment and considered his options. The two guys watched him closely. Jade slowly took out his pack of Luckies, and lit himself one. He snapped his Ronson shut, pocketed it, took a deep drag and blew the smoke toward the rafters. "You guys sure about this? Really?"

Valletti didn't say anything, but the cockiness had vanished from his face. "Please, no," Carbone sputtered. "P-please..."

"Okay. Here's how it's gonna go." Jade gave a palm-up motion with his hand. "Claude, bring 'em up."

Upstairs, mounted to a support beam, there was an oversized, heavy-duty crank that turned a series of gears attached to a heavy spool of chain, which led to a pulley rig over the center of the room. Claude nodded, and gave the crank a few turns. The gears and chain made a *clankety-clankety-clank* sound as Valletti and Carbone were lifted up by their shackled wrists. Finally, the tips of their shoes were about two inches off the ground. They dangled, back to back, their feet probing beneath them in vain.

"That's good," Jade said, and Claude stopped cranking. Jade crossed to the far side of the room, where a wide but short panel of the wall was attached to a rope that led up to another pulley and was wrapped around a wooden peg next to the crank. He pulled a steel rod from a locking latch. Then he returned to where Valletti and Carbone were suspended, grabbed Valletti by one arm, and gave him a good strong sideways push. The swivel chain holding them was well oiled. The two guys rotated easily.

Jade returned to the ladder. As he climbed he said, "All right, boys. I want to convince you that I'm completely sincere." Back on the walkway next to Claude, he unwrapped the rope from its peg, and pulled.

Across the room, the wooden panel slid upward. Sunlight spilled in, and lit up Valletti and Carbone's faces. As they spun around, each of them was afforded a brief, intermittent view of the open door. But it was enough.

"Boys," said Oscar Jade, "meet Buster."

"Ah, no no no..." Carbone muttered softly. "No no no no..."

"You have *gotta* be fucking kidding me!" Valletti said.

As adult alligators went (or so Jade had been told), Buster was a little smaller than average at eleven feet long and around six hundred pounds, but he nevertheless cut quite an impressive profile, looking greenish-brown in the bright sunlight, flashing his twin rows of razor-sharp white teeth in a death grin as he turned toward the interior of the warehouse.

"Buster lives here," Jade said. "And he's used to finding fresh food right where you two assholes are hanging right now. Plus he's smart, like one of those trained seals at the circus. Wait 'til you see it! All Claude has to do is blow that whistle he's holding, and Buster'll come running. I don't know when he had his last hot meal...Claude, how long since Buster had a good dinner?"

"Don't know, boss." Claude gave a faint smile. "Been a while, I think."

"I think so, too. Go ahead and blow the dinner whistle."

"No!" Valletti blurted. His eyes were riveted on the alligator. "It's because of Little Tom's sister! That's why we're here!"

"What the hell are you talking about?" demanded Jade.

"Connie Terranza! La Forno married her so he could get in tight with the old man...put himself in line to be Don! Little Tom couldn't stand it, he never trusted him like his pop did—"

"I asked you about Myrna Mallory."

"Gimme a chance, would ya? Little Tom loved his sister. He knew she wasn't happy bein' married to La Forno—the guy's a nut job! You know what happened with his two boys, don't you?"

"I know they were killed on the street."

"Yeah—but they were killed by his own guns! La Forno wanted to run the family after the old man died, so he was gonna hit Little Tom on Broadway, in front of God and everybody, to send a message to the other families. He sent some guys to shoot up his car when he knew he'd be on the way to a meet with the Sorrentos in Midtown. Thing was, Little Tom liked his nephews. He was trying to get them away from La Forno. So he *hired* them to be his personal bodyguards, and La Forno didn't know it, 'cause they never talked to each other anymore—hell, he never even talked to his own sons. Little Tom was sick that morning, and cancelled the meet, so the La Forno boys were the only ones in the car when it got hit. Crazy son of a bitch whacked his own kids by mistake!

"After that, Connie couldn't take it no more. She started drinking hard, and taking pills. When she died, La Forno got the hell outta town 'cause he knew Little Tom would want payback. And he does. I'm tellin' you, Jade, that's why we're here! We're supposed to shut La Forno down in Florida—hit everything. He's sweet on the Mallory broad. You know that, right? Little Tom wants her dead, and he wants La Forno to know he did it."

"That's as far as it goes with Myrna? You're just

supposed to kill her?"

"Yeah, that's right!"

"Then what?"

"Then we're supposed to bring La Forno back to Little Tom. He wants him alive, but he'll take him dead, if that's how it's gotta be. He just wants to see the body. But now it's different. Now he wants *you*, too."

"Why me?"

"Little Tom sent his own son down here so he could make his bones," Valletti said. "Kid just turned seventeen. You killed him."

Jade remembered the black stain on the Pontiac's back seat. No wonder he'd been able to draw and fire, or that he and Myrna were still alive. The kid had been too young to be pointing a gun at anybody—too young to be playing grownup games, for keeps.

"That's too bad," Jade said. "Tommy should have kept his boy in school. What were you doing with Horace Mallory?"

"Mallory worked for us," Valletti said quickly, still staring at the alligator. "His job was to tell us what La Forno was up to—how he was making his money, where he had his fronts."

"What happened at the Marmalade Club on Tuesday night?"

"I told Mallory the Vincennes girl was skimming off his take—and that she was a spy for La Forno."

"How did you know that?"

Valletti and Carbone had finally stopped rotating at the end of the swivel chain; they'd come to rest so that each of them had a sideways view of Buster, who was still staring implacably from just beyond the open rectangular doorway. If you hadn't seen the creature move at the moment the door panel had been lifted, it would have been all too easy to imagine it was a statue, so still and fixed was the reptilian stare of those opaque eyes. But both of them had seen the alligator turn their way. "Jade, please," Valletti said.

"How did you know she belonged to La Forno?"

"I can't—" Valletti began.

Jade took the whistle from Claude and gave it a good long blast. The alligator crossed the distance between the open door and the two men in less than a second—the blinding speed of a waking nightmare on four legs. Valletti and Carbone screamed. They were still screaming when Buster's advance came to a sudden stop, his huge snapping jaws just a foot from their flailing, dangling feet, and only then did it become apparent that he was restrained by a chain of his own; a collar and harness rig around his neck and waist. The tail whipped back and forth. The twin rows of teeth flashed. The mouth opened, and snapped furiously shut on empty air, again and again.

"Oh, God," Valletti screamed. "Oh my God!"

"Pretty neat, eh?" Jade had to shout to be heard over the yelling. "I told you he was trained. Now all I have to do is pay out a couple of feet of slack, and—"

"We got somebody on the inside," Valletti blurted out. "Somebody La Forno trusts."

"Who is it?"

"The cop!" he cried. "Connor! La Forno thinks he's got him in his pocket, but he's blood relation to

Little Tom."

Of course, thought Jade. So Tinsel had been right about a rotten cop in the mix after all, and he'd paid the price.

"So Connor works for Terranza," he said, thinking aloud. "What about Billings?"

"Who?"

"Captain Billings. Miami Beach P.D. What about him?"

"I don't know nothing about him," Valletti wailed.

"He's gone missing," Jade said. "I heard he was on the take, too. Is it true?"

"I don't know."

"Where is he?"

"I swear to God, I don't know. He's not ours. If he belongs to La Forno, that's his business, not mine!"

"Where's Connor now?"

Valletti had come unhinged; Buster continued to snap at his feet. "He's taking care of business—he's the one gonna make sure our guys get in!"

"When?" demanded Jade. "When are you making your move?"

"Today—right now. They just got into town!"

Jade lit himself a fresh Lucky. "How many men?"

"There was supposed to be twenty-five of us, counting Tommy Junior."

"Well, make that twenty-two, asshole," Jade said, "'cause you and Li'l Abner here won't be at the dance, either. Where's it going down?"

"At La Forno's place, after we take care of you," Valletti shrieked. "On Palm Island! We're supposed to move in quick, 'cause he's got a big yacht docked in back of his place—"

"A yacht?"

"Yeah, a big one, a cabin cruiser, like a forty-footer, maybe bigger. Little Tom figures he's gonna try to make a break for it—for Chrissake, Jade! Call this thing off me!"

Jade took a long, leisurely drag on his cigarette. "First," he said, "tell me *everything*."

Jade was doing ninety when he hit the causeway, weaving in and out of the oncoming lane of traffic, blowing past slower-moving cars. He checked his watch. It was already past two in the afternoon. Less than four hours until La Forno's deadline, but a few minutes past the time when, according to Valletti, Terranza's button men were due to start dismantling the South Florida operation of their former *caporegime*.

Claude had insisted upon going back to the Pelican, and making his stand there. That was understandable. There was nowhere else he'd be when the shit hit the fan. "I'll get there when I can," Jade had told him outside the old warehouse. "Call the cops and give them the particulars. They're gonna want to call in their off-duty boys."

The wild card was that there was no telling what Terranza's guys were going to hit first, or whether they were going to move in force or split up into smaller groups. The only thing Valletti knew for sure was that they weren't going to wait to hear from the advance guys. They knew Terranza's boy was dead, and they knew who'd killed him. Things weren't too tough to figure from there.

Oscar Jade slid the Pontiac through a left turn onto West Avenue, a right onto 12th Street, and then a left again onto Alton Road. From there he could already see the smoke, trailing blackly into the cloudless sky, and hear the sound of approaching sirens.

He came to the intersection with Meridian, braked hard, and turned right. He ran three stop signs, and came to the twin rows of apartment buildings, and the narrow courtyard where he'd gotten his ribs kicked in just a few hours earlier.

Greta Vincennes' apartment building was ablaze.

20
The Darkening Sky

Jade threw his shoulder against the door and forced it open. The blast of heat seared his face. Acrid black smoke caught in his throat and made him gag. His eyes burned and watered. The room was alight on all four sides—fire raced across the ceiling, roaring like the monster it was. The place was a tinderbox, and it wouldn't be standing for much longer.

He got down on his hands and knees, beneath the worst of the smoke, and shouted her name. There was no response. He crawled inside. His groping hand finally found an ankle on the floor, near where he remembered her sofa to be. Jade grabbed her and shook her. "Greta!" She didn't reply. He got to his feet and scooped her up in his arms, a hundred and thirty pounds of slack, drooping weight. Jade limped blindly for the door, his bad foot screaming. He tripped over a chair, nearly dropped her, and then found the way out.

He stumbled into the courtyard between the

buildings, and pitched through the wrought-iron gate onto the narrow strip of grass between the sidewalk and the street. By then, one fire engine was sitting at the curb, and a second was pulling up behind it.

Jade gently laid her down on the grass. Her head lolled to one side. She looked, even now, as utterly beautiful as she had the first time he'd seen her under the stage lights, projecting that subtle mix of sexual boldness and fragile, vulnerable melancholy. The Exquisite Miss Greta Vincennes. Her staring eyes, in death, conveyed that same deceptive fragility—but they also seemed somehow wiser, now, for the experience.

Jade's eyes watered and stung from the smoke. He wiped them with the sleeve of his suitcoat and checked her for a pulse, even though he already knew what he'd find. Then he spotted the single bullet hole, just above the generous soft swell of her left breast. The navy blue terrycloth bathrobe she'd been wearing mostly hid the blood.

He leaned back, and gratefully gulped a few lungfuls of fresh air. "Stupid bitch," he said. "You poor, stupid bitch."

A fireman leaned over them. "You okay?"

"I'm fine," Jade said. "She's dead. Better check the other apartments, and get everybody else out. The whole thing's gonna come down, and quick. It's arson."

He got back to his feet, and stumbled. The fireman steadied him. "Hold on a second. Who the hell are you?"

"Oscar Jade. When the cops get here, tell them

that's the car from the Pelican, yesterday morning." He pointed at the nearby Pontiac, which had jumped the curb, and its open driver's door. "You got that? The car from yesterday morning. And there are two guys in the trunk. Hand 'em over. They won't give you any trouble."

Jade didn't wait for an answer. He limped quickly down the street, to where he'd parked his roadster a hundred years ago, when he'd been a much younger man. The Flathead V-8 awoke with an eager growl. He threw it into gear, and left squealing-hot tire rubber on the street as he pulled away.

It was as if a broad front of storm clouds had suddenly formed over the city. The sky darkened as Jade navigated the oddly sparse traffic on Collins, alternately stomping on the gas and brake pedals as he urged the roadster on toward the Pelican. He'd taken a passing note of the sun passing behind the clouds, so it wasn't until he came upon the three fire trucks and the dozens of dazed-looking people blocking the street, and braked hard—bringing the car sideways—that he realized the Caribbean Hotel was burning.

Jade looked up. Sure enough, it was the fourth floor. Flames leapt from the windows. He threw the car into reverse, spun it around, and turned left onto 19th, left again on James Avenue, circling around behind the mess and a right onto Collins on the other side, just two blocks from the Pelican now, shifting smoothly through the gears and making sixty mph by the time he had to slam on his brakes at the intersection with 15th Street, which was when he heard the unmistakable, heavy bark of large-caliber automatic gunfire.

Jade turned sharply left onto the short run of 15th, along the outside southern wall of the Pelican—where a guy in a dark suit, holding a pump shotgun, had flattened himself after peeking around the corner and firing a blast inside. He had just enough time to see what was coming, but couldn't quite get the barrel of his weapon all the way around. There was an instant of an astonished, disbelieving face—two wide eyes and the flash of teeth—as Oscar Jade jumped the curb and swerved the roadster up against the side of the building, grinding the left fender against the stucco. The Ford's front end crunched heavily into the gunman and he was drawn down beneath the car with a moist thump. The roadster jumped a little as the tires rolled over him. His shotgun spun and clattered across the concrete.

There were more shots from the beachfront, and the answering bark of machine gun fire from inside. "How about *that*, you fucking Guinea sons of bitches?" Jade recognized Claude's voice. "How about some *more*?" Another thundering, measured burst from the Browning automatic rifle: bam-bam-bam-bam-bam-bam-bam-bam!

The driver's side door was jammed up against the wall. Jade exited his car from the passenger side, and pulled Valletti's .45 from the waistband of his trousers. He flipped the safety off, crept in front of the roadster, and crouched down as he peered around the corner.

Several panels of the Pelican's wooden frontage shutters had been splintered into toothpicks. Lying among these chewed-up ruins was another Terranza soldier, who'd been stitched from groin to neck with some of that big lead. He stared, unblinking, up at the red and white striped awning, a hint of smoke still curling up from the barrel of his Thompson in the sudden stillness.

A slight movement from the other side of the half dozen outdoor umbrella tables, near the far corner of the Pelican's ocean frontage, caught Jade's eye. He raised the .45 and lined up the sights on the edge of the building, where he could see the edge of a fedora's brim. A head peeked around the corner, looking in toward the old wooden bar. Jade fired the big Colt three times in rapid succession. The guy made a tiny sound and spun away headfirst, arms and legs askew, as his brains sprayed misty red-and-grey across a tabletop. One of his shoes, a polished black wing tip, came off and tumbled into the sand.

Quiet again. A strange kind of quiet, broken by the sound of emergency sirens coming from the direction of the Caribbean Hotel, and from farther away. A gentle breeze stirred the palms overhead. Jade called out Claude's name.

"In here, boss," came the reply.

The big bar mirror had been shattered, along with many bottles of liquor; the smell was richly pungent and sweet. Bullet holes peppered the wall. Claude had used the old wooden bar as a shooting platform, the Browning laid crossways over the dark hardwood. Slightly pale, he leaned on the bar behind the weapon. “How many?”

“Three.” Jade stepped through one of the wrecked shutters. “You all right?”

“Three?” Claude shook his head disgustedly. “Fuckers only sent *three*? Serves you right, you stupid fucks!” he shouted. “Look at you now!”

“Jesus, buddy.” Jade came over and helped Claude onto a stool behind the bar. “You’re hit.”

“Huh?” Claude looked down at his right shoulder. Several patches of red, each about the size of a dime, had blossomed across the tired fabric of his old brown suit-coat. There were a few speckles of blood on his face, and a small piece of his right ear, at the side, was gone. “Ah, it’s okay. I got down; he missed me.”

Jade nodded. “Sure he did…where’s your kit?”

“In the office.”

Claude told him that Terranza’s men must have been watching the place from somewhere close by, but he hadn’t seen anyone when he pulled the Dodge into the garage. He’d made the call to the police like Jade had asked him to do. Then, when he’d opened up a shutter panel on the beachfront and come out onto the street to look at the smoke in the sky, he spotted the guy with the shotgun coming around the corner of the building. He’d just managed to get behind the bar and duck for cover when the guy had gotten his first shot off. That was when a volley of machine-gun fire had punched through the shutters, from the direction of the beach, and then it was on. Claude had reloaded twice; the next thing he knew, Jade was there.

The big man shook his head. “Cops are spread

pretty thin. Too much goin' on. There's a big fire out at the dockyard, too. See all the smoke? People are gonna think the goddamn Japs are attacking."

Once he got Claude's coat off and gently peeled his shirt back, Jade was reassured. It could have been a lot worse. If he'd taken half a second longer to react, the shotgun blast would have caught him in the face, or square in the chest. As it was, everything was superficial. "A doctor's gonna have to dig some of these pellets out," Jade told him.

"Yeah, yeah."

"And that ear's never gonna look the same."

Claude grinned tiredly. "S'all right. Dames love the scars."

The telephone rang; Jade picked it up. "Pelican Bar and Grill," he said. "Sorry, we're closed—"

"Jade, this is Peter La Forno," the voice on the other end replied evenly.

"Greta's dead," Jade said without preamble.

"Yeah, I know." La Forno's voice couldn't have been more casual if Jade had just told him that the forecast called for rain. "She had it coming, though, didn't she? No great loss. She was just like her father: a lousy little thief who thought she was smarter than everyone else. Now she knows better. I'll be able to sleep at night."

"Terranza's men are in town," Jade said. "Lighting up everything you own. They're coming after you."

"That figures."

"They're gonna be on your doorstep any time now."

"Yeah, well..." There was a pause at the other end; something in the tone of his voice made Jade uneasy. "I'm not gonna be here much longer anyway, so that's all right. It's time to move on. Matter of fact, that's why I called. I just wanted to say thanks."

"For what?"

"For killing Little Tom's boy for me. That was nice. Saved me the trouble. And for keeping the rest of his guys busy while I get out of town. You know, usually I like to take care of my own problems. I hate loose ends. But in your case, I'm gonna make an exception. Tommy can have you."

"What about Myrna Mallory?"

"See, that's the best part, that's the kicker. I've had a guy working on that for a couple of days—and now I've got her. She's right here by my side, right where she belongs. And I didn't have to pay you a dime. How about *that*?"

A knot appeared, tight and very big, deep within Jade's stomach. "You're bluffing," he said. Next to him, Claude Applegate got to his feet and put his shirt back on.

La Forno laughed. "Oh, come on. I gave you a lot more credit than that. Guys like me don't bluff, Jade. We don't have to. Want to talk to her? Hold on a second." There was a pause on the line; the muffled commotion of the receiver changing hands.

"Oscar?" she said, and Jade's heart sank. "I just wanted you to know how sorry I am about all this."

"What the hell do you mean by that?"

"I should have told you sooner," she said. "I'm sorry. But this is how it's supposed to be. We're going to be a family."

"Myrna, is this what you want?" Jade asked quickly. "*Tell me* this is what you want."

There was a moment's hesitation. "It's what I want, Oscar. I should never have gotten you messed up in all this. You need to let me go, and worry about yourself."

"Myrna—"

"Goodbye, Oscar."

Another rustle of sound as the phone changed hands again, and the old Sicilian came back on the line. "Well, I guess that's it, Jade."

"You won't get away with this."

"You know what, Jade? I think you've gone soft for my Myrna. Can't say I blame you."

"Maybe it's my job. She paid me to protect her, and that's what I'm going to do."

"Whatever it is, it doesn't really matter. You lose again. She's made her choice, and it's the right one, so we're all through here. Good luck with Tommy—"

"Do you know Terranza's got a man inside your operation?" Jade said. "Somebody you trust? You're never going to get away, no matter how far you go. He's gonna rat you out as soon as you relax, La Forno. You're never gonna have a moment's peace as long as you live."

"Yeah, sure. You're the one who's bluffing now, kid."

"Think so? Then sleep tight, asshole," Jade hissed into the receiver. "'Cause I'm coming for you...if he doesn't get you first."

Another long, faltering moment. The line went dead at the other end.

Jade hung up the phone and looked at Claude. "He's got her," he said. "He's leaving town."

"The hell with that," Claude rumbled. "I'm sick of

that sonofabitch. We're going, right?"

"Absolutely."

"And I'm gonna kill him."

"Okay," Jade said.

They went to the office and opened the door to the weapons closet. Jade got himself another fresh .38 and some extra ammunition for Valletti's Colt .45, and loaded both pieces. Then he retrieved the two Colt Police Positives he'd taken from Mallory's men behind the Caribbean, and loaded them too. He placed one in each coat-pocket.

Claude stuffed a few extra clips for the Browning into a leather satchel, and tossed in a handful of .12 gauge shotgun shells. Then he picked up two items that looked like miniature black metallic pineapples. "Been savin' these for years," he told Jade with a grim smile. "For a special occasion. Hope they still work." He put the hand grenades into the satchel, draped the strap over his shoulder, and closed the compartment door.

It was when they emerged from the stairwell door, just as Claude picked up the Browning and they turned toward the torn-open frontage of the Pelican Bar & Grill—there was a half-hearted joke on the tip of Jade's tongue about locking the place up—that all hell broke loose.

21
Last Call

One of them must have had an itchy trigger finger, Jade thought as he and Claude crouched behind the heavy old bar, and the automatic and small-arms fire banged and popped. The few bottles of top shelf booze that had survived the first assault now shattered and rained their pricey contents down on them. *Somebody just couldn't wait to get in the first shot, and he blew it.*

As the sporadic pauses began for reloading, Claude laughed bitterly and swung up the Browning, laying the big weapon across the bartop.

"How many you think?" Jade asked him.

"More'n *three*," he muttered, and cut loose two short bursts—one each toward the far corners of the Pelican's frontage, where shadows in nice suits moved in and out of view in the fast-fading daylight of a December afternoon, the disinterested Atlantic waving gentle whitecaps behind them. "Better check the back, Oscar. They're gonna try and flank us, sure as hell."

Jade nodded, and crawled past him toward the stairwell door. He opened it, and glanced back at his friend.

"I'm okay," Claude insisted. "I'll cover you." He fired a sweeping burst toward the beach. While he did, Jade slipped through the door.

He moved down the short hallway in a running crouch, past the stairs and toward the door to the rear garage, the .45 in his outstretched hand. Before he opened it, he heard a precise, small sound—a distinct counterpoint to the angry exchanges of Claude's gun with those of the attackers—easily lost in the chaos of what was going on at the other end of the building. Still crouched, he eased open the door, and snuck down the right side of Claude's faithful old Dodge, where he could see that the business end of an axe had gotten all the way through the edge of the big garage door, about halfway down, and had made a ragged hole about the size of a basketball in the hinged wooden panel. The axehead was withdrawn. Then a hand, wearing a black leather glove and a tan-colored suit-coat sleeve, reached in and groped around blindly for the latch. Jade raised the Colt, took careful aim, and put a single, fat .45-caliber slug right through the wrist. Right at the point where all of those nerve endings and small bones came together, in God's masterful design, to make everything work. The hand was jerked away. Oscar Jade peered out the hole in the garage door. Behind the wrist, the shot had found the guy it was attached to, striking him in the throat. The button man briefly hovered on his knees, gulping like a gaffed fish and looking around in desperate stupefaction, his hat tilted comically back on his head, his good hand trying to catch the blood as it spilled from where his Adam's apple had been. A moment later, he fell to one side and expired, still looking completely bewildered by the situation.

There was more movement off to the right, on the side of the Pelican farthest from 15th Street. Through the hole in the garage door Jade saw two more of them, each holding a bottle of liquid with a burning rag tucked into its mouth. The first one let his fly; Jade heard a window shatter upstairs. He put the barrel of the .45 through the door and fired six shots at the second, who was slightly closer. The first three shots didn't hit him, but the fourth one shattered the bottle he was holding high, his arm cocked back and ready to throw—and the gasoline ignited as it cascaded down his arm and over his head, neck and chest. He shrieked and ran out of Jade's narrow field of vision, a human torch, his arms waving grotesquely like something out of a nightmare.

A volley of bullets thudded into the side of the Pelican. Some of them passed straight through the garage door near Jade's head. He ducked and backed away toward the door to the hallway. The slide of the .45 had locked back on empty; Jade fed the weapon another magazine, pulled back the slide and let it snap home. He heard two more upstairs windows shatter, and knew what the sound meant. There were just too many of them. *This is it.*

Claude glanced over at him as Jade came back through the door. "Do any good?" he asked conversationally as he rammed a fresh clip into the Browning and cocked it.

"Got a couple," Jade muttered.

"Think I got three, altogether." Claude fired another short burst.

"We gotta go," Jade said. "We gotta get out of here."

"We will. We just about got these assholes on the run."

"Claude." Jade grabbed his arm. "They've lit the place up. We're burning topside. We gotta get out."

There was a brief moment before this sunk in, and by then the fire could be heard overhead; the roar and crackle of old wood feeding a hungry animal. Smoke had already started to seep between the boards of the ceiling, and waft downward. The big man's face went soft and sagged at the edges, for just a moment, and then hardened back to its customary angular granite. His eyes blazed. "Fucking bastards," he said. "Fucking New York Guinea bastards." He looked around, as though seeing his old place for the first time. "I need a minute. Gotta clean out the safe, and do a coupl'a things."

"Okay," Jade said. "Make it quick." Somebody peeked around the edge of the frontage on the right, which was now completely open. Jade fired twice; the goon retreated.

"Hold on a second." Claude fished one of the grenades out of his satchel. "Give 'em a minute or two," he said quietly to Jade as they both crouched behind the bar. "Let 'em think we're out of ammo, and get in close. When I toss it, drop flat. You might wanna plug your ears." And they did wait, for a full minute, as the smoke from above continued to creep along the ceiling and fill the room. Finally, they began to hear footsteps approaching the bar.

Claude pulled the pin on the device and silently, resolutely held it for what seemed like far too long as somebody said, with a deep and distinctly Brooklyn inflection, "Where the fuck they go?"

Then Claude leaned around the end of the bar, and briskly tossed the little black pineapple so that it skipped heavily across the hardwood floor, *thumpety-thump-thump-thump*, toward the Pelican's beach frontage. Jade did as he'd been told and put his fingertips in his ears.

"Aw, no," somebody said.

"We're right here, you wop fucks!" Claude shouted.

The massive *bang* shook the place to its foundation. Then suddenly, bizarrely, the jukebox began to play "Doris Mae," by Bing Crosby, which provided an accompaniment to the moans and cries of the dying as Jade and Claude peered over the bartop.

Despite being completely shot and blown open along the wall facing the beach where the frontage paneling had once been, the room was filling with smoke—but this didn't obscure the carnage. It was difficult to tell how many Terranza men had been on the other side of the old bar when the grenade had gone off; only the coroner would know for sure.

"Doris Mae, oh Doris Mae…" sang Bing Crosby, from the 78 rpm record that was somehow spinning in the wrecked but illuminated jukebox. "With eyes as blue as a summer's day…you stole my heart, you stole it awaaaay…"

"Go do what you need to do," Jade told Claude,

who nodded and went back to the office. Jade held the .45 at the ready, the barrel squared up right in the middle of the opening on the beach, but saw no movement except for the palm trees and the ocean. One of the well-dressed, mangled hunks of meat moaned one last time, and then went silent.

"Without you, my world has been so blue," Bing continued, in his dulcet tones. "I'm hypnotized by your ev'ry smile…for the promise of a kiss from you, I'd walk a thousand miles…"

Claude returned a moment later, holding a canvas bank bag. "I'm gonna get the Dodge out," he said decisively, and Jade knew there was no use arguing the point. He nodded. Then Claude went over to the four draft beer taps near the center of the bar and opened each of them up in turn. He put large breakfast platters upside down over each rectangular drain-grate, so that beer spilled out across the bartop and ran onto the floor.

"See you outside," Jade said. Claude nodded, and went out the back door with the Browning.

Jade crept along the right wall in a crouch, toward the edge of the frontage, while Bing Crosby continued to gently croon, "Doris Mae, oh my Doris Mae…won't you please just look my way…you stole my heart, you stole it awaaaay…I'll love you forever, my sweet Doris Mae…" When he peeked around the edge of the wall, he was met with gunfire from a black Packard parked across the street. Hot lead zinged past him and struck the far wall, shattering the glass in the framed picture over the jukebox: a photo of Claude smiling and posing with the actress Joan Crawford, who had had a drink at the Pelican back in '34 while on vacation in Miami Beach.

Well, that makes sense, Jade thought as he ducked back. *Now that the joint's on fire, they'll just try to keep us inside until it comes down on top of us. Well, screw that.*

Jade transferred the .45 to his left hand, and reached around the edge of the wall to fire several blind shots in the general direction of the Packard. With his right hand, he retrieved the Colt .38 Police Positive from his jacket. When the .45 went empty, he simply tossed it away and rounded the corner, still in a crouch, firing three more shots at the Packard with the .38 as he climbed over the hood of his roadster and dropped into the driver's seat. There was a great crashing sound—metal against splintering wood—from the back end of the Pelican, along with the squealing of tires and several gunshots.

By the time he'd turned the engine over and put it in gear, pulling the car away from where it had ground up against the Pelican's wall, the Terranzas in the Packard (it looked like there were two of them) had begun to return fire. Jade crouched down in the seat as his windshield shattered, and other rounds thumped heavily into the side of his car.

Claude's old Dodge pickup screamed in from the right and broadsided the Packard where it sat, driving its right-side tires over the curb. Claude got out of his truck, carrying the big Browning. He walked calmly around in front of the Packard and killed both of the men in it with two short bursts through the windshield. Then he went down, grabbing his leg, and it was only then that Jade registered three distinct shots from a small-caliber handgun, like the cracks of a whip, that came from behind them on Ocean Drive.

Jade turned around in his seat and saw a young suit about thirty feet away trying to reload his little Saturday night special, fumbling in his haste. Jade fired a warning shot over the kid's head, but he was too stupid to take a hint—or even take cover—and clumsily struggled, instead, to thumb one last round into the cylinder. Jade shook his head and took careful aim, holding the .38 with two hands. He squeezed off his second shot just as the kid snapped the cylinder into place. Struck in the shoulder of his gun arm, the kid collapsed like a house of cards. He'd live, and he wouldn't be shooting a gun anytime soon. Maybe he'd consider a different line of work.

Claude was apologetic when Jade got to him. "Goddamn it," he said. "I'm no good to ya."

"Knock it off," Jade said. "How bad is it?"

"Ah, shit," Claude sneered with disgust. "Just a goddamn peashooter—went clean through. Ain't nothin' gonna kill me. I just can't walk too good right now, is all. Never mind that now…there's one more car full of 'em," he said. "Three guys. Maybe four. Around the corner, in front of the Wayfarer—they're holdin' back, waitin' to see what happens. Get me to the truck."

Jade tried to get him up, but the big man couldn't stand, so Jade dragged him over to the driver's side running board of the old Dodge. He was alarmed by the blood trail Claude left on the street. "Don't you dare die on me, you old bastard."

"Not a chance," Claude grunted. His face had gone as white as bathroom porcelain. "Devil don't wanna deal with *me* just yet."

Jade had known him for too long. "Jesus Christ. Hold on a second." He took off his belt and quickly looped it around Claude's thigh, just above the gunshot wound. He cinched it tight. The blood kept coming. He cinched it tighter.

"This is no good, Claude. You're gonna need a doctor, or else—"

"Gonna be fine, Oscar. Gonna be just fine. You need to go, or that sonofabitch is gonna get away."

Flames streamed from the windows of the Pelican's second floor, and black smoke poured into the sky. The fires burning all over town had brought an early nightfall. "Gimme the sack," Claude said. Jade did. "Okay. Now, you take this." Claude gave him the last grenade. "Remember, it's a seven-second fuse—takes forever to go off. But it'll do the job."

Jade stood up, and motioned behind him at the Pelican. "I'm sorry—"

"Don't be," Claude said. He took out his sawed-off shotgun and cradled it in his lap. "It's just a pile of wood and plaster. Don't mean nothin'." His eyes twinkled as he smiled with one corner of his mouth. "Go get him."

Jade turned and spared a last look at the old Pelican. The second floor was engulfed in flames. Inside, the four kegs of beer would be emptying their contents across that faithful old hardwood tavern bar. "Listen, old man. You need to let off on that belt every few minutes, or—"

"Go," Claude growled impatiently.

Jade climbed into the roadster, did a U-turn and didn't look back.

The Wayfarer was an older, small hotel just to the north of the Pelican on Ocean Drive. As he came to the intersection with 15th Street and did a slow roll through the stop sign, Jade saw the car Claude had told him about: a green, late '30s Mercury with three Terranza goons inside, its front end aimed toward him. *They've got to follow me, and forget about Claude.*

He gave them a distinct, unmistakable hand gesture and hit the gas.

The Flathead V-8's twin exhausts boomed along Alton Road as the roadster screamed southward at 70 mph, the wind in Oscar Jade's face through the shattered windshield, the green Mercury looming in his mirror. His left headlight was gone—smashed and torn away when he'd struck the guy outside the Pelican—and he hadn't gone very far when he realized that there was a problem with the front end, too. There was a shimmy, and a drag that pulled the steering to the left. It got worse the faster he went; Jade remembered the way he'd crunched up against the stucco wall—probably the fender rubbing against the tire, he guessed. Well, there wasn't anything to be done about it now.

In his mirror, Jade saw one of the Terranzas lean out the passenger window of the Mercury, aiming a revolver. The barrel flashed. The report was barely audible over the engines' roar—but the hiss of the round, as it cut through the air near Jade's right ear, sounded close. Jade pumped his brakes; the Mercury came up on him fast and slammed into the Ford's rear end. The roadster bucked and lurched. Jade reached around and fired the Colt .38 into the Mercury's windshield. A splintered spiderweb appeared in the glass. Jade pulled the trigger again; the gun clicked empty. He cursed and threw the weapon. It dented the Mercury's hood as it bounced and flew over the car's roof. The Mercury backed off.

Jade turned back around, hit the gas and swerved, first to the right—fighting the pull of the front end—and then back to the left, taking care not to fishtail as the rear tires skidded across the road. He accelerated, putting more distance between them. He grabbed the steering wheel with his right hand, and reached into his jacket pocket with his left and produced the second Colt .38. Transferring the revolver to his right hand, he turned and fired another shot at them—and got three shots back in reply. Jade fired twice more, and the Mercury's windshield shattered.

He ignored the honking horns and screeching brakes of the cars that got in his way. Jade ran a stoplight and veered sharply into the oncoming lane to avoid a line of stopped traffic waiting for the signal to change. He was doing over eighty when he came to a high spot in the road near the intersection of Alton and 7th Street, and all four tires left the ground for a split-second before the roadster's undercarriage slammed violently against the pavement as he landed. He continued to take gunfire from the Mercury, muzzle flashes from the darkness of the car's interior flashing above the headlights.

With their windshield gone, Terranza's men had a clearer field of fire, and they were taking full advantage of it.

He ran another light at 6th Street, and hit the brakes when he came upon cars at a dead stop in both directions. A shot fired from the Mercury thudded into the roadster's dashboard. Jade pressed the gas pedal to the floor and swerved onto the sidewalk, blasting his horn and shouting, "Get out of the way!" at pedestrians who scattered before him. He narrowly missed a two-wheeled vending cart on a street corner. In his mirror, Jade saw the Mercury jump the curb and smash through the cart. Bundles of magazines and newspapers flew apart.

Jade slid sharply right onto 5th, gritting his teeth as he fought his car's urge to go the other way. As he shot past the Miami Beach Chamber of Commerce building and veered left onto the Dade County Causeway—signs advertising charter boat services flashing by on either side—Jade saw that black smoke had started to billow from his ruined left front tire well. He could smell burning rubber. Biscayne Bay hurtled past on either side of him, gunmetal grey beneath a smoke-filled evening sky. The last hint of the sun, a slender paintbrushing of orange and red, was low on the horizon behind Miami as the causeway made a sweeping right turn.

The smoke—and the left-hand pull—was getting progressively worse. Jade eased off on the gas; the Mercury came up fast and rammed into the rear of the roadster once again. Jade fought the wheel, and corrected the spin before it happened. He turned around in his seat, and fired the last three shots in the Colt. He tossed the empty revolver onto the floor in front of the passenger seat. Then he had a desperate idea. It would depend on how long he could keep them close, without them being able to zero in on him. And whether he could hit what he aimed at. Jade fished Claude's hand grenade from his jacket pocket and stared at the Mercury in his mirror, swerving back and forth, from left to right and then back again, with more difficulty each time as his left front tire continued to smoke and he got less response from his steering wheel. He pulled the pin, and hit his brakes.

One one thousand, he silently counted as the Mercury filled his mirror once again. *Two one thousand...three one thousand...*

The big car rammed the roadster's back end. Metal buckled, and tore. Jade tapped his brake pedal, and yanked the wheel from left to right, and back again, to keep the Mercury behind him. *Four one thousand...*

The grenade slipped out of Jade's hand, and bounced around on the passenger seat. He groped for it. It rolled out of his reach. *Five one thousand...*

Jade swerved back to the right. The grenade rolled into his hand. He picked it up, looked over his shoulder, and gave the pineapple a backhand toss through the hole in the Mercury's windshield. Then he punched the gas pedal, and the Flathead howled. For a horrible moment, it felt like the two cars' bumpers had become entwined. *Six one thousand—come on, come on!* Jade began to pull away from them, and he could see, in his mirror, the crazed, grimacing faces of the two guys in the front seat as they groped frantically for the weighty black trinket that had dropped into their laps.

Jade crouched as low as he could in the Ford's driver's seat.

The massive *bang* cut through the chaotic wind howling in Jade's ears. Metal fragments hissed angrily through the air all around him as the force of the explosion tried to kick the roadster sideways. Sitting up in his seat, he fought the wheel as he had a brief but spectacular view, in his rearview mirror, of the Mercury pinwheeling around and lifting onto its front end, where it spun like a macabre ballet dancer in drunken mid-pirouette, its roof peeled back from the rest of the vehicle. It seemed frozen in mid-air for a moment, then it tumbled over the edge of the causeway, trailing black smoke and flaming pieces of unrecognizable matter. Its fuel tank erupted in a massive secondary explosion—feeling close and hot against the back of Jade's neck, even as he raced away from it—just before the wreckage splashed into the bay.

Jade gasped as he tried to get enough air, and the thunder of his own heartbeat pounded in his ears. He passed the turnoff to Star Island on the right; Palm Island would be next, not far ahead. He hit the gas, ignoring the wobble and the pull of his wrecked alignment. Would he get there in time? God knew they'd had plenty of time to clear out, more than enough time to be long gone.

He braked as little as he dared and took the right turn at speed onto the short road that led to the big-money real estate of Palm Island, where the houses were big and the manicured lawns, with their sculpted hedges and coconut trees, were bigger. These artificial islands had caused quite a stir when far-sighted developers had built them up with dollar signs in their eyes. Movie stars, senators and steel tycoons had houses out here. Al Capone, out of prison and rumored to be out of his mind, lived here too. And so did Peter La Forno, late of the Terranza family from New York City—at least until today. It was a nice place to live, and as good a place as any to die.

The access road formed a 'T' with Palm Avenue, which was the only street on Palm Island, with a cul-de-sac at either end. Jade had the address, but it wouldn't have been hard to guess where he was going. Not surprisingly, all he had to do was follow the smoke.

He turned left, and accelerated toward its source at the end of the pricey residential lane, where two large Cadillac sedans, one of which was on fire, had been pulled in front of the closed, six-foot-tall wrought-iron gates as additional makeshift barriers. Another car, also on fire, sat off to the left. Four bullet-riddled corpses were sprawled nearby. Guns opened up on him—muzzle flashes from the other side of the gate—and Oscar Jade laughed with relief. He wasn't too late! There was still time—but time for what? What the hell could he hope to do? His only chance was to hope that La Forno wouldn't just kill him outright—that he was as paranoid as Jade hoped he was.

He gripped the wheel tightly and built speed, gauging the slope of the semicircular ornamental red brick façade on either side of the pillared gateway, which rose from ground level to the eight-foot height of the pillars on either side of the gates. La Forno had defended against a head-on ramming attack, which the Terranzas had clearly attempted with no success, but if he was going fast enough, and came at it from an angle…

He was doing more than fifty miles per hour when his left front tire blew, some two hundred feet out. Shredded rubber and a chunk of his quarter-panel flew off as he fought the fishtail, aiming for the raised edge of the brick façade to the left of the gateway. He hit the curb and his front end jumped about two feet, scraping along the façade's curved incline. The undercarriage gave an agonized shriek as the roadster glanced off the red brick masonry pillar and crashed against the top of the iron gate, impaling itself midway along the underside of the chassis, and then suddenly Jade wasn't in the car anymore. There was a delirious moment of weightlessness, a blur of night sky and emerald grass lit by electric lanterns in the yard, and an ephemeral sense of his car crashing to the ground somewhere a million miles away, or more. Who cared? And then he landed, flat on his back, on a surface that both yielded to the weight of his arrival with gentle, outreaching branches, and stabbed him, brutally, in a thousand places at once. He bounced, tumbled and rolled. The air was crushed out of his body, and he felt something give, with a distinct and discernable *snap*, in his ribcage.

And somewhere, in the middle of it all, the lights went out.

22
Whisky-Breath

"He's alive," somebody said. "Crazy son of a bitch."

"I want him," said another voice, this one familiar. "Let me have him."

The darkness, once again, was soft and comfortable. Why couldn't they just leave him alone? But he forced himself up and out of it as he tried to place the voice. Hands roughly grabbed his arms, which didn't feel completely attached.

"No," he heard La Forno say. "He's coming with us."

"Boss, I'm telling you! This guy's trouble. You can't turn your back on him, not even for a second."

"Since he's here, I want to have a word with him. Then you can shoot him and toss them both overboard, for all I care. But not until I say so."

"But—"

"I'm not asking your goddamn opinion!" La Forno shouted. "What the hell kind of people do I have around me, here? Do what I tell you to do, and shut your mouth! Or do we have a problem?"

There was a long pause. "No. We don't have a problem."

"That's good, because today I'm solving all my problems. Get him up, and let's go."

His .38 was deftly plucked from its waistband holster. Jade was grabbed underneath his arms and hoisted up—and then the pain erupted in ripples along the left side of his ribcage, taking his breath away. A moan, that sounded to him as if it had come from someone else, escaped before he could stop it. He opened his eyes and saw his own feet being dragged backwards across the immaculately cut grass. Every movement, every step taken by whoever was holding him brought fresh waves of agony, as if his chest had been placed in a gigantic bench vise. *They're busted now, Claude*, he thought as he lifted his head slightly and took in his surroundings. His wrecked roadster lay on its side, just inside the iron fence. A number of bodies, at least six of them, all strewn in various poses of violent death, littered the front lawn like tasteless landscaping ornaments.

"Come on!" La Forno sounded like he was in a hurry, which wasn't surprising. It looked like he'd lost quite a few of his own men, and he'd have no idea how many more Terranzas were still out there. For that matter, neither did Jade. How many more could there be? According to Valletti, there were twenty-two altogether when it started. *God! Twenty-two!* How many people had died today? How many people had he, himself, killed…and for what? How much more blood had to be spilled before it was over, and if some of it was his—if he was about to die—what would his life have meant? Maybe nothing. And maybe that was all right. It would have to be.

Jade felt eyes on him. He looked up and to the left; Detective Rusty Connor, Miami Beach P.D., was bringing up the rear, his service revolver at his hip, the barrel trained squarely on Jade's chest as Jade was dragged along.

"Hey, copper," Jade said. "Proud of your work?"

"Shut up. You're a dead man."

"I'd say that makes two of us, Rusty," he said. "I'm fine with that. How about you?"

Connor's eyes widened, and he took a breath to speak as his hand tightened on his gun, but he must have thought better of it. He kept his mouth shut, and kept staring. Jade knew the cop was waiting for an excuse: *"He went for my gun! I had to kill him!"* Jade didn't plan to make it that easy. He was in no shape to put up a fight. *Might as well ride this train to the last stop.*

Behind the huge Spanish-style mansion was a kidney-shaped swimming pool enclosed within a concrete patio and trimmed in multi-colored terra-cotta tiles. A cocktail bar was nestled beneath the overhang of an upper-floor terrace. Jade could imagine the place on any other Friday night of the year: music playing under a starry sky, laughter and drinks around the pool, local political figures and businessmen—most likely with La Forno-owned girls like Greta Vincennes hanging on each arm, laughing with false amusement at every witticism—being gently but firmly leveraged by the La Forno machine for various concessions and protections, without even knowing how obviously they were being played. Or maybe knowing and not caring. But not tonight. Tonight there was only a small group of people moving quickly and nervously past the darkened pool area, guns out and prisoners in tow, ready to flee like the exiles they'd suddenly become, all other options played out.

Jade found it was getting more difficult to breathe. He dug in his heels, and pulled at the hands that restrained his arms, even though it caused a new surge of pain in his ribs. "I can walk," he said irritably.

"Let him walk," La Forno said. "We need to move. If he tries anything, shoot him. Rusty, use your cuffs."

The hands let go. Jade stood up, and breathed a sigh of relief as the pressure on his chest was lessened. Connor stepped in behind him and handcuffed Jade's hands behind his back with a decisive click. "Thanks, Rusty," he said. "You're swell."

Connor spun him around. Jade saw that there were only four of them altogether: himself, La Forno, Connor and Freddie, who glared at Jade over his bandaged nose with an eager hatred.

"Looking good, Freddie," Jade said.

They were at the top of a flight of wooden stairs that descended about ten feet to a grassy bank and an L-shaped dock on the water. There, gently rocking in the soft light of the lamps at either end of the dock, its motor already idling in a fat and bubbly purr, was a top-of-the-line Chris-Craft motor yacht. Jade recognized it from one of the famous boat-maker's brochures, which he'd once read while waiting for a haircut. He'd always tried to imagine what it would be like to have enough money to afford such a thing. With her spotless white hull, sleek lines and varnished mahogany cabin, she was a beauty, for sure, all money and styling. She was a big, floating piece of The Good Life, a life that didn't care about stock market crashes or wars being fought halfway around the world—or even the occasional small, solitary ruined life ground underfoot. Across the stern, in large elegant letters, the name "*Constance*" was painted in black and gold.

She's bigger than a forty-footer for sure. More like forty-eight. And probably with all the extras money can buy.

They stepped onto the dock. For an instant Jade had the crazy idea of shoving Connor and Freddie into the water and having a go at La Forno. Then he remembered his cuffed hands, and the pain in his ribcage. Even if he managed to get the other two guys off the dock, La Forno was still pretty fit-looking, despite his age. One good punch to the gut, and Jade would be in the drink too—unable to do anything except drown like an idiot. If he was about to die, he didn't intend to go alone.

The lounge was done in mahogany, hunter-green leather upholstery and polished brass. A small galley and bar lined the port bulkhead. Up ahead, by the helm, stood a tanned but slightly pudgy middle-aged guy Jade didn't recognize. He wore a white naval officer-style hat with an embroidered gold anchor over the bill, and a starched white shirt with decorative gold-braided black epaulets. A nametag on his chest said 'Leo.' He held a small semiautomatic pistol at the ready.

"Evening, skipper," Jade said wryly.

Connor prodded Jade past the clown in the make-believe navy getup, down three short steps and into a narrow passageway, then through the first door to port.

The tiny stateroom was dark. The air was thick, and smelled like stale bourbon. The cop gave Jade a hard shove in the back, and closed the door behind him. Jade tripped over something and pitched forward. He tried to twist as he fell, struggling in vain against the cuffs binding his wrists, to avoid landing on his chest. Still, the pain was such that Jade cried out.

"Uh," said a voice from very close. "Whaddahellizzit…"

There was another person on the deck right next to him, a sick moan wafting on a blast of cloying whisky-breath in the pitch-blackness. "Al?" Jade asked cautiously, blinking against the stench.

"Uhh…whowanna…dunno."

"Al! Wake up."

"Wha…whatizzit?"

"It's Oscar."

"Oscar?" Billings' voice was thick and garbled. There was a long pause. "Aw, Jesus, no…they got you too."

"Yeah. They got me." Jade's eyes began to adjust to the darkness. He could now make out Billing's face, just inches from his own. "So you're a drinking man again."

"I dunno," he said groggily. "Guess so…it's my fault, the whole thing. My fault."

"What is? What's your fault?"

"I dunno how it happened, swear to God I don't! One minute I'm talking to her, just following a lead Rusty said he got from vice. Next thing I know, I wake up in bed with her, an' neither one of us got any clothes on, an' I got that old pounding in the head. How the hell? I dunno."

"Take it easy—"

"Then she tells me she's got pictures." Billings groaned pitifully. "Pictures! She says she'll give copies of 'em to the commissioner, newspapers...give 'em to Sally..."

"So you turned a blind eye to the Caribbean."

"They made me into a liar! An'a cheater...Sally... Sally," Billings sobbed. "I looked her father in the eye, Oscar. I promised him...promised I'd take care of his little girl. Boy, I've taken care of her all right. Stood in front of God and her family and promised to be her husband...Christ. Promised everyone. Everything. Now it's all rotted from the inside out. The worms have got me."

"Are you on the take, or not?"

"Not for money! Jus' to keep the pictures quiet! No thirty pieces of silver for me. But the crows are coming anyway, bet your ass, Oscar, and they'll have my eyes—you know Rusty's dirty, right?"

The soft murmur of the boat's motor changed tenor slightly as it was put in reverse; the big Chris-Craft had to be backing slowly away from the dock. "Yeah," Jade sighed. "I know Rusty's dirty."

"He's innit with the girl, the dancer...shoulda known. I shoulda known!"

"Goddamn it, Al! Pull yourself together! I need your help."

"Rusty the boy wonder. How do you like that?" Billings' barely visible face had screwed itself into a grimace, tears streaming from his eyes. "A cop's all I ever wanted to be. A good cop. We all got dreams, don't we? You did too, Oscar. I know you did. You coulda been the best cop in the state, coulda been commissioner, instead of sneaking around behind the law, twisting it, tricking it. You shoulda held on…shouldn't'a given up—"

"That's enough."

"God gimme four good limbs. Nothing wrong, nothing misshapen. Everything right where it belongs, 'cept on the inside. When it's gnarled up on the inside, what you got? But that was never the real problem with you, was it Oscar?"

"Shut up."

"What's inside of you, boy? A foot can't keep a cop, a real cop, down! Y'know, you were always like a kid brother, Oscar…I remember I promised your folks, too. Told 'em you'd be alright—"

"Al, I'm telling you to shut the hell up."

"I was supposed to take care of you, too! Now look at us! We're gonna die on this tub."

"I can see why you quit the booze," Jade said. "You're a lousy drunk."

"What, you gonna feel sorry for me? Hell no, you're not! Whyn't just admit it? You blame me for what happened, you always did."

"That's not true, and you know it."

"The hell I know it! Don't feel sorry for me, don't you dare. Feel sorry for yourself, instead. Who else is gonna feel bad for the pitcher who blows the game…even if he *is* crippled." Billings laughed.

"Poor crippled pitcher, ex-cop, four-F—nobody loves me! No family, don't believe in the law, don't even believe in myself. Hell, boy, that's why God invented the bottle, ain't it?"

"I'm not going to talk to you until you sober up."

"We're gonna be dead by then," Billings said. "We're gonna sink. Sink together. All the way to the bottom. Drowning...drowning's nothing. Guess I been doing that for years. Didn't even know it. Can the worms swim, Oscar? I dunno." Suddenly, raggedly and woefully out-of-tune, he began to sing:

"When thou art lost, adrift on the sea
Will there be angels to guide thee?
Will we stranded sailors on ole Neptune's crest
Ever make port to find our rest?
Nay, nay, nay! cries your heart. And thou know that it rings true:
For all the wicked sins in your life, the sea will claim her due!"

The door to the stateroom swung open, bathing them in light. Freddie's hulking silhouette filled the doorway. "That's enough of that shit!"

"Go fuck yourself, you dago bastard," Billings spat.

Freddie stepped inside, drew a foot back and briskly kicked the cop in the back of the head. Billings bellowed another obscenity.

"Your turn's coming," Freddie told him. He moved over to Jade, grabbed him by the cuffs and pulled him up. Jade groaned as he felt his broken ribs rub against one another. "Boss wants a word with *you*."

“There you go, Oscar,” Billings said. “You walked ’em full, now. Bases loaded. Boy, you better make sure the next breaking ball breaks…now’d be a helluva time to leave one hangin’…You’ll get the hook! Back to the dugout, boy!”

“Get some sleep, Al,” Jade said as Freddie manhandled him into the passageway. “I’ll be back.”

“No, you won’t,” Freddie said.

23
Blood

Myrna Mallory sat meekly on a cushioned bench-style seat across from the bar. “Oscar!” She leapt up and moved toward Jade, but Connor stepped between them. “Oscar, I’m sorry.”

She had an angry purplish bruise and some swelling under her right eye. “What happened to you?” Jade demanded. She glanced immediately at La Forno, and then down at her feet.

“She was being stupid,” La Forno said. “That’s all. Sometimes even the best women have to be reminded when to keep their mouths shut.”

“Like Greta was reminded?” Jade said angrily. “They shot her and burned the place down. That’s a tough lesson.”

Myrna gasped, and looked at La Forno.

La Forno shrugged and lit a cigarette. “Well, she’s not going to steal any more of my money, is she? But anyway, it wasn’t my boys,” he said indifferently. “It was Little Tom’s.”

Jade looked Rusty Connor in the eye, winked at him and gave a cold smile. "Gotta tell you, it's getting pretty hard to tell the difference."

"Well, they did me a favor. I guess I've got a soft heart. Gave the girl too many chances. Have a seat, Jade," La Forno offered congenially. As if to punctuate the point, Freddie roughly pushed him down onto the bench next to Myrna. Jade groaned as the pain flared across his chest. "And like I said, don't make a fuss, and you'll live a little longer."

The dock lights had receded in the darkness astern, their silver reflections dancing in the churned-up water.

Jade kept silent and looked over at Myrna. She tried to smile, but didn't quite make it. Then he saw something in her eyes—she glanced down. She was trying to tell him something. He followed where she was looking, but could only see the front of her blouse. He looked at her questioningly, and she looked down again: a pointed, deliberate movement. Jade looked around the lounge. La Forno had gone to the bar and was pouring himself a tall shot of bourbon. Both Freddie and Connor stared intently at Jade. He gave Myrna a gentle shake of his head, and tested the fit of the cuffs around his wrists. They didn't give an inch.

"Knock it off," Connor said. "Whatever you're doing, knock it off."

Once they'd been under way for a few minutes, La Forno let out a deep breath, and seemed to relax. By the time they'd passed underneath the causeway bridge into Government Cut, and headed into the open water of the Atlantic, he was positively gregarious. He raised a glass and beamed at Connor. "So much for Little Tommy, eh Rusty?"

"That's right," Connor replied quickly, *too* quickly, staring at Jade.

"So what now?" Jade made the question conversational.

"The Bahamas." The old Sicilian was sanguine. "I've got a nice little place there, and more than enough money for my retirement." He smiled at Myrna. "You're never too old to start a new life."

"Retiring again? I thought you were already retired."

"This is different."

"Really? Looks to me like Terranza ran you out of New York, and then he ran you out of Miami. What makes you think this'll be the end of it? How do you know he won't run you out again…or just finish you off next time?"

The smile faltered. "You're on borrowed time, son. The water out there's gonna get real deep pretty soon. They'll never find you. You oughta be more polite."

"Sorry." Jade motioned around the lounge with his head. "But it sure looks like you're running away. How many men did you lose back there at your house? Most of 'em, right? Terranza lit up everything—your warehouse on the docks, the Caribbean, your garbage collection business, your stables out at Hialeah. He probably killed your horse, for Christ's sake! You can't tell me that doesn't matter to you!"

La Forno stared past Jade, out the door of the lounge and past the stern of the boat. The scattered, muted lights of Miami Beach—because new blackout guidelines had been imposed since Pearl—had begun to fade away in the night, along with the telltale smoke of multiple fires. His face grew ashen and stiff. "Sometimes you've got to cut your losses. I've got a score to settle there, but that's for someday. Meantime, he's gonna know he's been in a fight." He looked at Jade. "I'm guessing you bloodied him up a little, yourself. Am I right?"

Jade looked into those black shark's eyes. "I did," he said.

La Forno smiled. "I bet you did. Good for you. You know, Jade, it's really too bad. You're just the kind of guy I like to have around when things get dicey—"

"Things are dicey right now, Mr. La Forno," Jade said. "Nothing's over with, not even close—"

"That's just a bunch of bullshit," Connor interjected. "Boss, he's just trying to buy himself time. He's going to say anything that—"

"How much does Myrna know about your wife?" Jade pushed on. "Does she know why everything you own is named after her? Does she know about how she died? She really ought to, so she knows what she's getting herself into. Otherwise, all you're doing here is kidnapping her. Isn't that right?"

La Forno calmly, deliberately put his drink down. He took a last drag on his cigarette, and put it out in the ashtray. Then he crossed the narrow lounge in three steps, drew back his right fist and punched Jade in the mouth. Jade rolled with it as best he could, and tasted fresh blood.

"Don't!" Myrna cried out. "Peter—*don't*. Please."

La Forno ignored her and absently rubbed his knuckles as he told Connor, "Take her up front and put her in her room. Make sure she stays there."

Connor angled a thumb toward Freddie. "Why can't he—"

"Do what I tell you!"

The cop scowled but took Myrna by the wrist; she jerked it away. "Don't touch me!" she hissed. But she rose from the bench of her own accord and walked ahead of Connor past Leo in the cockpit and through the hatchway. When they had vanished into the starboard stateroom, La Forno said, "You had that one coming, boy."

"I guess I did," Jade mumbled. He felt blood spilling down his chin. He knew he didn't have much time. "How did you know I killed Little Tom's son?"

The question seemed to take La Forno by surprise. "The cop told me," he said.

"Which cop?"

"That's funny." La Forno took a drink of bourbon. "You know goddamned good and well which cop. The one that isn't about to take a ride on a boat anchor, that's which one. Don't get me wrong; Captain Billings has been a big help lately. But I had to use some leverage to secure his services."

"So I hear."

"Just a little something extra in his coffee," La Forno said. "That's all it took. After that, a little booze goes a long way. The pictures will be mailed to the mayor and the newspapers. And since it was *his* gun that shot the bookie, it won't be too tough for the police to figure out why he skipped town. Permanently."

"Very neat," Jade said. "But that doesn't answer my question. How did Connor know I killed Little

Tom's boy?"

"Oh, yeah. I see what you're trying." La Forno shook his head. "And it's not going to work. Connor's been on my payroll a long time, Jade. I trust him."

"Do you?"

"Yes, I do."

"Do you know he's a blood relation to Little Tom?"

La Forno gave a short laugh, which sounded harsh and artificial in the closed space. "Yeah, sure."

"That would change things, though, wouldn't it? And Nino Valletti would know, wouldn't he? I've got him under lock and key right now. He told me the whole story. And it's a doozy."

Near the door to the lounge, Freddie shifted uncomfortably and adjusted his grip on the gun in his hand.

"Listen, Jade. Connor works for *me*. He's got connections from up north, sure. But he tells me everything. Hell, he's the only reason I knew Tommy was about to make a move. He could have put a bullet in my head anytime he wanted to, the last year or so—especially today. Like I said, nice try."

"So he's the one who told you Terranza's men killed Greta."

"That's right." La Forno's brow drew down, forming horizontal lines across his tanned forehead. He glanced over his shoulder in the direction Connor and Myrna had gone.

"And he'd have no reason to lie about that, would he? Unless he had something to gain from it."

"What the hell are you saying?"

"I'm saying you need to ask your cop buddy about

who actually killed her," Jade said. "Maybe it doesn't matter to you. Maybe you don't care...but I would. I'd want to make sure the people I trust aren't shitting on me when my back is turned. Think about it: Terranza's men had to be spread all over town—from the docks all the way to Hialeah—besides having at least ten or eleven guys at the Pelican. With all that happening at the same time, how the hell did Connor know what was going on at Greta's place?"

"Because I found her there." Connor was standing next to Leo, who was holding onto the boat's wheel and staring at the cop in astonishment. Connor's gun was out, and aimed squarely at Jade's head.

"Rusty, calm down." La Forno's voice was even and smooth. "Just relax."

"*I'm* the one who found her," Jade said, "and I got her out. But she was already dead. What did you do, just walk away and leave her in there with the place on fire? No—I'll tell you what happened. Greta offered me one of those keys to let her go. She said it was worth five grand. I'll just bet she offered you one, too. But instead, you just killed her and took them all for yourself. Right?"

"You're a goddamned liar," Connor said.

"Valletti told me it was your job to get rid of her. It's pretty sad: she figured you were her insurance policy. She lived just long enough to find out how wrong she was, didn't she?"

"Shut up!"

"Mr. La Forno, ask your cop buddy about all that money Greta stole from Mallory—your money. She put it in lock boxes all over town—the train station, bus stations. She was about to fly the coop on you, and this guy knows it. Why don't you ask him if he has any of those keys in his pockets right now? I'm telling you: he's a Terranza. And if you keep trusting him, one of these days he's gonna kill you in your sleep."

"I don't know what he's talking about." Connor's voice had gotten a little higher, tinged with an edge of desperation. "Boss, please..."

There was a long silence, filled only by the hum of the boat's motor and the soft slap of water against the hull. "Rusty," said La Forno, still in the same dangerously matter-of-fact tone of voice. "This is easy. Why don't you put your gun away and empty your pockets, and prove Mister Jade wrong? Then you can shoot him, or tie him to the anchor with Captain Billings and throw 'em both overboard, and we'll all be friendly business partners again. But right now, I'm afraid it's something I need to know. I'm sure you understand."

"Mister La Forno," Connor said plaintively, "I swear to God, I've been loyal to you! I told you this guy'd do anything—"

"Give me the goddamned gun." La Forno held out his hand, all pretense of good humor gone. "And empty your pockets. Otherwise, we're about to have a different kind of conversation."

Connor kept his gun centered on Jade's head. The knuckle of his trigger finger whitened.

"Freddie," La Forno said, "Shoot the cop."

Connor swiveled, and shot Freddie in the chest. Freddie pitched backward through the doorway and out onto the fantail of the boat as Jade launched himself across the small space and buried his head in Connor's gut.

Jade and Connor landed on the deck. Jade screamed in agony through clenched teeth as his hands pulled against the cuffs, but he used his legs for leverage and continued to drive his head into the cop's stomach, bearing down as if to drive a hole all the way through him. Connor's elbow caught him in the side of the head once, twice, three times, but Jade ignored the blows, keeping the pressure on.

"Leo!" Jade heard La Forno shout out, and suddenly there was a wet, crunching sound. Jade glanced up; the heel of La Forno's expensive leather shoe had come directly down on Connor's face, smashing the cop's teeth in and flattening his nose. La Forno reached down and grabbed the gun out of his hand. "Okay, Jade," La Forno said. "I got him."

Jade rolled off with a groan.

'Captain' Leo, comical in his make-believe navy officer getup, stood over Connor and aimed his little automatic at the cop's head. His eyes darted nervously from La Forno to Connor and back again. La Forno fished through Connor's pockets, and then opened his hand to examine what he found. There was a handful of loose change—and four keys, each with a numbered brass tag. He put it all into one of his own jacket pockets, and then stood up.

"I guess I owe you an apology, son," he told Jade. Then he grabbed Connor by the lapels of his suitcoat and lifted him up from the deck with an ease that belied his age.

"N-no," Connor mumbled. "'S'not what you think."

"Sure it's not," La Forno said as he hauled the

cop out to the fantail. He shot him once in the head, and pushed the body over the side.

Jade used the bench to get to his feet. He went outside and knelt down beside Freddie, who looked at him in hopeless desperation. The kid opened his mouth to say something, but it never came out. Instead, a bubble of blood appeared, and then popped like a circus balloon. He gasped again wetly, then writhed and twisted with an impotent, grunting finality. He died staring up, past Jade, at a brilliantly starry night sky.

La Forno turned around, holding the cop's gun. "Get back inside, son. Let's not have this get any worse."

Jade looked out into the darkness and caught a glimpse of Detective Rusty Connor, Miami Beach P.D., floating face down in the black water. In the next second, he was gone.

"What are you waiting for?" Jade asked. "Why don't you just shoot me too?"

"Is that what you want?"

Jade thought for a second. "Why not."

"Don't!" screamed Myrna, from the doorway of the lounge, staring in horror at Freddie, and the gun in La Forno's hand. "Please, Peter! Don't."

Behind her, Captain Leo had his little gun nervously held in a ready position at his hip, one hand on the wheel.

La Forno looked down at Jade—who was still on his knees next to Freddie's body—for what seemed like a very long time. The *Constance* gently rolled on the calm sea. Then he motioned with the gun. "Get up," he said.

With great difficulty, grasping the railing behind him with his cuffed hands for support, Jade did. They went back into the lounge. Jade gingerly sat down on the bench.

"Myrna, dear." La Forno's voice was gentle. "Please go back to your room. Mr. Jade and I have some 'man talk' to discuss."

"Peter, please don't hurt him any more. He wouldn't even be involved in any of this if I hadn't gone to him for help. It's my fault he's involved—"

"Myrna." His voice was suddenly as sharp as a blade. "Go back to your room. Leo, put her away."

Looking apologetic and embarrassed, Leo gestured with his gun. Myrna gave La Forno a baleful last stare, and retreated through the passageway into the starboard-side stateroom. Leo resumed his place at the wheel.

La Forno took a seat on one of the bar's two stools and rested his gun hand on his thigh, keeping the weapon aimed. He took a drink. "You know, Jade, that was a real cheap shot you took, that stuff about my wife."

"I didn't mean to insult you," Jade said. "Or your wife."

La Forno took a drink of his bourbon. "I loved my wife; she meant everything to me. Tommy never understood. He killed my boys, did you know that?"

Jade nodded carefully.

"Antonio and Mario." The old man gave a drawn, washed-out smile that quickly disappeared. "I never wanted them in the business. I wanted them to stay in school, be doctors or lawyers. Anything but *this*." La Forno motioned around him. "I wanted them to keep their hands clean, and their souls, too. But with them it was always, 'Uncle Tommy' this, or 'Uncle Tommy' that. 'Uncle Tommy took us to the ball game.' 'Uncle Tommy taught me how to play poker.' My boys never even knew what I did for a living until they were almost men—because I'd promised Connie I'd keep them out of it. She made me promise, and I'm a man of my word. They thought I ran a trucking business...but they knew all about Uncle Tommy and his guns, and his card games, and his rackets. Uncle Tommy was a hero to them. When they started to work for him, they never told me.

"Tommy knew there was a hit out on him. That's why he used my boys as decoys. They didn't know any better—they were probably happy to get to drive Uncle Tommy's car across town." La Forno's face was an impassive mask as he drank down his bourbon and poured himself another.

"I heard it was your hit," Jade said.

"It doesn't matter who gave the order!" La Forno spat the words. "If it hadn't been me, it would have been somebody else. Tommy had no business running that family, the Don's son or not, and everybody in town knew it. But he made goddamned sure it cost me everything. My boys..." His voice trailed off in a deep sigh. He stared haggardly at his drink. "And my wife." He took another drink; Jade watched closely. The old man was beginning to get drunk.

Finally La Forno said, "Times have changed. Where did honor go, Jade? And respect? In the old days, a man respected who he worked for. Everybody knew his place, and everybody made money. Everything worked. When I was young, I never even considered stealing from my boss. Sure, you made a little dough on the side, everybody expects that. But this is different."

"So in the old days, a guy just killed his boss and took over, right? Like with Sal Gagliardo."

La Forno was shaken from his reverie, and stared darkly at Jade for a long moment. Then he chuckled. "You're pretty good. I'll give you that…but yeah. Old Sal had it coming. He got fat and lazy. You can't just screw everybody around you and not expect it to come back on you eventually."

"Maybe he should've quit while he was ahead," Jade said. "Maybe he should have retired to Florida."

His grip tightened on Connor's gun. "You really do want to die, don't you, son?"

"Times don't change that much, Mr. La Forno, that's all I'm saying. And neither do people. The cop killed Greta, and that was okay with you, right? Even though he did it for Terranza, not you. And then he stole her money. But that money wasn't really hers. She stole it from Mallory…and he got it by skimming off the Caribbean. Did you know that Mallory was a stooge for the Terranzas, too?"

La Forno's gaze wavered. He didn't reply.

"So it all comes back to Mallory stealing from you…and you knew he was stealing from you. Why'd you put up with it? Why'd you keep him around?"

"Because he paid me back," La Forno said, with a crooked smile. "Or, he's about to."

"What do you mean, he paid you back?" Jade thought for a moment. "Oh, my God. You don't mean—"

"That's exactly what I mean, smart guy." La Forno finished the bourbon in his glass, and poured himself another. Some of it splashed across the top of the bar. His grip on the gun had gone slack again. He took another drink. "She's a fine-looking lady, isn't she? Don't tell me you haven't noticed. Not like a movie star, or anything...but she doesn't know how good-looking she is, and those are the best kind, you know what I mean? Not like Joe Vincennes' girl, who figured everybody owed her something, just because she took some hard knocks, and had big jugs. Girls like that are a dime a dozen...

"Mallory told me he was going to send her to the post office to mail some letters one day, so I got there early and waited for her. After that it was easy. Mallory treated her like dirt. She was ready to be treated like a lady again—dames like that deserve to be treated like a lady—they appreciate it when they get what they deserve...and *then* they give you what you want."

"And you want a son," Jade said.

"That's right. And I'm going to get one. And I'm not going to make any mistakes this time. He's going to live a good life. He's going to be a good man. Something good's going to come out of all this, I swear to God."

"'He?' What if it's a girl?"

La Forno chuckled. "He won't be."

"How can you be so sure?"

"Some things you can be sure about." La Forno took another long drink. "It's in my blood. No man in my family has fathered a girl in more than a hundred years. That's just the way it is. This time, I'm going to do it right."

"Well, that's tidy," Jade said bitterly. "You know, if you'd been a better father to your own sons they'd probably still be alive, and so would your wife, and you wouldn't have to ruin so many other lives just to make sure your name gets carried on."

"What the hell do you know about it?" La Forno shouted. He leapt off the barstool, brandishing the revolver wildly. "You don't know what it's like to never have any peace! To never know when somebody's going to come gunning for you, and take everything you have left!"

"The only reason your sons got killed is because you couldn't leave well enough alone with the Terranzas," Jade shot back. "You couldn't just leave town. You had to try to kill Little Tom, and you killed your own boys instead! You deserve everything that's happened to you."

"You're dead," La Forno snarled.

"I hear that a lot," Jade said. "And I'm getting bored. Do it already, you crazy son of a bitch! I dare you."

La Forno steadied the gun, lining up the mouth of the barrel between Oscar Jade's eyes.

Jade stared up at the old man's face, and waited for it. "Fuck you," he said.

There was a single gunshot, sudden and loud, but it came from up forward. Both Jade and La Forno looked toward the wheel, where Captain Leo staggered away from the controls, clutching his chest. Blood, bright red against the crisp starched white of his shirt, poured out from between his fingers. The *Constance* began a turn to starboard, the untended wheel in a slow spin. The boat rocked gently from side to side as she came astride the shallow troughs between waves.

Standing in the passageway was Myrna Mallory, holding a .38 snubnose that Jade immediately recognized as his own, a wisp of smoke curling up from the barrel. She aimed it at La Forno. Her lovely, freckled pixie's face had contorted into a dangerous and unfamiliar scowl, her brow furrowed into a deeply etched 'v'-shape.

"Horace gave me over," she hissed, "as *payment*?"

"Myrna, sweetheart." La Forno's voice was velvet-smooth, his gun still pointed at Jade's head. "It's not polite to eavesdrop. You misunderstand what I said…put that down. I don't want to have to kill your friend here, but I will if you make me."

"Answer me!"

"Myrna, it's complicated. I don't expect you to understand. Maybe it started out that way…but you have to believe me, everything has changed. I'm going to take care of you—"

"Shut your mouth! Shut your filthy, lying mouth! You're nothing but an animal! What was I thinking? What was I thinking?"

La Forno seemed to swell with indignation, puffing from within. He stood up to his full height, his gun hand steady on Jade, his black eyes locked on her. "Myrna, I *will* kill him if you don't come to your senses. Come now, you know you won't shoot me. You're not that kind of person."

"You don't know me," Myrna said, tears streaming down her cheeks. "You don't know me at all."

"Myrna my dear, we're going to be a family," La Forno said. "We're going to put all this ugliness behind us and start a new life—"

"Horace took out a life insurance policy on me!" Myrna said. "You planned to kill me once I had your baby!"

"That's not true," La Forno said. "Who told you that? Him?" He nodded toward Jade. "It's a lie."

"Peter, I saw the insurance policy!"

"Then that was your worthless bastard of a husband, not me!" La Forno shouted. "Myrna, I swear to God! I'd never hurt you in a thousand years. I did this for you, can't you see that?"

Slowly, uncertainly, Myrna lowered her gun hand.

La Forno smirked at Jade. "See? She's a sensible woman." He looked back at her. "Now, give me the gun, darling."

Suddenly, Myrna put the barrel of the .38 against her own stomach, and pulled back the hammer with her thumb. "I'll kill us both," she said, sobbing. "But I'll kill your precious little son first. I swear to God, Peter, I will. I won't bring your little monster into the world, not like this. Drop your gun."

"Myrna, you aren't going to do that—"

"*Drop the goddamned gun!*"

La Forno did. The piece thumped on the deck at his feet. "I love you," he said simply.

Myrna Mallory shot him twice: once in the groin, and—as he bent over and clutched at himself in incredulity—once between the eyes. Then she calmly strode over to where he was sprawled, at Jade's feet, and emptied the gun into his chest. She continued to pull the trigger as the hammer fell onto empty casings, and the cylinder rotated with each click… click…click…click…

"Myrna," Jade said. "Myrna!"

Slowly, very slowly, she turned to look at him. There was no recognition in those big brown eyes, not at first, as the tears spilled over.

"He's gone," Jade said. "It's over."

She dropped the gun and threw her arms around him. The sobbing began, deep wracking convulsions, her breath sweet and warm against his neck, her hot tears flowing like they might never end.

Myrna found the keys to the handcuffs on the key ring La Forno had taken from Rusty Connor's pockets. Jade rubbed his chafed and bloody wrists, trying to get circulation back into his hands. Then he took control of the boat's wheel and brought her around until the compass showed them on a westerly heading. They'd gotten far enough out that there was no sign of land to the naked eye, but Jade had a pretty good idea where they would be. He throttled back to just above idle, put Myrna at the wheel, and told her to keep the compass needle where it was.

"I was lying when I told you I wanted to go with Peter," she said.

"I figured," Jade said.

"And I wouldn't have done it. I wouldn't have killed the baby. You know that, don't you?"

He nodded. "How did you still have the gun?"

"When Detective Connor came for me...he never searched me, except for my purse."

"I can't believe it," Jade said.

"He never would have looked for it...where I hid it," she said.

Jade shook his head. "I'm not going to ask." He went to the bar and took three long, grateful swallows from the bourbon in La Forno's crystal decanter. He checked on Billings in the portside stateroom. The cop was sound asleep and snoring in leisurely, regular breaths.

Jade unlocked the cuffs and rolled him onto his back. He put a pillow beneath the cop's head.

Then he went aft to do some grim business.

He found the *Constance*'s spare anchor. It was tough work, but Jade gritted through it. By the time he had all three bodies laid out on the fantail, tied together with all the spare rope he could lay his hands on, he was sweaty and faint from the exertion. It took everything he had left to get the anchor over the side. It vanished into the black water with a heavy splash, and then, one by one, they followed: Captain Leo, then Freddie, and finally Peter La Forno—each of them staring in blank, passive accusation at Oscar Jade as they were pulled out of sight and into eternity.

Jade stood there for a moment, breathing in the cool night air as deeply as his broken ribs would allow. There were a lot of decisions to make, a lot of things to do, before he could get the cops involved. Already a part of his mind was formulating the answers to what he knew would be a series of difficult and uncomfortable questions, asked by people in authority—some of them friends, most of them not—who would be looking for as many scapegoats as they could find. He began to count the number of markers he'd have to call in, and the fresh debts he'd owe before the ledger sheet was balanced out. It was going to be a near thing.

He went out onto the bow. The *Constance* pitched slightly, from aft to forward, as the gentle waves overtook her in the slow race toward the scattered lights of home.

Quite unexpectedly, just then he caught a glimpse of something off to the left. Something out of place—straight, man-made and purposeful where such a thing didn't belong. A brief, silvery vertical reflection of the faint lights of the city, right on the surface of the dark water, and a tiny pinpoint of reflected light lost in the halfhearted whitecaps of tranquil, moonlit night seas…there and gone. Had it lowered out of sight? He peered into the darkness: nothing. The harder he tried to find it, the more pointless it became.

Oscar, you've lost your mind. You haven't eaten or slept in…what? Two days? Three? You're seeing things. Enough is enough. Forget about it.

Jade went below and took the wheel. He told Myrna to lie down and get some rest; they'd be home soon. He told her everything was going to be fine. She believed him.

What he didn't tell her, after some careful deliberation, was what he thought he'd seen in the water.

24
Ashes

Oscar Jade stood on the threshold of what used to be 3062 Aviation Avenue, in the stark light of day, and surveyed the remains. Whatever Connor had used—gasoline, most likely—had done its job. The place had burned cleanly to the ground, while police and fire departments chased bigger fires all over the Miami metropolitan area. All that remained was the brick outline of the foundation and a few blackened skeletal struts, which stood futile guard over the ashes and debris. In his mind's eye he could still see the rooms and the walls, the lives and memories within them, now seemingly as distant—and irrevocably gone—as ancient Rome. He was struck, most of all, by how small the space looked, now that it had been opened to the rest of the world.

What was left of the Pelican Bar & Grill had looked that way too, with an important difference: the old place hadn't completely burned to the ground, although the rearmost half of the second floor, and the roof above it, had collapsed into the garage area. What was left standing would need to be torn down, but not before an important part of it was salvaged—a result of what was already known, by locals in the know, as 'the miracle.'

As Jade understood it, this was thanks to 'Babe' Baker and Paulie Ryan, the morning drinkers who had been the Pelican's most faithful patrons since the early thirties, invariably washing down the breakfast special with the first draft beers drawn from the tap on any given business day. On Friday morning they had gone to the Pelican for breakfast, as always, and found the note, in Claude's sprawling and unmistakable hand, thumb-tacked to the closed and locked door: "Closed due to personal business. Will be back soon. Sorry for the inconvenience." They had gone glumly to a nearby diner for a beer-free breakfast, wondering what was so important that their favorite bar was closed on a Friday morning for the first time in ten years.

These ruminations had brought them back to the Pelican in the afternoon, only to find that the joint was still locked up. They propped themselves up at the Wayfarer's hotel bar and tried to get back on schedule. Then, just as the sun began to go down, they heard the gunfire.

Babe and Paulie came out to find dead bodies in the street, the Pelican engulfed in flames—and Claude Applegate lying against the running board of his old Dodge pickup, bleeding out and detachedly watching his place burn down. Paulie, who'd been a medical corpsman in the Great War, laid Claude on the street and elevated the leg with the gunshot wound while Babe made a frantic circuit of nearby hotels and businesses. A sizable volunteer bucket brigade soon hauled seawater up from the beach, as longtime friends and total strangers rallied to fight the fire. Garden hoses were aimed at the flames. When a fire truck finally arrived on the scene and the fire was brought under control, the building was judged to be a total loss. But the old tavern bar itself, carved from old hardwood from the Black Forest in the last century, and stubbornly purchased during prohibition—despite having some blackened edges and several new bullet-holes—had survived the blaze. Claude refused to go to the hospital until Babe and Paulie promised to camp out in the Dodge overnight to keep an eye on what was left of the joint. He promised them free beer down the road, and they were duly deputized. Then, and only then, did the big man allow himself to be loaded into the ambulance and driven away.

A squad car cruised slowly down Aviation Avenue and turned into the driveway behind the Chevrolet sedan Jade had borrowed from Kelly's Comfort Cabs. Allen Billings climbed out, his tie uncharacteristically loosened at the collar, and a folded newspaper tucked under his arm. He nodded at Jade, who nodded in reply.

"Smoke?" Billings offered.

"Sure," Jade said as he accepted the offered cigarette and a light. Then the cop handed Jade that morning's copy of the *Miami Herald*.

Jade unfolded the paper. The headline proclaimed: GANGLAND ARSON AND VIOLENCE COMES TO MIAMI. Directly beneath were pictures of the burning Caribbean Hotel, and the wreckage of the Pelican. A caption read: *Gunshots fired on Ocean Drive and Palm Island. Many alleged New York crime figures among the dead.* The article went on to name "reputed mob boss Pietro La Forno" as being "sought by authorities." Jade refolded the paper and gave it back without comment.

"Jesus," Billings said finally, after they'd spent a half-minute together, nursing their smokes and gazing at the ashes in silence. "Claude okay?"

"He's going to be fine."

"That's good...Oscar, I'm sorry about all this—"

"Did you tell Rusty where to find her?" Jade asked.

"I must've." Billings looked away. "I don't remember. Listen, Oscar...I don't expect you to forgive me—"

"Let it go, Al."

"I can't let it go. It's my fault."

"La Forno knew what he was doing," Jade said. "He picked his marks. It's done with. You need to let it go. That's what I'm going to do."

"Are you?"

Jade looked at him. "How's Sally?"

"She's fine now. She thought I was dead." Billings hesitated. "She...doesn't know about—"

"Maybe that's the best thing."

"Yeah. Listen, Oscar—"

"What did you turn up on Connor?"

Their eyes met. Billings nodded, and swallowed. "Nino Valletti's singing like a canary," he said. "What did you do to him?"

Jade shrugged. "I have a way with people."

"Well, he says Rusty is related, and it checks out all right. His mother is Gaetano Terranza's sister. They moved down here about fifteen years ago. But Rusty always spent his summers up in New York. Turns out he was pretty close to La Forno's sons."

"Figures," Jade said.

"He did a good job of burying the family connection—falsified his application to the academy, paid off all the right people. God only knows how many of these guys there are on the force, all over the place. And some of them are probably even legit. You know, Oscar," he said reluctantly, "I don't understand any of it. He *was* a good cop, I swear to God. Best arrest record in the state. You're the only one who ever made detective younger than he did. I'd've trusted him with my life."

Jade gave a tight smile. "So did La Forno."

The following Monday, Jade pulled some strings with a guy named Jack Spradlin, who owned a local construction company. Six months before, Spradlin's nubile young wife had started taking up with his foreman whenever Spradlin was out of town. It had been one of those jobs—peeking through windows with a camera, taking pictures of two people who had every right to believe that nobody was looking—that left a bad taste in Jade's mouth, but he'd saved Spradlin a significant alimony payment. The last thing he'd told Jade was: "Anytime you need something from me, just ask."

So Jade did. He'd probably never have gotten the job otherwise, given his busted ribs and reduced capacity to do heavy work, except that he was owed a favor, and promised to work for cheap—that, and the fact that more than half of Spradlin's men had volunteered for military service in the days since the attack on Pearl. With a dozen sites across the Miami area to pick from—including what was left of the Pelican—Jade volunteered to supervise the cleanup of the burned-out apartment building on Meridian Avenue.

It was dirty, uncomfortable work. Unlike most supervisors, Jade insisted on being right in the middle of it, shoulder to shoulder with his crew, using shovels to load debris into wheelbarrows...especially in the general area where Greta's sofa had been. It was tricky because the wooden floor had burned through to the crawlspace, and there were a million places for them to have fallen where they'd be easily overlooked by anyone who didn't know what he was looking for. This was also true of her bedroom, where there was little clue as to where her dresser and chest of drawers would have been located. While he'd had the eyes of a good detective, Connor wouldn't have taken the time, after killing her, to do a thorough search.

Fortunately, Jade had both the eyes and the time. And he took it. Buried in six inches of damp ash on the ground of the crawlspace, mixed in with a fist-sized jumble of charred costume jewelry, were three more keys with little blackened brass tags to go with the four that La Forno had fished out of Rusty Connor's pockets.

A view from the beach is like having a good, long look at forever. The sea and sky meet at the horizon, somewhere distant, and you aren't meant to see what happens beyond that point. But you stare anyway, not necessarily because there's any fresh wisdom to be found in that great, bending expanse, but because of the time it gives you to *think*—to breathe the sea air, feel the breeze, and weigh things out. Oscar Jade appreciated that kind of time, and he took it when he could. From here, sitting in the same chair he'd been sitting in exactly two weeks before, when a woman named Myrna Mallory had come to him with concerns about her husband, it was just the kind of time he needed.

The breeze felt especially good on his face, where beads of perspiration had been raised by the job at hand. He'd done quite a bit of physical work lately, and his body had responded well—although he still couldn't swing a hammer without discomfort, it was tolerable. Besides, he couldn't remember a time when he'd been completely free of physical discomfort. It was one of the ways he confirmed that he was still alive.

He took a long swallow from a bottle of cold beer, his first of the day, and gazed down the narrow beachfront stretch of Lummus Park. It was two days before Christmas: even with the noontime sun high in the sky it was a little too cool to be swimming, but there were small groups of would-be bathers there anyway, running down to the water's edge, and then retreating from the breaking waves in laughter when they turned out to be colder than expected. Jade smiled.

A voice behind him said, "Mind some company?"

Jade turned around. Allen Billings held a napkin-wrapped hamburger in one hand and a bottle of Coca-Cola in the other. Jade offered a chair with a wave of his hand; the cop sat down. "It's coming along real good," Billings said.

Jade looked back in the direction where the Pelican had once stood. The wreckage had been hauled away. Under the focused attention of six shirtless, suntanned bricklayers, the foundation was in the process of being expanded by twenty feet to the north and five feet toward Ocean Drive to the west. Along the lines of the old foundation that wouldn't be changing, Jade and young Ben Tuttle, along with two other hired hands, had begun to erect the wooden framing for the east and south walls. In the middle of this activity, completely covered by a huge piece of tarpaulin secured with rope, and further sheltered by a tent, the old tavern bar awaited the roof that would eventually make it an indoor fixture once again.

"Gonna be a big job," Jade said.

Nearby, on crutches, Claude was doing a busy trade from a makeshift cart he'd set up on the sidewalk, grilling hamburgers and bratwurst over a bed of coals in a converted fifty-five-gallon steel drum cut in half and mounted on wheeled legs. He sold bottles of beer and soda from a wooden barrel filled with ice, while Charlie Bechelli stood nearby and supervised. A wooden placard next to the little enterprise announced: "FUTURE HOME OF THE *NEW* PELICAN BAR AND GRILL." Two tables over from where Jade and Billings sat, Babe Baker and Paulie Ryan happily drank their lunch.

"Claude's taking it all in stride," Billings observed.

"Well, that's what he does," Jade replied. "Always has."

"I hear La Forno's Palm Island place burned down."

"Yeah," Jade said. "I heard that, too."

"Do you suppose it was the Terranzas?"

Jade looked over at Claude, and watched as some burger grease caused the coals in the makeshift grill to flare up. Charlie whispered something in Claude's ear, and the two old reprobates shared a laugh as Claude sprayed some water on the flames. Charlie's laugh wafted across the beach: "Hee, hee!"

Jade smiled knowingly. "No, I don't think so."

Billings met his stare, but not for long. The cop cleared his throat. "Um…what about the boat?"

In truth, the *Constance* was safely under wraps at a boatyard in Fort Lauderdale, but it wasn't the *Constance* anymore. It was in the process of being scrubbed clean, from its name and registration number to the bloodstains on its mahogany deck. By the time it saw the light of day once again, the only thing it would have in common with La Forno's motor yacht was the fact that it, too, was a top-of-the-line Chris-Craft with dubious ownership.

"I've inherited a boat from a long-lost uncle," Jade said. "The paperwork checks out. Take my word for it."

"Um, yeah. Sure." After a long silence the cop said, "You know, I talked to the commissioner. The offer still stands."

"I'm not a desk man, Al."

"Yeah." Silence again. "So you're gonna stay in business, then?"

"That's right."

"Might be a good idea, I guess," Billings said. "Read the paper lately? Miami's gonna be a boom town again. The army's gonna start sending recruits down here for training…a *lot* of 'em. Might be some work in it for you."

Jade remembered how he'd felt just two weeks ago, when the government had told him 'no thanks' in no uncertain terms. There wasn't any room in the new war for a guy with a bad foot and a long run of bad luck. On that day, he'd given some hard thought to the future. Myrna Mallory had shown up on his doorstep and he hadn't wanted any part of it—but now everything was different. Circumstance had pushed him far enough—it was time to get off his ass and push back. If you don't make your own moves, life has a way of moving on you.

Billings seemed to understand that Jade wasn't in the mood for a visit, and excused himself after he'd finished his hamburger.

Jade went back to work on the new south wall, and didn't pause again until late afternoon when a taxi dropped Myrna Mallory off next to Claude's hamburger stand. Jade wiped his hands with an old towel and walked over to them as the big man gave her an affectionate bear hug that clearly took her aback. Claude winked at Jade. "Take a break, boss," he said. He opened Jade's second beer of the day, and handed it to him.

Jade and Myrna sat down at the table. "How are you?" he asked, lighting a cigarette. He didn't bother asking her if she wanted one; he knew she'd quit.

"I'm fine," she said distractedly.

"You're a lousy liar."

She smiled. "I never lied to you, Oscar...well, almost never."

"It's nice to know somebody who isn't very good at it," Jade said. "People like that are getting rare."

"Oscar, I just wanted you to know that I feel terrible about—"

"All you did was come to me for help, Myrna. And I agreed to help you. Everything after that belongs to other people, not you." He took a drag from his smoke and washed it down with a long drink of his beer. "You *can* do me a favor, though."

"Anything," she said.

"For God's sake, be *extra* careful when you pick your next man, would you?"

She gave a short laugh. Their eyes met, and she reached across the tabletop to take his hand in a firm grasp. "I promise."

Jade returned the squeeze. When she didn't remove her hand he said, "Myrna..."

"Oh, all right," she said, finally letting him go with a roll of the eyes. Her smile faltered, and a single, stubborn tear worked its way down her cheek. "I'm sorry. I'm so sick of crying."

"What is it?" he asked.

"I'm going to lose the house," she said. "Horace borrowed against it back in August, and never made a payment."

"They won't work with you?"

She shook her head. "They're going to foreclose. And the bank won't hire me back. Everybody knows I'm expecting...and they know it's not Horace's baby." She gave a halfhearted smile. "I'm damaged goods, Oscar. Bad news. I don't know what I'm going to do."

Not so long ago, she'd asked him how long a person was supposed to pay for a mistake. He hadn't had a good answer then, and he still didn't. Maybe it wasn't meant to be that simple. Sometimes, fairly or not, payment came due for other peoples' mistakes and misdeeds as well. It was a chain of other peoples' mistakes and misdeeds, after all, that had led her to him, Oscar Jade, out of a clear blue sky. Sometimes blood was spilled, and things burned down, and now a man named 'Little Tom' Terranza from Brooklyn, New York, would be biding his time, waiting for the right moment to come back down and square things, once and for all, for the death of a son. This wasn't the end of anything. It was only the beginning.

Jade remembered what he'd said to Greta Vincennes: the problem with blood money was that you could never get the blood off.

It had taken several days, but he'd been methodical: the train station in Miami first, then every bus stop in the Miami area, then expanding outward. On a hunch, Jade had made a trip to Hollywood, Florida—not the Hollywood to which poor Greta had aspired, but as near as she was destined to ever get—where he'd found the two rental lockers to match the last two keys, numbered #38 and #49, at a bus station on the southern edge of town. It wasn't quite the windfall he'd hoped for. There had been enough to rebuild the Pelican—and, maybe, just enough to drop the customized Flathead V-8 into the chassis of another '35 Ford he'd found in a junkyard in Port St. Lucie.

And after all the blood money had been spent, the only remaining question was: what would grow from the ashes? And could he ever possibly be worthy of it?

The answer came to him, with quick and unsettling clarity: maybe not.

Jade shook off the feeling and forced it back into the recesses of his mind, into a lockbox he'd kept safely tucked away there for some time now, a box that already seemed overcrowded with ugly things... but there always seemed to be room for more, didn't there? Maybe later he'd take them out—later, yes, that was it, later, when he had time—and look at them in the safe light of day.

Maybe he wasn't worthy. Maybe he never would be. But he had to try.

He finished his beer, and gave Myrna a mischievous grin.

"Can you type?" he asked.

Author's Note & Acknowledgments

"I think you should write an old-fashioned private eye story."

It was the summer of 2007, and my father and I were sitting in my parents' family room, as we sometimes do late on a Sunday morning. My father is a fan of the classic-style mystery novels, and had just finished reading *I, the Jury*, by the great Mickey Spillane. He observed: "They don't write books like that anymore...and people still want to read them."

The moment is burned permanently into my memory, since—although I didn't realize it at the time—it was the moment that Oscar Jade was born, and the book you're now holding in your hands is the direct result of that particular moment in time.

I suddenly realized I was about to write a private detective mystery—and it would be an intentionally 'retro' affair, taking place back in the time when some of these great stories were first conceived and written by giants like Dashiell Hammett and Raymond Chandler. It was a time before DNA experts, cell phones and Internet databases—when a gumshoe's toolbox was limited to shifty street contacts, his skills and his nerve...and, when the time came, the gun in his hand.

Choosing the period was the easy part. Next came the more difficult decision of where my hero would ply his trade. Hammett's Sam Spade had San Francisco, Spillane's Mike Hammer owned New York City, and Chandler's Philip Marlowe haunted the expanse of Golden Age Los Angeles. Keeping this in mind, and looking at a map of the United States, there was clearly a territorial opportunity in the Southeast.

Researching the history of the area provided an epiphany: at the beginning of World War Two, Miami Beach was on the cusp of a new age of expansion, facing a massive influx of military personnel (taking advantage of the tropical climate to be able to train year-round), along with the ongoing presence of gangsters, industrialists and movie stars—all of whom made the beach their personal playground. It was an arena of infinite possibilities. The fact that my father had been born in Florida, and had lived a fair portion of his childhood on Aviation Avenue in Coral Gables, was the deciding factor. It will be news to anyone outside my immediate family that my dad (born in February, 1939) actually has a cameo appearance in chapter one of *Blood & Ashes*, along with his three older brothers, his older sister and my grandmother, who turn up as bathers on the beach in front of the Pelican Bar & Grill.

Once I was in the midst of it, I realized that I had grabbed a tiger by the tail, and all I could do was hold on. Things got more violent than I'd foreseen, but that's what happens when you're just an observer, in over your head and just trying to stay alive…

As much care as possible has been taken in preserving the accuracy of Miami Beach in December of 1941: the overall geography has been replicated based upon maps of the era, to include street names and the general layout of various neighborhoods. That being said, real estate development has been relentless over the past seventy years. The Miami Beach of 1941 (to say nothing about South Florida as a whole) is long gone, and some artistic license has admittedly been taken to serve the story being told. Aside from Hialeah Park, virtually all businesses and buildings depicted herein are figments of my imagination, and any resemblance to actual businesses and buildings is strictly unintentional. The events depicted as occurring in and around Miami Beach on Friday, December 12th, 1941, never actually did—and, to the best of my knowledge, Bing Crosby never recorded a song entitled "Doris Mae"… but he should have…

Specifically, I *am* aware that the Drake Building has existed at the corner of Ocean Drive and 15th Street, in Miami Beach, since the 1930s—therefore, the Pelican Bar & Grill exists only in my mind and on these pages, and I hope that we might all continue to 'pretend.'

If you'll indulge me, I'd like to take this opportunity to thank a few of the many people without whom this book would never have been written. First of all, my parents: Tom and Janice Loeffelholz, who have been unceasing in their love and support…

My sister, Lori Kish, whom I *never* defeated in one-on-one basketball…

My brother Michael, upon whom Oscar Jade's physical appearance is partly based, and whose assistance in naming my hero was instrumental…

My lovely and long-suffering wife Cindy, who has been by my side since 1986, when we sat in a rented Ford Mustang behind George Ranks' bar and talked about my dreams…

My sons Ian and Alec, without whom my life would be unimaginable…

Joe Hackett, my sixth-grade teacher, who once wrote the lyrics to the Beatles' "Hey Jude" on the classroom blackboard and told me I could be a writer, if that's what I wanted to do…

Ian Fleming, who came along around the same time and showed me just how electrifying the printed word can be…

Erin Stropes, my editor, whose thoughtful and tireless work has helped me realize who Oscar Jade actually is…

Mike Williams, who helped me arrive at the title *Blood & Ashes*…

Daren Hatfield, for his brilliant cover art…

The moderators and members of ajb007.co.uk, whose friendship and encouragement have been invaluable (and without whom I'd *never* have met Mike Williams or Daren Hatfield)…

And, finally but perhaps most importantly, you the reader—since Oscar Jade can't *really* exist unless and until his exploits are enjoyed by others. Thank you so much for being there. I plan to do everything I can to keep you interested. If you enjoyed this story, please tell a friend!

There's a lot about Oscar Jade I don't know yet: exactly where he's been, or where he's going. He's a moody and tight-lipped fellow, and doesn't respond well to persistent questioning. Recently, he's threatened to punch me in the mouth if I keep bothering him. All I can do is keep an eye on him, and follow him wherever he goes. He has always managed to surprise me, and I trust he will continue to do so.

There's only one thing that I can be reasonably sure about.

Oscar Jade will return.

- M.L.
Springfield, Illinois, May 2010

LaVergne, TN USA
29 August 2010
194970LV00001B/3/P